MURDER AT
THE BEACH

MURDER AT THE BEACH

HELEN GOODMAN

W🌐RLDWIDE.

TORONTO • NEW YORK • LONDON
AMSTERDAM • PARIS • SYDNEY • HAMBURG
STOCKHOLM • ATHENS • TOKYO • MILAN
MADRID • WARSAW • BUDAPEST • AUCKLAND

Recycling programs
for this product may
not exist in your area.

Murder at the Beach

A Worldwide Mystery/August 2017

First published by Alabaster Book Publishing

ISBN-13: 978-0-373-28421-4

Copyright © 2016 by Helen Goodman

Printed in U.S.A.

MURDER AT
THE BEACH

ONE

THE BEACH HOUSE at 327 Shoreline Drive shimmered in the late August heat. Its paint, the color of strawberry ice cream, seemed to be melting onto the surrounding sand and shrubs. The stretch of beach in front of the house was nearly empty. It usually was during much of the day on Friday. During school vacation time, most of the weekly rentals in this area were from Friday to Friday.

Departing tenants packed up their wet swimsuits, their beach balls, their sunburned kids, their happy memories, and left fairly early Friday morning. This made time for housekeeping cleaning crews to sweep out the sand and wipe up the dust. It didn't take them long to get ready for the next batch of sun worshipers. By noon the empty beach houses were always ready for their next occupants even if most of the expected newcomers wouldn't arrive until late in the day.

Although the lifeguards were still on duty, they were relaxed—chatting, strolling, talking on their cell phones, paying no attention to the water in front of them or the houses in back.

The pink two-story house behind the lifeguard stand was actually three stories high since it was built over an open basement/garage area. The architect probably figured if the sand dunes in front of the house didn't stop storm surges spawned by hurricanes, then hopefully, the water would stay on the basement level. Today, though, there were no hurricanes on the horizon as the Atlantic Ocean waves lapped lazily against the shoreline. Likewise, there were no movements on the street behind the house.

Inside the supposedly empty house, though, there *was* movement. Quietly, stealthily, an intruder was methodically searching every room—an intruder on a mission.

The closed blinds blocked out the afternoon sunlight as well as any prying eyes that might happen to come along the sidewalk in back or on the beach in front. And instead of turning on the lights, the intruder used a small flashlight.

Eager fingers, encased in thin surgical gloves, reached behind and under every drawer, pushed aside pots and pans to explore kitchen cabinets, removed sofa cushions to dig into crevices for hidden treasure only to find an abundance of lint, searched air vents and toilet tanks—always careful to replace everything back in perfect order. There was no noise except for the air conditioner and the muffled sound of opening and closing doors and the light scraping of wood on wood as chairs were drawn up to reach the top shelf of closets.

Having had no luck in the living area or bedrooms on the ground floor, the intruder headed up the stairs— two more bedrooms to go.

The dying man's mocking voice taunted the intruder's brain. *"You won't find it. You'll never find it, Slink."* The nickname had been a joke between friends—but that friendship had ended last night. An ending the greedy fool should have seen coming. Did he actually think he could double-cross his partner and get away with it? The butt end of a gun at the back of his head proved him wrong.

"And I will find it," Slink declared to the empty room. "I only need to think where I would hide wads of cash where no one else would accidently find it." The narrow beam from the flashlight flitted into every corner of the upstairs bedroom, behind and under the bed, behind the drapes and blinds. Using a slender jackknife, the intruder peeled back the felt lining on the bottom of the bedside lamp only to find the neatly coiled electrical wires. Then Slink's eyes lifted upward, gaped at the overhead light fixture and figured the opaque globe might be a good hiding place. Dragging a chair up to use for a stepladder, it took only seconds to remove the screw, lift down the globe and to reveal its contents.

Disappointment swept the seeker when the contents of the globe consisted only of two old fifty-watt bulbs, one of which was burned out.

It would have been a lousy hiding place anyway. If the light were left on all day, the bills would probably catch on fire. I've got to be more logical. But I will find it. I have to. I just have to have more time. I didn't kill a man to end up with nothing.

IT WAS NEARING two when Dave Aldridge and his buddy from NC State, Neil Stone, drove through the town of Beacon Heights, crossed over a bridge and arrived in the small coastal town of Beacon Beach, North Carolina. The soft feminine voice that had guided them all the way from their summer counseling jobs at Camp Kanoka in the mountains now instructed them to turn left in four-tenths of a mile onto Shoreline Drive.

Dave slowed the car, made the turn, and continued

driving at a crawl. Neil propped his right elbow on the armrest and studied the houses as they drove by. "What's the number of the house?"

Dave grinned. Apparently, Neil wasn't content to wait for their guide to inform them they'd reached their destination. "327," Dave answered. "Only a couple more blocks."

"Imagine renting a big beachfront place during top tourist season. Must have cost your folks a pretty penny. When I was a kid and my family went to the beach, we hauled a tent and pitched it in a crowded camp ground." He paused. "Not that I'm complaining. It was really great fun."

"I'm sure it was," Dave agreed. "But we might as well enjoy a little luxury when we can. I have no idea how much this vacation is costing, but I think Mom and Fred just wanted Connie and me to have a good time before starting back to school." Dave felt there was no reason to mention about his mother's recent inheritance from her aunt. The fact that his great-aunt Leona had been murdered, seemed to make the money a burden to his mother. She refused to use any of it on herself, but did pay off the mortgage on the house as well as both his and Connie's college loans. Since she no longer had the mortgage payment, it meant a little more spending money. He was just glad after all her years of scrimping as a single mom she was now able to afford some luxuries. He was also thrilled she'd found happiness in her marriage to Fred Sawyer last year.

Dave had always felt protective of his mom, and with him and Connie both in college, he'd worried about her living all alone. Now that worry was behind him.

"Yeah," Neil said, "I can see why they would want

to plan a great vacation for the family, but there's something I can't figure out."

"What?"

"Why they told you to invite a friend along."

"Pure self-protection."

Neil's eyes scrunched up in puzzlement. "Protection against what?"

"Me. They probably figured if I had a flunkey along, I wouldn't keep bugging Fred to go surfing with me."

"Well, thanks a lot. When did I get demoted from friend to flunkey?"

Dave reached his right hand over, patted Neil on the shoulder. "When you started asking too many questions. Just relax and enjoy the week. That's what I'm going to do."

"Fine. But may I ask one more question?"

"Sure," Dave said. "Fire away."

"Does Connie's friend, Trina Moffat, come under the heading of flunkey, too?"

Dave roared, slowed the car, and gasped for breath. "I guess so," he finally managed to say, "but don't tell her so. I think her functions are to lie in the sun with Connie and keep her company on shopping trips, thus freeing up Mom to spend quality time with Fred."

"Sounds like a good deal all the way around." Neil seemed to suddenly remember his current duty of checking out house numbers. "Hey, that's 325. Must be the next house—the pink one."

Slamming on the brakes, Dave screeched to a halt, bent his head to get a good view and howled, "Who in the world would paint a house Pepto Bismo Pink?"

"I kind of like it. It looks like the dollhouse my kid sister used to have and she had pink dishes to match."

"I'm not sure I want to hear about how you used to play house with your little sister."

Neil jerked away from the window. "I didn't say I played with her. Just making an observation. No need for you to get snooty about it."

Grinning, Dave said, "Believe me, if I had a snooty bone in my body, I wouldn't be friends with a commoner like you."

"Just so we understand each other." Neil's gaze went back to the pink house, and when Dave made no move to pull into the drive, he added, "So—are we going to park or just sit here gaping?"

"I'm parking, I'm parking." Since there was very little space in the backyard, Dave drove into the basement area. As with all houses that lined the beachfront, the rear of the house was street-side while the front had a view of the waves and sand.

Sliding out of the car, Dave ran around to the front of the house. "Let's check out the beach."

The berm of sand at the edge of the front yard limited their view of the water, so Dave headed toward the steps on his left. He took the short flight of stairs to the front porch in two leaps, swiveled his head around due east and gave a rapturous sigh. "All that water, all that sand…and no girls? No bikinis? Something's wrong with this picture." He turned puzzled eyes to Neil. "What's going on?"

Neil raised his eyebrows, gave him a look that plainly indicated Dave had asked a particularly stupid question. "Not to panic," Neil cautioned patiently. "It's early yet. Probably the weekend doesn't officially start until tonight. By tomorrow the sand will be littered with so many sun-bronzed beauties you'll have to shovel your way to the water."

Dave gave a sigh of relief. "You're right. Maybe we better get in some swimming while we can. We might be too busy getting acquainted tomorrow."

"But let's check the house out first," Neil said. He opened the screen door, jiggled the knob on the inner door. "It's locked."

"Of course it's locked."

Neil held out his hand with the palm up. "Well, give me the key."

"I don't have the key. Fred will pick it up at the rental agency when they get here."

"So just where are we supposed to change our clothes?"

"In the garage. There's no one around to care," Dave said. "Don't tell me you're getting prissy all of a sudden."

"It's not being prissy to want a little privacy. The garage isn't exactly a locker room. What if somebody comes down the street?"

"If it makes you feel any better, I'll keep watch while you change."

"Fine. And I'll do the same for you."

"Then let's go. We've got a good hour to swim before the rest of the gang arrives."

SLINK WAS HEADING for the other upstairs bedroom when the sound of screeching brakes, a car turning in, and loud voices floated through the closed and shuttered windows. *What are they doing here already? Check-in time for these houses is three o'clock. Someone at the agency must have given the key out early.*

Gliding noiselessly down the stairs, Slink heard someone try to open the front door and then ask for the key. The intruder was relieved when the other kid answered that he didn't have the key, and in a few seconds, more reassuring words drifted in, "...hour before the rest get here."

Good. I have another hour to search. But maybe I'd better get out while I can. The others might come early, too, and they'll probably have a key. I'm not giving up, though—and I'm not waiting another week until these people leave. I can watch them. They'll all go fishing or swimming or something, and I'll come back. I'm going to find what's rightfully mine.

Not able to resist the temptation, Slink stepped in behind the window drape and slowly lifted one slat of the blind. The two boys standing on the porch didn't quite match their voices. They had sounded younger— teens, maybe. But these were solid young men, probably early twenties, muscular. They may act like silly kids, but they weren't to be taken lightly. And they definitely weren't brothers, too much difference in their looks. The six-footer with the frowsy, coal-black hair had soft, almost childlike features while the shorter one had blond hair and a square chin.

The tall one repeated, "Let's go." The two of them bounded off the porch and disappeared for a few minutes into the basement area. When they reappeared, the tall one was wearing bright blue, low-riding swim trunks emblazoned with mean-looking white sharks. The other kid, who apparently was less daring, had on faded khaki trunks. They swatted each other with towels and headed for the water.

Not knowing how long the two would be in the water, Slink knew the smart thing to do was to leave right away.

Dressed like an ordinary vacationer with hair hidden by a cap and eyes hidden by shades, Slink slipped out the back door, made sure it was locked, and moseyed on down the street.

TWO

THE "REST OF the gang" Dave had referred to were in Fred Sawyer's van creeping South down US Highway 40. As the traffic started slowing down, each one of the occupants had their own theory as to what had happened up ahead.

Fred's opinion reflected his years in law enforcement, "Some loony tried to pass when there wasn't enough room and smashed some fenders."

"Or maybe someone's car overheated and stalled," Allison said. "It wouldn't surprise me in this heat."

From the seat behind Allison, Trina chimed in, "Could be texting and driving. That causes a slew of accidents."

Connie finished the round with, "Might be cops checking drivers' licenses."

Allison knew it made no difference to them what the reason was. They were stuck in traffic, and there wasn't a thing they could do about it. The others soon seemed to come to the same conclusion. Fred relaxed his grip on the steering wheel, Connie pulled out a deck of cards and Trina cleared the seat between them.

Leaning her head back on the seat, Allison let her thoughts roam. It wasn't the upcoming week of vacation that flitted around her brain, though, but rather the following week when the new school year would start. She'd been teaching at Madison Middle School for years under the name of Allison Aldridge and would continue to do so even though she'd been Mrs. Fred Sawyer for over a year. It'd been a mutual agreement between her and Fred for her to keep being Ms. Aldridge to her students and to the school board, while being Mrs. Sawyer in her private life. The decision had been made to avoid confusion since Fred was now an employee of the same school district where Allison taught. His title sounded a little more important than hers. She was known as the Health Teacher and the Girl's Gym Teacher/Basketball Coach. Fred's official title was the School and Law Enforcement Liaison. Unofficially, he was the school cop.

Fred's part-time job fitted well into his retirement plans. After thirty years in a county sheriff's department, he'd needed to get away from catching criminals and put his energy into trying to help young people stay safe and to avoid certain pitfalls that might lead to trouble. He gave short lectures on safety, bullying, drugs, as well as the importance of having long-term goals. He became friends with the students and let them know he was there to help. Allison was proud of how well he'd made the transition and how well he'd been received by both students and faculty.

She glanced over to her left, studied her husband's profile. He was distinguished-looking rather than handsome: high forehead, firm chin. His dark hair was thinning on top and threaded with gray; his face, neck, and arms were the color of October acorns. She knew, though, his tanned skin ended at his neckline. Ever since he'd left the hospital the previous year he'd never gone without wearing some kind of high-necked shirt. It wasn't that he was ashamed of the scars left from the bullets that'd pierced his chest, and the subsequent surgery, but he didn't want to remind himself or anybody else of how close he'd come to dying.

His recuperation was long and painful, but their wedding went on as planned. Since then they'd spent every day together except for one terrible week last winter when she had to go to the mountains to bury her beloved aunt, and he'd been stranded by a snow storm in Dallas. During that week, she'd been stalked, kidnapped, and held at gunpoint by a killer. But all that was behind them now, and they had a marvelous beach vacation to look forward to.

The girls seemed to be engrossed in their card game so Allison took advantage of the situation to stretch up, lean over and give him a private kiss on the cheek. He turned his head; his eyebrows shot up; his hand slid over the console and squeezed her thigh. She smiled. They'd become quite adept at silent communication.

After several more minutes the traffic started moving faster and it wasn't long before they went by two cars parked on the side of the road, both with crumpled fenders.

"Told ya," Fred crowed.

Connie responded first. "Lucky guess."

As Fred picked up speed, Allison sounded a note of warning, "Don't try to make up lost time now by going too fast. It won't matter to the boys if we're a little late."

"Oh, it'll matter, all right," Fred said. "Remember, we have all the food."

Trina laughed. "And neither one of those guys can go more than a couple of hours without eating."

"Maybe I ought to call Dave, assure him we're on our way," Connie said.

Allison shook her head. "I doubt he'll answer. They're probably in the water."

DAVE AND NEIL came out of the water after an hour of swimming, running, dunking each other, and doing what most parents would call "tomfoolery." Although both had passed their twenty-first birthdays neither had any desire to act like an adult.

Flopping down on their towels, they sighed in contentment. That lasted a total of two minutes. Dave sat up, stared back at the pink house. "Wonder what's keeping them. I'm hungry."

"Me too. And I didn't even see a hamburger joint when we drove through town."

"We'll give them another half-hour and then we go looking for sustenance."

"You're going to have to talk to me then," Neil said, "to keep my mind away from food."

"What do you want to talk about?"

"Tell me about your stepfather. I only met him once and he seemed nice, but what's he really like?"

Dave squinted in the bright sunlight, brushed sand off his hairy legs, coughed a couple of times. He knew the answer, but had never tried to put his feelings toward Fred into words. Maybe it was time he did.

"He's a great guy," Dave began. "Easy to get along with, a good listener, respects Connie and me. Most of all he loves my mom and makes her happy." He paused. *If I go any further, I might get pretty sloppy, but Neil had asked and he deserved a complete answer.* "Remember when he was shot in the line of duty shortly before they were married?"

"Yeah. You called and told me about it. Shot and

left to die in the parking lot. That must have been some kind of scary."

"I probably told you how worried I was about Mom, how much she would be hurt if Fred died, but that wasn't the whole truth. I was just as worried about how much I would miss him. You see, when he asked Mom to marry him, he knew he was taking on the entire family. He started right off being like a dad to me: interested in my classes and asking about my friends, building me up. I never had that from a man before." Dave sat up, leaned back on his towel, and dug his toes into the sand for a bit before going on. "You knew I grew up without a dad—right?"

"Yeah, sure. You said your folks were divorced, and that you seldom saw your dad."

"Make that never. He took off when I was two and Connie was four. Mom explained it to me when I was old enough to understand. I guess he never looked back as we didn't see or hear from him again."

Neil sat straight up, shook his head. "Bummer."

"Yeah, but Fred makes up for all that. So, saying that he's a nice guy is like saying... Mount Mitchell is a nice hill."

Flopping back, Dave added, "And since Fred enjoys eating about as much as I do, you can be sure his van is loaded with goodies. Let's relax and think good thoughts about the monster sandwiches we'll have when they get here."

FRED SLOWED THE CAR as he drove over the curved bridge that spanned the distance from the town of Beacon Heights to the coastal community of Beacon Beach.

The space beneath the bridge, which at one time might have been an estuary from the ocean, was now filled with railroad tracks and small commercial buildings. The bridge was constructed so the eastward view from its highest point would send out a special welcome to the passengers of each car that crossed over. The, "ahs" and "ohs," from Allison and the girls in the back seat, was proof the beach area met with their approval.

Exiting the bridge, Fred noted several signs informing visitors of the delights that awaited them from ice cream parlors to souvenir shops to surf board rentals. The sign he was interested in at the moment, though, was the one reading, *Beacon Beach Realty Office*. He parked in front of the office and opened his door.

"Just have to pick up the keys. I prepaid, so it shouldn't take long."

As soon as he entered the realty office, a voice from his right greeted him. "Good afternoon, Sir. May I help you?"

He smiled at the gray-haired woman who spoke and nodded. He noticed a youngish man at another desk, who apparently was busy since he didn't look up. The third desk in the room was empty. Approaching the elderly woman, he gave his name and after she found his reservation on her computer, she produced two keys. As she handed them over, she gave a slight smile, "We welcome you to Beacon Beach, Mr. Sawyer, and hope you have a fine vacation." It was evident the "we" was meant to include the man in the greeting even though he never even glanced in Fred's direction.

Reading her name tag, Fred nodded again, "Thank you, Mrs. Platt. I'm sure we will."

AFTER LEAVING THE pink house, Slink strolled slowly around the block hoping to get a glimpse of the other members of the rental party when they arrived. *It'll help if I know who they all are. That way I can better plan my next excursions into the house. It would be nice if they were all college age, then they would likely stick together and go out at the same time.*

That hope was dashed when the intruder saw the brown van drive up and a middle-aged couple get out. The two girls that followed appeared to be in their twenties, a little more mature than the fellows. *Looks like I'll just have to keep close tabs on the house and wait until they all go their separate ways. That's all right. I can be patient. The prize will be well worth it.*

DAVE AND NEIL must have been watching for them, Fred thought, because as soon as he drove in the boys ran up. Fred gave them their instructions. "Help the girls unload the cars while your elders take a stroll on the beach."

"Yes, Sir," Neil said. "Just leave everything to us."

"But," Dave put in, "don't go until you tell us which boxes contain the food."

"Doesn't matter. You're going to take every box and every suitcase in before you start scrounging for edibles."

Fred had decided early on this vacation was especially for Allison. She'd been teaching for decades and he knew that each year the kids, even in the middle grades, became more sophisticated, more volatile, and often harder to reach. He intended to pamper her this week so she'd be well rested before starting the school year.

They took their time walking along the edge of the water, and when he and Allison returned thirty minutes later, Fred saw the suitcases and duffel bags from both cars dumped unceremoniously in the middle of the living room, while the coolers and boxes of food were placed carefully on one end of the plank dining table. Fred smiled. Maybe these kids had their priorities straight after all. Food first, work later.

One end of the table was crowded with four young people making sandwiches or munching on chips or slurping tall, cool drinks. "Mind if we join you?" he asked, as he ushered Allison up to the makeshift buffet.

"Be my guest," Connie said. "Sorry we didn't wait for you, but we didn't know how long you honeymooners would be gone."

Allison grabbed a banana, nibbled a bit before turning to Fred. "And here I thought our honeymoon would be over after the first year."

He bent and kissed her on the forehead. "It's never going to be over, Hon."

Dave let out a loud, "Ugh." Neil smirked. Trina giggled. Connie pretended to swoon.

Fred ignored all of them.

Allison finished her banana and made an announcement. "While you're eating, Fred will go over the house rules with you. And you might be more comfortable in the living room."

Four heads jerked up. Mouths dropped slightly open. Eyes darted back and forth. No one said a word. One by one, they picked up their paper plates and headed for the couches.

Fred took his time smearing mustard on bread, positioning the ham, cheese, and lettuce just right, and, to prolong the suspense, he carefully cut his sandwich into four pieces. When he looked up, Allison motioned him to a chair next to hers.

Setting his plate on the coffee table, he leaned back in the chair, crossed one knee over the other, gave them a secretive smile—the cop in control pose he'd used for thirty years.

Connie smiled back. Her deep brown eyes danced as she played with her ponytail. He could tell she'd caught on to his "pretend to act tough" charade.

Dave still looked a little worried, and the two guests seem to be studying the carpet.

He relented, uncrossed his legs and said, "The first rule for this week is…to have fun."

Talk about an ice breaker! Connie started the clapping and was soon joined by the others. Allison allowed it go on a little while before raising a hand for their attention. "I don't think Fred was quite through." She turned to him, asked pointedly, "Were you, Dear?"

"Not exactly. The other rule is that Allison and I are doing no work this week: no cooking, no dish washing, no sweeping sand out of the house. It'll be up to you four. You can work together, divide the tasks, take turns—any way you want to do it."

For the first time, Neil spoke up. "You can count on us, Sir. You and the Mrs. deserve a real vacation. And I happen to be a very good cook."

"Me too," Connie said. "It'll give me a chance to try out some new recipes."

Trina raised her hand and her voice, "And I happen to be a very good sand-sweeper-outer."

Dave shook his head at all of his peers. "If you think that leaves me as dishwasher-in-chief, think again. I know to how to cook and sweep, too."

Allison stood up. "I suggest you have a meeting and iron out your schedules. But to ease your minds about tonight, I fixed a beef stew to warm up. And your cooking chores will only be for dinner. All of us can manage breakfast and lunch on our own."

"And I'll take everyone out one night," Fred added. "I heard about a fabulous fish and steak place on the other side of the bridge. That will leave only five dinners you need to do."

Leaning over the coffee table, Fred tossed out some money. "Look over the staples we brought, decide your menus, and buy what you need. I was told the grocery store is at the south end of Shoreline Drive." Smiling at Allison, Fred said, "And as soon as I finish eating, we honeymooners are going to put on swimsuits and go play in the sand."

"In that case," Allison said, "I'm going to put my suit on now. I can't wait to start this vacation."

Fred took a big bite of his ham and cheese. "I'll be right behind you, Babe."

On their way to the beach, they stopped on the porch to apply sunscreen. Fred admired Allison's one-piece light green swimsuit as he lathered her back and shoulders. She may be in her late forties, he thought, but she still sported a fine figure—much better than his own. And since he wore his usual tee shirt, he had only to apply the lotion to his arms and legs. That job finished, they linked hands, skipped down the steps, ran to the sea. Fred didn't feel a day older than the kids left behind in the house. The day was beautiful; their lives were beautiful.

OPTING NOT TO build sand castles, Allison tied her beach towel around her waist and suggested they walk to the fishing pier a bit north of them. Fred agreed, tossed his towel around his neck, took her hand again. The beach was beginning to fill up as tourists arrived, claimed their rentals, and like them, made a dash to start enjoying their week in the sun. Toddlers started filling up new sand buckets; gangling youngsters dashed in and out of the waves; teenaged girls ogled the beefy lifeguards while the boys studied the array of bikinis.

Allison breathed deeply of the salt air, raised her eyes to the sky, and thanked the universe for its goodness. Everything was right in her little corner of the world.

Alternating between squeezing sand between her toes and wading in water, she was in no hurry to get anywhere.

When they came close to the pier, Fred nodded toward the steps, "Want to go up?"

"Sure. Probably a great view from there."

At the top of the steps, Allison was surprised to find the pier deserted except for one lone fisherman under a striped beach umbrella. He was lolled back in his folding chair with a silly grin on his face. It was evident to Allison he'd found his own version of heaven.

At the end of the pier, they staked claim to a wide bench, wallowed in the peacefulness of the waves and the clouds and the endless horizon.

After a while, they ambled back down the pier with Allison's eyes darting from side to side to look at the houses, the condos, the high-rise hotels. As they neared the stairs, she stared over the opposite railing at some trash. "How can people be so thoughtless? Just look at those drink cans and food wrappers. Absolutely disgraceful!"

"We could go in the bait shop here," Fred said, "get a plastic bag and pick the trash up—our good deed for today."

Allison heard him, but her attention was now on something else. "Fred," she said, There's somebody on the ground under the pier. He looks funny. Maybe he's sick." She pushed back from the railing, started running down the steps. "We need to check on him."

Not waiting for Fred, Allison hurried to the recess under the pier to where it abutted the adjacent building. She scrambled toward the man she'd spied. From this angle, he was lying with his back toward her. Stepping closer she saw the hair on the back of his head was matted with blood. She leaned forward, saw no movement on his chest, placed two fingers on his neck and felt no carotid pulse.

She backed out slowly as Fred came up. "He's not sick," she said. "He's dead."

THREE

SINCE NEITHER OF them had brought their cell phones, Allison sprinted up the steps to the bait shop to have someone there call the local police. Meanwhile, Fred patrolled the perimeter of what he knew had to be a crime scene. He kept a proper distance from the body, but his detective genes were on full alert. Being in retirement didn't mean he could be oblivious to the clues that were bombarding his brain. The dead man's wound, his position on the sand, the absence of any weapon, his matter of dress, and even his grooming, were all important indicators of his life as well as his death.

It seemed apparent to Fred that the man had been struck on the back of the head, maybe repeatedly, with…what? A piece of driftwood? The butt of a gun? A blackjack? He quickly searched the area from the edge of the building down to the water, but whatever the weapon had been, there was no sign of it now.

Turning his attention back to the victim, Fred's first impression was that the dead man was no beach bum. The logo on the blood-splattered shirt, the numerous pockets of his cargo pants, and his contoured sandals were indicative of upscale shops. Bending down, he noted the tan on the man's left lower arm was interrupted by a narrow band in a slightly lighter shade, obviously from a watch—probably an expensive one. No evidence of a wedding band.

Fred guessed the victim to be in his late twenties or early thirties. He had light brown hair and, in spite of the blood, Fred could tell he'd had a recent haircut since the back of his neck showed some white skin above the tan line. He was slim and not particularly tall. As far as he could tell, there was no evidence of a struggle. Maybe his attacker had surprised the man.

Fred doubted there would be any ID on the body, but a man who appeared to be somewhat affluent probably wouldn't remain unidentified very long. There may already be a missing person bulletin out for him.

Staring at the victim, Fred had the feeling that he imagined an old racehorse might have—the itch to be back on the track, to be back in the thick of things. When Allison raced down the steps and informed him the police would be here soon, he tried to smother the urge to be involved. He was on vacation, and besides, he had retired from detective work over a year ago.

"I called Connie, too," Allison said, "told her we might be delayed and to heat up the stew when they got hungry."

"You didn't tell her why?"

She shook her head. "I couldn't do that. I couldn't spoil their first day of vacation."

Fred knew the delay getting back to the beach house might be quite a while since they would both have to give their statements and their contact information to the responding officers. While they waited for the police to arrive, Fred did his best to keep the curious bait shop people and the few others on the beach away from the crime scene.

When the onlookers had backed off, he explained to Allison his deductions about the victim.

"I agree," she said. "He certainly isn't a bum. Probably a vacationer—robbed and killed by someone who smelled a big wallet. His family must be worried sick."

Before they could discuss the victim further, a police car drove up to the parking lot. Two uniformed officers waved to the locals they knew, urged them back further.

They turned to the half-dozen or so people in beachwear, and the taller officer asked, "Who reported the victim?"

Fred stepped closer, his arm around Allison. "We're the ones who noticed him under the pier. We went down to see if he needed help, but could tell he was dead."

The officer got their names and then introduced himself as Vince Tucker and his partner as Jack Hendrick. Fred thought neither of them looked much older than Dave, but they were polite and professional. After asking them and the others to stay around, Officer Tucker suggested they could stand in the shade of the bait shop while he and Officer Hendrick examined the scene.

Fred watched with interest as the officers circled the body, being careful not to disturb anything, and put up the crime tape. They extended the tape from the edge of the building down both sides of the pier to the water's edge.

When that was done, Officer Tucker came back to where Fred and Allison stood, while his partner started taking names and interviewing the other people in the area.

Tucker asked Fred to explain how they'd found the body. The officer listened carefully and made notes as he and Allison told their stories. Fred assured him neither he nor his wife had touched the body other than

Allison checking for a pulse, and they hadn't disturbed the crime scene in any way.

"Good," Officer Tucker said. "Now I'm going to ask you stick around while I notify the county's sheriff department."

"So you don't have a city police department?" Fred asked.

"Not exactly," the lead officer explained. "Beacon Heights, the town on the other side of the bridge has their police department, but Beacon Beach is an unincorporated town within the county. We're known locally as the town cops, but our job is mainly to enforce local ordinances and take care of any minor disturbances. The sheriff's office handles the crimes."

"Yeah, I understand how that goes," Fred said. "We had the same kind of arrangement in our department."

Fred noticed Officer Tucker looked at him in surprise, started to say something, then shook his head, moved a distance away, and made his call.

Ending his call, the officer walked back to Fred, gave him a quizzical look. "Your department? You're in law enforcement?"

Fred gave Allison a quick glance before answering. He knew she'd heard the question and since she had a half-smile on her face, he interpreted it as a go-ahead.

"Was. Recently retired from thirty years in the Webster County Sheriff Department—the last several as detective."

"Homicides?"

"A few."

A grin lit up the officer's face. "Hey, Jack," he called over to his partner, "come here a sec."

Jack Hendrick looked up, put his pen in his pocket, ambled toward them, and asked, "What?"

"Mr. Sawyer here is a homicide detective. How great is that?"

"Yeah?" Officer Hendrick turned to Fred. "Where?"

"Webster County. Over two hundred miles from here. And it doesn't make any difference anyway. Like I told your partner, I'm retired—out of the game."

But Fred could tell Tucker wasn't buying his story.

"Sure. And I've got a retired bloodhound, but old Wilbur still likes to sniff around. Your input could be helpful to Ed."

"Who's Ed?"

"Ed Tuttle—the detective on his way here. He's good, but we don't have many homicides for him to practice on."

Fred knew Allison had been watching and listening to their entire confab, and he gave an inward shudder as she stepped forward. Clad only in her green swimsuit and with her flimsy beach towel tied around her waist, she appeared small and fragile, but the determined look on her face worried him. They hadn't been married quite long enough for him to completely read her mind, but he imagined she was going to insist he stay out of the investigation.

Her first words were not what he expected. "Fred did make some astute observations of the body which, I'm sure, he'll be glad to share with you and Ed."

The officer's gaze went from Fred to Allison and back again. "Oh," he said to Fred, "such as?"

So, while waiting for the county detective and crime techs to arrive, Fred explained his impression of the victim: his high-end clothing, his recent haircut, no apparent sign of a struggle, a missing watch, and no evidence of a wedding band. "However," Fred went on, "him standing under the pier, as opposed to simply strolling along the beach, may indicate he was planning on meeting someone there."

Tucker nodded. "Maybe someone he knew—or had a business deal with."

"That would be my guess, Officer Tucker."

The officer slapped Fred on the back. "Just call me 'Tuck.' Everybody does."

"Well then, Tuck, I have one other observation."

"And that is?"

"I expect the time of death was probably during the night. I said I hadn't touched the body, but that isn't exactly true." Fred paused, took a deep breath, and hoped his admission didn't get him in trouble with the local authorities. "While my wife was inside asking someone to call you, I did use my foot to move his right arm—only to determine if he was still in rigor. He wasn't."

Tuck nodded. "Yeah, he's been here quite a while—actually I could have told you that just from the aroma. Not that I've had much experience, but my guess is a dead body wouldn't do well in this heat."

ALLISON STOOD AND stared at the two cops as they wandered together across the sand: talking, getting acquainted, apparently sharing stories, bonding—and leaving her out of the loop. It wasn't exactly what she had in mind when she suggested Fred share his observations.

It was obvious he was enjoying himself, but she wasn't. Her stomach growled, her swimsuit itched, and her patience grew thin. The waning sun went under a cloud, the air started to turn cooler, and Allison was more than ready to head back to the beach house, jump in the shower, and get dressed. She wasn't accustomed to standing around for long periods of time in nothing but a bathing suit and a beach towel. When she couldn't decide whether to keep her butt or her boobs covered, she ran after her mate and his newfound friend. When she caught up with them, she snatched Fred's towel from around his neck, wrapped it around her shoulders, and said in her sweetest voice, "We really need to be getting back, Hon. The kids are going to be worried."

No need to explain to Tuck that the kids were all in their twenties and were probably too busy having a good time to worry about the old duffers. But the ploy got Tuck's attention for a few seconds. That attention, though, was instantly shifted when a car from the county sheriff's department pulled into the parking lot.

Allison forgot her discomfort as she watched a tall, lanky woman in beige slacks and a short-sleeve white shirt exit from the passenger side of the car and head in their direction. As she approached closer, Allison noted the reddish hair pulled back in a loose bun seemed to glisten with a few strands of silver and there appeared to be faint wrinkles between her eyebrows. Smiling, Allison thought, *Finally, here's an officer who isn't fresh from the cradle.*

The woman was followed by a bulky man probably in his late thirties who looked as if he was a regular in a gym. Both of the detectives had determined expressions. Allison took an instant liking to them.

Tuck did the introductions as he motioned to her and Fred, "Mr. and Mrs. Fred Sawyer, vacationers who found the body, and who have been most cooperative." Reversing his arm motion, he went on, "Detective Sheila Davidson, been with the department for years, best bowler in their league. And Detective Ed Tuttle. Don't let his brawn deceive you; he also has a few brains."

With their handshakes completed, Detective Tuttle got right down to business. "Let's see the body. The techs will be here soon to do their thing."

Thirty minutes later, the detectives had studied the crime scene, had heard all the information Tuck, Jack, Allison, and Fred had to offer, and of course, had learned about Fred's background in law enforcement. The last piece of information brought the same response as it had with the city cops and soon everyone was on a first name basis. The difference was that this time Allison was included in the clique when Fred mentioned they had first met at a murder scene. Then he went on to brag about her help in solving cases.

When the county crime techs were finished with their work and the body was ready to be transported to the morgue, Sheila smiled and said, "Thanks for your help, Allison, Fred, and be sure and let us know if you think of anything else that's pertinent."

"Will do," Allison agreed.

Ed shook Fred's hand. "I'll be in touch."

Tuck stepped forward, put his hand on Fred's back, "I'll drive you two back to your cottage. You've had a long afternoon."

Since darkness was already beginning to creep in, Fred readily accepted the ride and Allison sighed in resignation. It wouldn't be the first time she'd been escorted home in a police car. As she tried to relax in the back seat, she knew there would be no getting away from telling the kids about finding a murder victim since the death was sure to be discussed on the TV news. A reporter had arrived on the scene shortly after the county officers. He had either been alerted by someone or had overheard the police scanner.

Allison had hoped to sneak into the house under darkness and not explain immediately about their mode of transportation. It wasn't to be. Dave and Neil had turned on the back-porch light and were shooting baskets into a hoop affixed above the basement entrance.

The police car slowing down at their drive got their attention, and when the young officer jumped out and opened the door for Allison, they were momentarily speechless. But by the time Dave tossed the ball to Neil and rushed to her side, his power of speech had returned along with his wicked sense of humor. "Hey, Mom, what kind of trouble are you in now? I thought I told you to behave yourself on this trip."

Tugging the towel tighter around her chest and holding up one hand, Allison croaked out, "No questions until I shower and dress."

Fred waved goodbye to their driver without making any introductions. He called out, "See you later, Tuck."

Without another word, Allison marched up the steps. Fred hurried behind her, caught up in time to open the door for her. Out of the corner of her eye, she saw Fred motion to the boys to keep quiet. *Bless him*, she thought. *He knows I have to have some quiet time.* The thought of maybe being involved in another murder investigation had struck a raw nerve.

As she entered the kitchen, the comforting aroma of simmering stew started the soothing process her tired body and mind needed. Connie's smile and quick hug helped, too.

The healing took another leap when Trina said, "If

you tell me which bedroom you and Fred want, I'll carry your bags for you."

Through their college years, Trina had almost become like another daughter to her and could probably pass for one. She and Connie were both brunettes, statuesque, athletic. They'd shared dorm rooms, friends, angsts. Upon graduation, though, their interests parted. Trina took her BA into the art world while Connie entered med school. Allison was glad they'd been able to hold on to their friendship.

Turning her mind back to the matter at hand, Allison asked Fred. "Any preference?"

"Doesn't matter as long as it has a double bed and a bathroom close by."

Dave, apparently sensing it would be all right for him to open his mouth again, said, "Since I've scouted out the whole place, I can tell you the two choices. The rear bedroom upstairs has a queen-size bed and adjoining bath. The one downstairs next to the kitchen is a duplicate."

Allison pointed one finger toward the stairway. "Up. I want to get as far away from the kitchen as possible. I know the midnight appetites you kids have and I don't want to hear the refrigerator door opening after I'm in bed."

"Then," Dave said, "I assume you don't want to hear late-late-night TV either, so the younger generation will take the two rooms downstairs and leave the entire upper floor to the old folks."

Nodding, Allison said, "You could have worded that a little more nicely, but I agree with the conclusion. And right now, I need all the peace and quiet I can get."

"Up it is then," Trina said, grabbing two matching suitcases.

Connie found her mother's overnight case and snatched a bunch of towels from the linen closet. "Follow us to your boudoir, Madam, and when you complete your ablutions, dinner will be served."

Allison tried her best to get back into a better mood. "Boudoir? Ablutions? Have you been boning up again for a rematch Scrabble game?"

"Absolutely. I intend to regain my crown as reigning champ in the family."

After Connie left her, Allison took her time unpacking her bags, finding her pajamas and robe, laying out her creams and lotions. Even though her hands were busy, her mind was busier—remembering the dead man, how spongy his skin felt as she tried to find a pulse and how blood from his mangled head made dull red streaks through his blondish hair.

She grieved for whoever the gentleman was and for his family. Then, very selfishly, she grieved that his death had somehow tarnished what was meant to be a perfect vacation for their own family. Trying to put the tragic murder out of her mind, she headed for the shower. Maybe she could wash away at least some of the memory.

ONCE CONNIE CAME back downstairs, and Fred heard the water running upstairs, he gathered all the kids around him and quickly explained about finding the dead man and that he'd obviously been murdered.

Trina's dark eyes became darker, and one hand flew up to her mouth as if she were about to upchuck. Her voice trembled as she repeated, "Murdered? You mean there's a killer running loose on our beach?"

Fred immediately realized his mistake. In an effort to explain why they'd been detained and why Allison was upset, he'd upset the entire household. All four of the young people stared at him. Connie and Neil joined Trina with looks of distress although theirs were more subdued.

After an initial reaction of stunned unbelief, Dave mustered his usual bravado. "You mean we get to be in on another murder investigation?"

"Absolutely not. We're not getting involved." Even as he was saying the words, Fred's mind skittered back to when he was propped up in a hospital bed with Dave hanging over the side rails and the two of them going over all the clues to find a killer. The kid really had a keen mind, Fred thought, and would probably make a great detective. But on the other hand, he was glad Dave had decided to follow his mother into the education arena— much safer choice.

He should have known, though, Dave wouldn't give up easily and the boy's next words proved it. "But you let me get involved before."

"But that was personal. This incident has nothing to do with us. And don't say anything to your mother about it. This has been hard on her," Fred said. "Probably brought back some memories she would like to forget. We'll watch the late news tonight to see if the police have an identity yet, and it's bound to be a topic of conversation on the beach, but we're not going to spend time discussing it in this family." Turning to the girls, he went on, "And you have nothing to be afraid of, so don't let it spoil your vacation."

FOUR

THE LATE-NIGHT TV news from the Wilmington station spent very little time reporting on the body found at Beacon Beach. Even though the information was skimpy, all six people in the pink house on Shoreline Drive listened intently. Fred sipped a cup of black decaf coffee; Allison nibbled on lightly salted almonds; the young people devoured bags of high caloric, high cholesterol, highly salted chips. Allison sighed remembering the days when she could do that with impunity.

The perky woman newscaster had put on her serious face as she reported a possible homicide at Sammy's Pier. "According to the police report, the victim was found by a couple walking on the beach. To date, there had been no identification of the man and no missing person bulletin that fits the victim's description." That was followed, not with a photo of the dead man's face, but rather with a sketch of what he probably looked like when he was still in the land of the living. "If anybody has any information about the man's identity or of the crime, please contact the local police department."

Allison slipped over closer to Fred. "Nice-looking fellow. Was he simply in the wrong place at the wrong time? Maybe been flashing money around and got someone's attention?"

"Could be. Or he met someone he thought was a friend and found out otherwise."

"Or," another voice joined in, "he'd arranged a drug buy, but the dealer upped the ante."

Allison stared at her son and shivered. "Dave, I don't even want to hear what you know about drug buys."

He shrugged. "Fine. I won't mention drugs again, but I do have a question about the report."

"And what is that?"

"Why did the reporter say, 'possible homicide'? The guy couldn't very well have hit himself on the head."

"I guess it could have been an accident," Trina said. "Maybe he had an argument with a friend, and he fell and hit his head on a post."

"And the friend left him there to die?" Neil said. "In a case like that, I think it's called negligent homicide—or something like that."

Fred lowered the TV volume, rose, reached his hand out for Allison. "I suggest all of you forget about the unfortunate man, no matter how he met his death, and concentrate on a game of rummy or Monopoly or something. You can stay up as late as you want as long as you keep the racket to a minimum. We old folks are heading for bed."

He squeezed his bride's hand, gave her a wink. Her lips curled up in a smile as they climbed the stairs hand in hand.

A chorus of "good nights" followed after them as Connie set up the card table.

SLINK WATCHED THE late-night news along with most of the other residents and visitors in the coastal community. When the reporter mentioned about no ID, Slink nodded. *And he probably won't be identified for a while. No family around here and no ties. And I doubt anyone*

*will remember seeing us together. I'm home free, and
all I need to do now is find the blasted money he hid
in the pink house.*

FRED AWOKE TO find the other side of the bed empty, but
the pillow still had the imprint of Allison's head and a
faint scent of her shampoo. The bedroom door was open
and the clang of something apparently dropped in the
kitchen echoed up the stairs as did the laughter of young
voices. He lay there and savored it all. He was still getting used to having a family. Although he and Allison
had been married over a year now, the kids had either
been in school or on summer jobs. It was great having
them and their friends here for the week. As his mind
flashed back to finding the dead body the evening before, he declared to the empty room, "And no murderer
is going to spoil this vacation."

Pulling on his walking shorts and a fresh tee shirt,
he hurried downstairs. Allison greeted him with a peck
on the cheek, Dave handed him a cup of black, regular coffee, and Neil gave him a comic salute. The girls
weren't in sight, but he could hear stirrings in the back
bedroom.

Looking out the front windows at the cloudless sky,
Fred announced his approval. "Going to be a good one."
He turned to Dave. "You and Neil have any plans for
this morning?"

"There's a good breeze, so we thought we'd go to the
Surf Shack, rent some boards, and try our luck. After
breakfast, of course."

"Of course," his mother echoed. "My boy has never
been known to miss a meal."

Ignoring the interruption, Dave went on, "After a

couple of hours of riding the waves, we figured that there ought to be some life on the beach, like of the female variety." He paused a second and when no comments came from the sidelines, he went on, "and I really need to make some friends this week. You know, widen my horizons."

Fred nodded. "A noble ambition."

After pouring a heaping bowl of crunchy cereal, Dave started to reach for the milk when he suddenly seemed to remember the manners his mother had tried to instill in him through the years. He stopped, turned to Fred and asked politely, "What are you and Mom planning for today?"

Before either one could answer, two bathing beauties emerged from their bedroom. "Fred," Connie asked, "are you going to be using your car this morning?"

Fred stared at the scanty suits, and knowing he would sound like a protective father, said anyway, "And where do you plan to go dressed like that?"

Connie's eyebrows shot up while Trina let out a tiny giggle.

Dave yelped, "Way to go, Pops!"

Fred waited for Allison to stop laughing and for Connie to regain her composure. Connie was the winner as she patiently explained, "Right now we're going to lie on the beach, catch some rays, and maybe take a dip. However, after that, we'll return here, eat a bite and put on some decent clothes. After which, we were hoping to use your car so we could check out some antiques shops. Since Trina is now working at a museum, she's trying to educate me about artifacts of past cultures."

"Oh, okay," Fred said, hoping his tan was deep enough to cover up any blushing he might be doing.

"No problem. And when you leave we'll give you a house key so you can get in just in case the rest of us are gone."

"Good." Connie tugged at Trina's arm. "Come on. I need you to unfasten my top so my tan doesn't get messed up with strap marks."

Fred shook his head as the girls snickered on their way out the door.

Wearing only his swimming trunks, Neil entered the room with a wide grin, "Gee, Dave, I guess that means we'll have to put shirts on when we go to church in the morning. I don't want your pops to disapprove of how I dress."

Fred threw up his hands.

ALLISON DECIDED SHE'D better cram a donut in her mouth before she said something that might embarrass Fred even further.

Dave, also, was ready to move on. "That reminds me that Neil and I are going to need a house key, too. We're planning on checking out the arcade later, see if they have any games for mature fellows. Then if the beach is barren, we may prowl the coffee shop in search of companionship. And since the girls have dinner duty tonight, I don't know when we'll be back."

"The trouble is," Fred said, "the rental agent only gave us two keys. I guess I'd better go down there and get another one for the older generation."

"Wait a little bit and I'll go with you," Allison said. "I want to call Clarisse first and check on Elmer and Lancelot."

Dave looked up from his cereal bowl and shook his

head. "Mom, don't tell me you foisted those two on your nice neighbor."

"Of course not. I wouldn't do that." Allison paused. "Clarisse volunteered to look after them. She loves animals."

"What am I missing here?" Neil asked. "Who are Elmer and Lancelot?"

"Strays that Mom picked up in her travels. Elmer is a shepherd with so much hair he needs an air-conditioned doghouse, and Lancelot is a tomcat who hates men. Go figure."

Allison knew Dave was just baiting her, but she went along with the game. "Elmer's dog house is not air conditioned. I simply asked Fred to install a ceiling fan. After all, he's a mountain dog and not accustomed to our hot summers." She turned to Neil to explain further. "He belonged to my aunt who lived near Asheville and when she died, I naturally had to take care of her dog. And as for Lancelot, the cat does not hate men. It just takes him a while to warm up to them, and Dave's not home enough to make friends with him. Lancelot and Fred have actually become quite close. Now, if you'll excuse me, I'll go out on the porch to call Clarisse and inquire of their welfare."

"Tell Clarisse to give them my love," Dave called after her.

As she went out the door, she heard Dave remark to Neil, "I wonder what pet she'll take home this trip."

She smiled at Neil's answer. "Seems to me her choice would be between a seagull and a crab. I'm sure both would make a great addition to your household."

When she came back in after her lengthy conversation with Clarisse, Fred had finished eating and the boys were cleaning up the kitchen area.

Fred motioned her toward the back door. "Ready? Let's get that extra key and check out downtown."

The realty office shared a building with a fishing equipment store with ads about boat rentals in the window. After parking the car, Fred said to Allison. "You go ahead and get the key. I want to check out the boats and stuff."

Allison hesitated before getting out. "But what if people are talking about the dead man at the pier? What if they ask me something?"

"They probably have already discussed it up, down, and sideways among themselves, but they're not going to mention it to visitors. They wouldn't want to scare off any of their paying customers. And there's no reason for anybody to ask you about it as our names weren't mentioned on the news at all."

"Right. Guess I'm just a little nervous." She sighed, smiled, got out, and headed for the realty office while Fred aimed for the fishing store.

Since Fred had picked up their keys when they arrived, Allison wasn't sure which of the three people in the room she should talk to. The three desks were placed somewhat like a semicircle. To her left sat a thirtyish man with sandy hair and a bored expression while next to him was a thirtyish redhead with a fake smile. The remaining desk was occupied by a sixtyish woman with gray hair and a mildly pleasant face. She knew she was playing the age game again. As she grew older she had a tendency to categorize business people she met into groups roughly labeled as: too young to understand her problem, too occupied to care about her problem, and lastly, busy but willing to listen to her problem. Even though getting another key really shouldn't be a problem at all, she settled on the gray-haired woman wearing a gray sweater and gold-framed bifocal glasses. The woman reminded her of a fellow teacher—old enough to retire, but not ready to give up the geniality of the working place.

The air conditioning was a welcomed relief from the outside temperature, but it must have been a little too cool for the woman because she tugged her sweater tighter. Her name tag identified the woman as Naomi Platt. Allison gave her a warm smile and slid into the chair in front of the desk. "Good morning, Ms. Platt. We're renting one of your houses and we need another key."

The pleasant look vanished and a high-pitched voice seemed to hurl an accusation across the desk even though it was posed as a question. "You lost a key already?"

Allison took a deep breath, gathered her dignity around her, and answered. "No, Ma'am. We still have both keys, but…"

"Well, if they don't fit, then you must have been too rough with them. We'll have to charge you to replace them."

Allison had always been respectful of her elders, but she quickly decided that rude people came in all age groups. Before she could make a retort, the one in front of her asked, "What's the address?"

Answering louder than necessary, she said, "327 Shoreline Drive."

"Oh, yes, one of our more popular houses. You're lucky to get it. Someone called and asked for that house specifically right after you made your reservation. It seems the least you could do is take care of the keys."

"We have taken care of the keys, but you only gave us two and we need three."

Mrs. Platt's gaze went back to the key rack. "But there are three keys gone, so obviously, we gave you three keys."

"No, Ma'am. My husband said he was given only two keys."

"Then he must have gotten careless and lost one."

"My husband is not a careless man." Allison was having a hard time keeping her voice and her temper under control.

She turned her head as she heard a movement at the next desk. The redheaded woman stood up and crossed the room. She apparently had heard their conversation and was going to intervene. She tapped the older woman on the shoulder. "I can do this, Mrs. Platt."

Naomi Platt glared at the interloper for a few moments, sputtered, "But I always do the keys."

"I know, but you seem a little upset. Why don't you take a break? You might feel better after a cup a tea."

Mrs. Platt slowly rose to her feet. Lifting her chin up and pulling her sweater even tighter, she carefully positioned one heel against the base of her rolling desk chair and pushed it backward. The chair shot across the tile floor and slammed into the water cooler right behind her. Both Allison and the redhead stared as the water cooler trembled slightly and its contents sloshed against the inside of the large plastic bottle on top. Mrs. Platt seemed to take no notice as she marched to a room in the rear of the building and slammed the door.

After the water stopped gyrating and the slamming

door stopped reverberating, Miss Redhead, or as her name tag read, Meg Freeman, smiled apologetically. "I'm sorry. Mrs. Platt gets upset sometimes because of all the young people coming in here saying they've lost their keys."

Allison's ruffled feathers gradually fell back in place. It was almost worth the rudeness to be thought of as a "young person."

Ms. Freeman reached down, fingered a lever on the desk chair and lowered it until her eyes were even with the computer screen. Allison felt a moment of empathy with the tall woman, although Meg's problem was just the opposite from Allison's. Being short, Allison always had to adjust her desk chair upward if anyone else had used it, whereas, Ms. Freeman, being usually tall for a woman, had to lower the chair.

Meg Freeman became all business. "You said 327 Shoreline?"

"That's right."

After typing a few strokes, she looked up, asked, "And the renter's name?"

Allison knew Meg had the name in front of her, but the agent wasn't about to give a key to someone off the street without verification.

"Fred Sawyer."

Nodding, she looked over at Allison again. "And you're?"

Quickly filling in the blank, Allison answered with, "Mrs. Fred Sawyer."

The very competent agent nodded and held out her hand. "May I see your receipt for the house?"

"Of course." Allison reached into her handbag, pulled out a crumpled piece of paper had Fred had given her earlier, and handed it across the desk. "There you are—327 Shoreline Drive—signed by N. Platt."

As Meg Freeman handed the receipt back, Allison accepted it in one hand and held out the other for the expected key, but the agent wasn't quite through with her yet.

"And your ID."

Allison sighed. She disliked people who apparently needed to show their authority by making others turn cartwheels. Then she immediately rejected her rash judgment of the woman behind the desk. Ms. Freeman was merely following protocol and there was no need to get prickly about it. Reaching into her bag, she pulled out her driver's license, and handed it over.

The agent glanced at the license, paused, frowned, studied the picture, and handed it back. "The picture is you, but it's made out to Allison Aldridge."

Allison cringed, gave a little laugh. "I can explain that. You see Fred and I only recently married and I decided to keep my previous name for professional purposes." Noting the doubt in the woman's face across the desk, Allison became defensive. "It's not that unusual. Lots of women have a professional name different from their married name."

Meg Freeman smiled. "Of course. I understand. If I ever get married, I'll keep that option in mind. Although most married women I know are glad to change their names."

The comments surprised and irritated Allison. Since Meg looked to be in her mid-thirties and was definitely attractive, Allison wondered briefly why the woman was still single—but it was none of her concern. As to why she kept using her professional name, that was certainly none of the realtor's business and there was no need for Allison to have to explain it further.

Retrieving her license, she jammed it back into her purse and to forestall any other questions, Allison explained, "And the reason we need another key is that there are six of us in our group and we often pair off to go in different directions."

"Certainly. I understand. Young people these days like to take off on their own." She reached behind her, opened the correct drawer, pulled out a shiny new key. "There you are, and I hope all of you have a lovely week."

Pocketing the key, Allison headed toward the door, but was stopped by the man who'd sat at the third desk in the room. Apparently, he'd listened carefully to both conversations because he called her by name. "Mrs. Sawyer, I want to add my apology for your unfortunate encounter with Mrs. Platt. I'm Clyde Johansen, the manager."

His right hand levitated in front of her face and she noted the long, thin fingers, the perfectly manicured nails, his lily-white skin, the emerald ring that seemed to shimmer in the sunlight streaming through the window. It was a moment before she realized he was waiting for her to shake his hand. She did so and mouthed the expected words, "I'm glad to meet you, Mr. Johansen." She wasn't the least bit surprised to find his hand was as soft as the proverbial baby's bottom. His man, she thought, hadn't done a day's hard work in his life or played tennis or gone sailing or participated in any sport that might raise a callus on his fingers. On a more positive note, though, his hands might be perfect for holding a winning poker hand or performing a healing massage.

She'd only glanced at him upon entering the office, but now tipping her head back slightly, she got the full effect of his Nordic blue eyes and hair blond enough to make a Clairol model envious. She glanced quickly away as his mouth started to move again.

"I assure you I'll deal with the situation."

Allison was instantly alarmed. She certainly didn't want poor Mrs. Platt to get fired over a minor lapse of manners. "Don't worry about it," she said. "We all slip up from time to time."

She tried to maneuver around him, but the long fingers of his right hand caught her arm while his left hand held out a piece of paper. "I want you to have this from our agency."

Frowning, Allison reached up and took what looked like a grocery coupon. When he released her arm, she stepped back, quickly slipped on her reading glasses, and studied the slip of paper. Her voice cracked a little as she read out loud, "Free lunch entrees at Masuki Japanese Steak and Seafood House, Beacon Heights." *Fred Sawyer* had been written in the name space, followed by the numeral *6* and the date was for the coming Monday. It was signed by Clyde Johansen.

"We can't accept this," Allison protested. "It's too much."

Clyde smiled. "Nothing is too much to protect our good name. We hope you and your family will come back every year and share your vacations with us. And you might even like to recommend our agency to your friends who are planning a beach vacation."

"Thank you. We probably will come back. It's a lovely beach area." Allison pocketed the coupon as she hurried out the door. She appreciated the manager's effort to establish goodwill with his clientele, but still thought the gift was a little over the top. And she had absolutely no plans to recommend the agency to anybody. Her suspicious nature kicked in. Was he afraid she would file a lawsuit over a little rudeness? Or was Mrs. Platt's behavior her norm and he wanted to whitewash it? Or did his employee have some kind of hold over him that she could get away with being rude to their renters?

Allison knew her suppositions were probably way off base. She should simply be glad about the peace offering and surprise Fred with a free lunch.

As she walked down the sidewalk Fred came out of the fishing/boat store with a million-dollar grin on his face. "Look what I got!"

That was exactly what she'd intended to say to him, but since he beat her to it, she asked as if she were really interested, "What?"

"A deep-sea fishing cruise for the boys and me."

It took a second for her mind to register the fact that her dearly beloved husband had just committed a sexist blunder. She reared back, put her hands on her hips, and said softly, "And you didn't think the girls and I would be interested in deep sea fishing? Or didn't you think we were capable of it?"

Her sarcasm didn't faze him. "Yes, I thought you might be interested, and yes, I know all of you are extremely capable. But, I heard the three of you on the way down making plans to shop the outlet stores and since you seemed to infer that the males in the household wouldn't care to join you, I figure we men would have to come up with something ourselves."

"I see." Allison's features relaxed. "Well, that's different." Inwardly, she was glad to have been excluded from the fishing trip. She enjoyed fishing in small lakes, but didn't relish the thought of hauling in something bigger than herself. However, she wasn't yet ready to let Fred know that. "And," she asked, "what day did you plan for your escapade?"

"Wednesday morning."

She smiled. "Good. I'm glad it's not Monday because I have plans for everybody then, and it won't cost us a pretty penny."

"That sounds good. What is it?"

"Lunch paid for by the realty manager." She waved the coupon in front of his face.

He grabbed it and took his time reading it, and said, "Free lunch? What did you do to deserve this? Pick a lucky number? Smile at the gentleman especially nicely?"

Poking him in the arm, she snatched her prize back. "Just for that I think I'll ask Mrs. Platt to take your place."

"Who's Platt?"

"A very unpleasant elderly woman who works there." Allison explained the whole bizarre episode with Mrs. Platt, the rescue by Ms. Freeman, and the apology from Mr. Johansen, the manager.

"Oh, yeah," he said. "I remember the old lady. She's the one who gave me the original keys. She was nice to me. Too bad you had to rile her."

"I did nothing to rile…" Allison stopped in mid-sentence when she realized Fred was just trying to get a rise out of her. "Anyway, just remember, this is my treat. You're still on the hook another day for the steaks you promised everybody."

"Oh, I haven't forgotten. In fact, I think we'll do that Thursday evening—before our moonlight cruise."

"Moonlight cruise? What are you talking about now?"

Fred put his arm around her waist and propelled her toward the door he'd just exited. "Come on. I want you to meet Ben."

They had to transverse the entire length of the store to get to the counter in the back. Allison saw more kinds of fishing poles and tackle gear displayed than she ever imagined existed. Behind the fishing paraphernalia were pictures of several boats with all the pictures showing results of a successful day of deep-sea fishing. One showed a man grinning at a six-foot marlin hanging upside down and another was of a group of guys with enough fish on their strings to feed their families an entire year. Allison shuddered at both of them and hoped fervently that Fred and the boys didn't bring back anything nearly that big or that much.

When they reached their destination, she tore her eyes away from the pictures and focused on the person behind the counter—and blinked in amazement. The man Fred was introducing as Ben Johansen appeared to be a replica of Clyde, the realty manager, as far as his facial features and height went. But that's where the resemblance ended. This man was many years older, his skin bronzed and crinkled by the sun, and his blond hair streaked with gray. When Allison shook his extended hand, she noticed the same long, thin fingers, but instead of a recent manicure, Ben had dirt and/or grease under his nails and rough calluses on his palms.

And instead of Clyde's carefully modulated voice, Ben's came out loud and boisterous. "So you're the beautiful blushing bride Fred wants to take on a romantic moonlight cruise." Ben stopped just long enough to give her a quick grin before continuing his palaver. "I got to admit the old boy has mighty good taste."

Allison laughed. "And I thought the Irish had a monopoly on flattery."

"No way. Us Vikings know a lovely woman when we see one, too. That's about the only thing my son and I have in common." He drummed his fingers on the counter, nodded his head. "Fred said you were next door, so I guess you met him."

Pretending innocence, Allison said, "Oh, is Clyde your son? When I saw you, I figured he might be a younger brother."

"Hey, you're not only beautiful, but diplomatic as well. Of course, I know I don't look old enough to have a son that's over thirty, but that's because meeting good-looking women keeps me young."

"Okay, you two," Fred interrupted with a shake of his head, "enough dancing around. I'm surprised some jealous husband hasn't already shot you, Ben. Just tell her about the cruise so we can get on with our day."

Ben snapped to attention. "Yes, Sir, cruise info coming up."

Allison smiled; Fred rolled his eyes.

Pointing to a picture on the wall behind him, Ben said, "Let me introduce to the newest member of the fleet, *The Jolly Weigh,* a boat meant for pleasure cruising, sight-seeing, romantic getaways, and moonlight fantasies."

"It's lovely." She nodded her approval of the sleek, blue and white vessel as she wondered how much a boat like that cost. She figured Ben must do a really good business here to afford it. Allison went on, "I was afraid I might be going out in a smelly fishing boat." She slammed a hand over her mouth, then quickly said, "Not that there's anything wrong with fishing. I've done some fishing myself, it's just that…" Unable to find the right words, she glanced at Fred for help, but he was laughing too hard to come to her rescue.

Ben patted her hand. "I understand. At the end of a long day, the stench of dead fish, rotting bait, and sweating anglers can be overpowering—and no amount of scrubbing can get rid of it. Which is exactly why we invested in this new boat which will never be used for fishing."

"A wise decision," Fred said.

"I think so. It can carry ten passengers. My partner and I will alternate as captain just as we do with the fishing boat, and since the store will be closed as usual in the evening, my assistant here will do the wining and dining of the passengers."

Ben called over to a young man who was restocking shelves with presumably items no avid fisherman could resist. "Wes, come here. I want you to meet somebody."

Wes turned in their direction, shrugged, and slowly headed down the aisle. Allison figured he was still in high school, that this was a summer job, and that he really wasn't enthused with the whole boating bit. Nevertheless, he went through the correct motions, shook hands with Fred, assured Allison she would love the cruise.

She gave the kid a reassuring smile and said, "Sounds like a perfect evening. I'm looking forward to Thursday night."

"And I'm looking forward to having such a charming passenger."

Allison threw her head back and gave a laugh would qualify for a TV show sound track. "The Chamber of Commerce in Beacon Beach must give all its male citizens lessons in chivalry. I haven't heard that much blatant flattery in years."

Wes shrugged. "Just following orders." He gave her sly grin. "Did it work?"

"Absolutely. And it'll work even better on my lovely daughter and her friend. They'll enjoy meeting such a handsome gentleman." Allison knew neither girl would give the kid a second glance, but she, too, could play this flattery game.

Fred was relieved to hear Allison's approbation of his plans, but now he had a question for Ben. "You hadn't mentioned a partner before. Does that mean you might not be the one that takes the boys and me out fishing Wednesday or on the cruise Thursday?"

Ben laughed. "Hey, I'm a pretty tough guy, but I can't work all the time. Have to have a little relaxation myself."

Fred grinned. "Well, I certainly wouldn't want you to work too hard on my account."

Wes, who'd leaned over the counter apparently waiting to be dismissed, added, "No danger of that. Ben takes off any morning or afternoon whenever the urge hits him."

"Why not? I figured that's what bosses are supposed to do." He shooed Wes away and turned his attention back to Fred. "Not to worry, though, you'll like Zack. He's bulldog ugly, but a real sweetheart—when you get to know him."

Smiling, Fred went along with the joke. "He can't be

much uglier than you, so I guess we'll be friends. See you later—or not."

He hustled Allison toward the door. It was time to get on with the day. The kids could go any direction they wished while he and his bride relaxed on the beach.

It turned out to be a lovely morning. The temperature was comfortable, the ocean breezes refreshing. The younger set took off in separate cars—with separate keys. Fred locked up the house with his own key, lugged beach umbrellas and folding chairs through the sand and set up his post near the lifeguard stand. Allison carried the towels, a bag of snacks and drinks, and another bag filled with an assortment of reading material and her cell phone just in case one of the kids called.

The day was a splendid mixture of staring at the waves, imagining faraway lands, quick swims, long naps, quiet chats, holding hands from adjoining chairs, and languid reading. The beach filled up: youngsters squealed as they ran in and out of the water, teens flirted, lifeguards blew their whistles. It all added to the ambience.

It was mid-afternoon when Fred stirred, rose, brushed off some sand, and said, "Want to take a walk?"

Allison squinted, seemed to think about it. "Not really."

"Mind if I do?"

"Not at all. Just don't get lost." She closed her eyes again, murmured, "Where you headed?"

"Thought I'd check in on Tuck."

"But you said last night the case has nothing to do with us."

"It hasn't. Just call it professional curiosity."

She dropped back in her chair. "Fine. Just promise

to tell me everything you learn. As you know, I can be a little curious, too."

Her last remark made him shudder. Her curiosity last February had gotten her kidnapped and nearly killed. It was one thing to want to follow the investigation from the sidelines, but it something entirely else to get personally involved. He may give his professional opinion if asked, and Allison might even offer her own opinion, but that was as far as it would go.

IN THE LATE AFTERNOON, Slink ambled by the pink house, noted both cars were gone, no sign of anyone being home. *Maybe I should take a quick look, check out that last upstairs bedroom. Or not. Some of them could return unexpectedly. I'll wait until Monday, but no longer than that. I'm going to continue my search. I've got to find the cash that my dearly departed friend hid. I guess I shouldn't have hit him so hard. If I had controlled my temper, I might have slowly tortured the information out of him. But there's nothing to do now except keep looking—and nobody better get in my way.*

FIVE

EVEN THOUGH IT was Saturday, Fred knew the local police wouldn't be taking any part of the weekend off—not with a dead John Doe on their hands. He figured the town cops wouldn't mind if he wandered down to the station to chat a bit. In fact, Tuck had told him to come back anytime. So why not take him up on the invitation?

Tuck had told him yesterday the police station was on a side street only a couple of blocks north of the crime scene pier. Fred had learned the name of that pier, which was on the north side of the Beacon Beach town limits, was called "Sammy's Pier" while the one in the other direction was named "Mammy's Pier." He had no idea who Sammy and Mammy were or if the names had just been drawn from a hat. At any rate, they were easy to remember. The pink house his family had rented was just about halfway between the two piers.

Carrying his sandals, Fred scuffed his feet in the sand with an occasional venture into the splashing waves. He also got unexpectedly splashed by two rambunctious boys racing each other into the water. He reveled in all of it and for a few moments he felt completely at peace.

That peace was shattered as he approached Sammy's Pier. As expected, though, all evidence of any crime happening under the pier had been removed and the area raked over. But it wasn't so easy for Fred to erase the picture of the young dead man whose head had been bashed in. Even after years in law enforcement, he hadn't become hardened to the brutality of murder.

Two pretty little girls, probably five or six played in the shadow of the pier, busy erecting their own version of a medieval castle. A few feet away, a teenager—either their big sister or a baby sitter—lounged on the sand, her eyes glued to an ebook reader. He sincerely hoped she would look up occasionally to check on her charges. Since he'd taken on the fatherhood role, Fred had become more aware of potential dangers that surrounded children everywhere. He was glad his new job in the school system gave him a chance to perhaps mitigate some of the dangers.

Crossing over to the public parking lot, Fred slipped on his sandals and hurried down the block, anxious to hear if there'd been any developments in the case. As he approached the station, Fred could see Vince Tucker through the window, bent over his desk, flipping through papers. The young cop looked up as the door opened, smiled, waved in his visitor. The officer rose and headed toward the door. They met in the middle of the room, shook hands.

"Good to see you, Fred. Glad you stopped by."

Fred nodded to his counterpart of thirty years ago: green, eager to please and, judging from his haggard look, feeling a bit overwhelmed. "Thanks for letting me," he said. "I really don't have any business here."

Tuck motioned him to a chair, sat back down behind the desk. "I'm beginning to think I don't have any business here, either. In fact, I'm really glad the county detectives are doing the investigation. Murder is a little out of my league."

"Does Ed keep you posted?"

"Oh, yeah. And Jack and I have been doing a little legwork for him: passing around the sketch of the victim, checking motels in the area. No one seems to be missing a guest, and at this point, no one in the nearby restaurants will admit to seeing him."

"So no luck at all on IDing the man?"

Tuck shook his head. "Ed says his prints aren't in the system. They're checking stores around that carry his brands of clothes. Nothing so far. No abandoned car found yet, but he certainly didn't look like a hitchhiker. Ed sent the sketch out to all law enforcement departments in the surrounding states. No missing person reports that match, but we did get a sketch in return from Atlanta."

"Oh?"

"Yep. Seems that our man somewhat resembles a guy seen at a liquor store robbery back in the winter. There were two of them, both wearing ski masks, but the store owner struggled with one, got a glimpse of his face before the perp shot him."

"But he survived and gave the police a description?"

"Sure did," Tuck said, "and it pretty much matches our John Doe. But since the liquor store case is still open with no leads, it doesn't help us much."

Fred put on his thoughtful face, ran a hand through his thinning hair, wiggled in the less than comfortable chair.

Eyeing him across the desk, Tuck gave an exasperated sigh, "Well, are you going to say something, or just sit there looking wise?"

Fred grinned. "No one's ever accused me of looking wise, but I rather like the idea. It sure would be helpful when I'm counseling some recalcitrant students. Maybe I need to practice looking wise in front of a mirror so I can be sure to get it right." Before Tuck could made a retort, Fred went on. "But I guess you're not interested in that. Now what were we discussing?" Fred paused just long enough to get a slight smile out of the young officer. "Oh, yes, that liquor store job. I'd like to postulate on that case a little."

Leaning back in his chair, Tuck waved a hand at his visitor. "Go ahead. Postulate. But keep it simple. I don't have a dictionary in the office."

Fred was liking the young officer more by the minute. He could take a little teasing without getting mad. That was important in police work.

"All right. This is how I think it went down. The robbery probably took place right at closing time on a Saturday night which was before a big Sunday TV football game. And there was a full cash register because fans were stocking up on their refreshments, and the owner hadn't had a chance to get to the bank."

"Bingo!" The young officer stared in admiration at Fred for several seconds before he apparently realized what had just happened. "That was no guess." His voice oozed disappointment. "You'd heard about the robbery when it happened and remembered it."

Fred laughed. "Almost got ya."

Tuck pulled out the two sketches from beneath his files, handed them to Fred. "Well, if your memory is so good, how come you didn't recognize him as the Atlanta perp when our sketch was shown on TV?"

After studying the two pictures, one from the crime scene and the other from Atlanta, Fred bobbed his head. "They are a lot alike. I should have caught it."

"So, any ideas of why a big-city crook would be hanging around our little town?"

"Sure. Get away from traffic. Work on his tan. Eye the beach babes. Or, how about this—hire a boat to whisk him away to Bermuda."

"In other words you haven't the faintest."

"That's about it. Anything else you can tell me?"

"The prelim autopsy is about what you would expect. Healthy, early thirties, organs and teeth in good condition. Apparently, he hadn't led a hard life. Would be interesting to know what led him to a life of crime. No needle marks or other signs of drug use, but it'll take a while to get the tox screen back. Death between midnight and four. Hard to pinpoint because of the heat. At least two blows on the head with a heavy object—most likely the butt of a gun. No big driftwood in this area. And it seems that he might have taken a while to die."

Fred held up a hand to halt the recitation. "Why would they think that?"

"The ground underneath the body was pawed, as if he'd tried to get up."

"Oh, right. I think I noticed that, but it slipped my mind." Wiping a hand over his mouth, Fred posed his next question. "But if he died during the night, isn't it strange his body wasn't noticed until late afternoon?"

"No. Very few people on this beach during the day on Fridays. Outgoing renters leave in the morning and the others don't come in until later."

"Okay. I get that. And there were no footprints of the guy and his attacker or any indication of which direction they'd come from?"

Tuck shook his head. "Dry sand doesn't really hold

footprints and the high tide would have wiped out any by the water."

Standing up, Fred walked around, pondered the information, came up with another comment. "I noticed railroad tracks west of town. Any passenger trains come through here?"

"Just freight as far as I know. If there are passenger trains they certainly don't slow down. Probably the closest station would be Wilmington. Some Greyhounds go through Beacon Heights, on the other side of the bridge, with groups going to Myrtle Beach, but none make regular stops there."

"Then here's the dilemma as I see it," Fred said. "You have a man killed in your lovely little town with no ID on him, who no one claims to know, with no means of transportation, with no rented lodging and who doesn't eat out. Your conclusion?"

"Okay, I'm going to take a wild guess. He rides in with a friend, maybe his partner from the Atlanta job. They don't need a room because...?" The young cop looked to Fred for help.

Fred shrugged.

"Because," Tuck plowed bravely on, "they do know someone here who is going to put them up, feed them, show them a good time. But something goes wrong. The partner or the host kills him and then both of the others skip town. How does that sound?"

"It's as good as anything I can come up with. Of course, he could have driven in, parked his car in a residential area, and no one has complained about it yet. But I'm sure that Ed and Sheila will have something soon."

Glancing at the office clock, Fred headed for the door. "I've got to get out of here before my wife issues a missing person bulletin on me." With his hand on the door knob, Fred made a quick U-turn, reached down to the desk, and picked up a scrap of paper. Jutting down some numbers, he said, "I know I don't have a bit of right to be here, but if you think I can be of any help, just let me know."

He handed the paper to Tuck. "My cell."

CONNIE LOWERED HER packages to the front porch floor, unlocked the door, and motioned Trina in. Both of them dropped their loot on one couch and flopped down on the other.

"Whew. I'm ready for a nap," Trina said. "Too bad it's our night to do the cooking." When Connie didn't respond, she asked, "You want to do the salad or put the cookies in the oven?"

Connie shook her head. "I don't care."

"What's the matter? You worried about something? You haven't said a word since we left Madame de Hoya's Antiques. You want to take your lucky bookends back that you bought?"

Shaking her head again, Connie said, "Of course not. I've already gotten fond of them, although I probably did pay too much for a couple of old horseshoes."

"Horseshoes that Madame assured you were lucky and hinted they were from the Wyatt Earp era and had somehow made their way here from the Wild West."

Connie smiled. "The woman did come up with quite an imaginative story." She drew her treasures out of their bag, examined how the horseshoes had been welded on to heavy pieces of metal to form bookends. "These things are strong enough to hold *Gray's Anatomy, Diseases of the Circulatory System,* and the *Complete*

Pharmacopoeia. They'll look great on the top of my bookcase. And they had better be lucky because I'll need all the good luck I can garner to get though the next few years."

She placed them on a small table by the stairs and stuck a couple of fishing magazines between them. "There, my pretties. You sit there and start stirring the good luck brew for my next year in med school."

As she headed for the kitchen, she called back, "Well, come on, Trina. You said we had to get dinner started. I'll do the meat loaf and salad. You can do the sides and dessert."

By keeping Trina busy, Connie hoped she would forget the question she'd asked earlier. It didn't happen, although Trina did wait a little bit before bringing it up again.

The chocolate chip cookies came out of the oven, wafting their tempting aroma throughout the kitchen. Connie resisted grabbing one as she lowered the oven temp, let some of the heat escape and then slid in the meat loaf.

It was then her friend made her move. "Okay, you've fretted long enough. If you suck on that lower lip any longer, you'll lose all your kissibility."

Connie shook her head. "You know me too well."

"I should after four years. Now tell your soul sister what's bothering you."

"The body."

Trina scowled, walked over to the cooling cookies, chose one, took a bite, and swallowed before continuing the conversation. "You're referring to the dead body found under the pier by your mother. Right?"

"Right."

"But Fred said the murder had nothing to do with us."

"At this point it doesn't have anything to do with us. But think about it. Fred is a detective and Mom has an ingrained snooping gene when it comes to mysteries. Neither one of them will be able to let it go. They're going to nose around, pick up some information, and in the process, put themselves in danger."

"I don't follow. Why would they be in danger?"

Trina jumped as Connie slapped her hand against the counter. "Don't you see? There's a killer in town. He's watching the police. He's listening to the gossip. He's heard the story about who found the victim. Believe me, he knows what's going on, and if he feels threatened, he'll kill again."

Instead of Trina pooh-poohing her fears as Connie expected, her friend gave her a hug. "Then you and I will just have to keep a close eye on them," she said, "and keep them reined in."

Connie appreciated the support, but she also knew that Trina's suggestion was impossible. No one had ever kept her mother reined in.

WHEN FRED GOT back to where Allison was sitting, he filled her in on the investigation of the murdered man. Of course, there wasn't much to fill her in on—just the fact that their John Doe may resemble a suspect in an Atlanta robbery several months ago. "But let's not say anything to the kids about how the investigation is going, or rather that it's not going much of anywhere. Don't want them to worry."

"I agree. Let's just have a good dinner and catch up on what they've been doing today."

It was during dinner an event scheduled for Mammy's

Pier the next morning was mentioned. Neil brought it up. "Seems like I was wrong. One doesn't have to wear a shirt for church here."

Fred blinked at the ruddy, blond kid on his right. "Would you care to explain that rather odd statement?"

"Gladly," Neil said. "In between our surfing and arcading and ice cream eating today we met some girls who invited Dave and me to church tomorrow."

"And?"

"And we accepted after we learned the location and the dress code."

Fred knew Neil wanted to be begged to tell the complete story so he obliged. "Please, kind sir, tell me the location and the extent of the dress code. Some of the rest of us might be interested in going."

Before Neil could answer, Connie piped up, "Wow, that's a novel way to pick up fellows—inviting them to church. We may have to try that, Trina."

"I'll make a note of it."

Neil cleared his throat. "As I was about to explain, the location is beach side at Mammy's Pier. And in case you don't know, that's the pier on the opposite end of the beach from the murder site. It's closest to downtown." He paused, but since no one commented, he went on. "The time is eight—make that a.m. The dress code is anything short of nudity."

"Let me see if I have this straight," Allison said. "There's a church service scheduled to be held on the beach in the morning, and one can attend in a swimsuit if so desired."

Neil nodded. "Exactly."

"And tell me," Allison went on, "what kind of swimsuits were the girls wearing when they invited you?"

Neil shrugged. "I didn't really notice. Did you, Dave?"

"Not at all. I was more interested in their spiritual attributes than their bodies. And I'm truly looking forward to the worship service in the morning."

Connie nodded her head. "That figures." She turned to Trina to explain.

"He loved going to Sunday School when we were kids because the teachers would pass out treats in brown paper bags. But I imagine the treats tomorrow will be dressed in something a little more attractive."

SIX

WHEN ALLISON CAME down the stairs Sunday morning, she was surprised to see the boys already at the table slurping giant-sized pancakes smothered in syrup. She was even more surprised to see that, instead of swim trunks, they both were dressed in neat shorts and shirts. Admittedly, neither shirt would win any fashion award, but at least their manly chests were well covered. She even rather liked the wild geometric figures on Neil's shirt, but the scarlet hibiscus Dave was sporting seemed a little over the top. But who was she to criticize? The important thing was the red light on Mr. Coffee was shining brightly that indicated her morning brew was ready.

Not accustomed to small talk before her first cup of caffeine, Allison merely stated the obvious, "You boys are up early."

"Cindy will be there early," Dave said. "We're going to help her set up."

"Cindy? She's one of the girls you met?"

He nodded. "Along with Gail and Suzette and..." Looking across the table, Dave asked, "What was that other gal's name—the one with the long braid?"

Neil sighed. "Angela. Lovely Angela."

"Two questions," Allison said as she filled her coffee mug. "One, didn't you meet any guys in your travels yesterday?"

"Oh, sure. Some really nice ones. I just didn't get their names."

"That makes sense. Now question number two. What needs to be set up? Don't people bring their own chairs or towels to sit on?"

"Yeah, but the band needs a mike and amps."

"Band? Why am I getting the impression this isn't going to be like the 'little church in the dale' where I grew up?"

Dave gave her his sweetest smile, "Think of it as broadening your horizons, Mom."

After the boys left, Allison lolled back on the couch, took her time finishing her second cup of coffee and watched the other tribe members straggle in. Fred dropped a kiss on her forehead while the girls preened for inspection. Over their bikinis, they each wore a lacy thigh-length swim robe. It did little to hide the flesh underneath, but Allison smiled her approval. What else was she to do?

Connie and Trina took off down the beach saying they would eat breakfast later. Stepping out on the porch, she could already hear the sweet twang of a guitar, the roll of a drum, and a cornet filling the air with the soaring notes of *Amazing Grace*.

By the time she and Fred started making their way to Mammy's Pier, the migration was well under way. The tourist population of Beacon Beach seemed to be coming from all directions as if following a lure of nature. Allison understood the pull. She'd often experienced the tug of a higher power when surrounded by the sight and sound of beauty—whether at the seaside with the lapping waves, on a mountain as an eagle soared, or in the forest listening to the flutelike song of a wood thrush. "Come on," she urged Fred. "We want to get a good spot."

They ended up close to the sand dune, well away from the action, but that was fine with Allison. She had a wide view of the audience and from this point, the music probably wouldn't be quite as ear shattering.

"Bigger crowd than I expected," Fred said.

The large lady next to him in purple shorts and a Braves baseball cap must have thought he'd spoken to her. At any rate, she answered, "Oh, this is nothing. You ought to see it the week of the Fourth. Not even room to spread a towel."

Fred didn't respond, so Allison leaned over to continue the conversation. She figured the woman must be a local resident, and this might be a chance to learn more about the town and about what was being said regarding the dead man. But before veering off to that topic, she kept on the present subject, saying in a loud voice, "Is this a weekly event?"

Ms. Purple Pants shook her head. "Once a month during the summer, is all. This will be the last one since school starts back soon, and the town will shrink back to normal proportions."

"Then you live here?"

"Most of my life. My husband and I run the only grocery store this side of the bridge. We charge a little more than the chain stores on the other side, but most folks don't mind paying for convenience." She sat up a little straighter, said proudly, "We do all right for ourselves."

"I'm so glad." Thinking this might be a good time to switch gears, she climbed over Fred's legs, pushed him gently aside and leaned close to the woman. She said, "I hope the recent tragedy doesn't adversely affect your business."

"Tragedy?" The woman frowned, and then apparently made the connection. "You mean the dead guy?"

Allison's head bobbed up and down. "Terrible thing to have a murder in your own front yard. Think the cops will find out who did it?"

"Well, first they have to figure out who the poor bugger was. No one I talked to ever seen him."

The background music stopped; the crowd quieted down, and Allison knew her inquiries would have to be put on hold. A gray-haired stout woman dressed in a green cotton pantsuit approached the microphone.

The grocery store lady bent close to Allison's ear. "You'll like our preacher. She's really down-to-earth."

The preacher welcomed all the congregants, asked them to bow their heads for a short blessing on the event.

After the prayer, she introduced the band and singers as being the youth group at their church. There was a spattering of applause just before the lead singer blasted out the words to *How Great Thou Art,* accompanied at intervals with drum rolls. This version was jazzed up a lot as it was faster and louder than Allison had ever heard it, and the phrase, *awesome wonder,* was repeated over and over. The final two renditions of, *how great thou art,* was a crescendo, and Allison had to admit it was certainly awe-inspiring.

The singers followed up with several modern gospel songs that were sometimes referred to as "Seven Elevens"—seven words repeated eleven times. But the message of God's goodness was clear.

Allison not only liked the preacher, but the modern

music and the ambience. She decided having church on the beach with no dress code was an absolutely grand idea.

From time to time, she scanned the crowd for her crew, but never spotted them. Not only was the ground covered in a wide swath, but dozens of people hung over the railing of Mammy's Pier to take in the service.

The thought crossed Allison's mind that a killer could be among the worshipers. But all thoughts of evil left her brain when the band leader invited the audience to join in singing "When the Saints Go Marching In."

The drums, the singing, and the hand clapping were so loud that Allison knew there couldn't be anybody still asleep in Beacon Beach.

When the music died away, a hush fell over the crowd, and the minister approached the microphone. Her sermon was brief and positive, extolling the beauty of nature and the brotherhood of mankind—a message everyone needed to be reminded of from time to time. After the closing prayer, the mass of people started moving like slowly awaking moths coming out of warm cocoons: shaking off sand, testing out legs, stretching shoulders, breathing deeply—and smiling widely.

As Allison was folding up her towel, the grocery lady leaned toward her. "We got some nice fresh peaches in yesterday. You better get some before they're all gone. We're open from noon to six on Sundays. I'm usually there all afternoon. Come on in."

Well, Allison thought, *I may have just made a friend in town—one who seems to like to talk.* "I will. I love fresh peaches."

SLINK SLOWLY AMBLED from the downtown area and joined the crowd on Mammy's Pier during the brief sermon, smiled when the preacher started the, "love your neighbor," nonsense. *I'm not much of a church person, but right now I'm all for it. It was mighty handy for the singing to cover up the gunshot. It'll be at least an hour before the body is discovered. Plenty of time for me to be somewhere else. But I get so tired of hearing the crap about loving others. In my world, it's everybody for themselves. And when my neighbor gets too greedy—or too nosy, I'm going to put a stop to it.*

FRED AND ALLISON made their way back to the pink house, holding hands and dragging their feet. There was no hurry. Fred knew the kids would stumble in when they ran out of entertainment or got hungry. Allison and he had no plans for the rest of the day except lounging, reading, and perhaps napping.

They were in the midst of brunching when they heard the siren of a police car.

At the first wail of the siren, Fred's hand stopped in midair, his forkful of cheese omelet dangled dangerously close to his new white tee shirt, and his pulse speeded up. It was a conditioned response. At his retirement party, he'd been kidded about, "once a cop, always a cop." It was true.

He took a deep breath, forced himself to relax, started eating again. But his mind zeroed in on his new friend, Vince Tucker. Fred had taken a liking to the young officer and hoped the call was only to quell a small disturbance or to stop a car going forty in the twenty-five-mile zone. Of course, Tuck may not even be on duty since it was Sunday. However, he knew, since the town of Beacon Beach had only a two-man police force, that meant either Tuck and his assistant, Jack, were on call. At any rate, the siren and whatever misdemeanor it indicated had nothing to do with him or Allison.

Sipping the last of his coffee, he glanced over to his bride. He sometimes still wondered how an old bachelor like him had gotten so lucky. And if they were blessed with the opportunity to grow old together, he would continue to think of her as his bride.

She was curled up in the recliner, had a big yellow book in her lap and her reading glasses on. The glasses tipped him off that she was settled in for some serious down time.

He went over, gave her a peck on the cheek. She responded with a soft, "Hmm," but didn't lift her head.

"I saw a newspaper stand a couple of blocks from here who carried out-of-town papers. Think I'll walk down, get a Sunday paper—catch up on the ball games."

"Good idea."

"Be back soon."

"Okay."

The vendor had papers from several large cities in the state so visitors could keep up with news from home. Fred picked up ones from Raleigh and Charlotte. They both had good sports sections and he could find out how the Atlanta Braves were faring. He was on his way back to the pink house when his phone rang. He didn't check the ID since he figured Allison must have thought of something she needed from the news stand.

Instead, it was a worried young cop. "Fred, I could use some input from you."

"Sure, Tuck. What's the matter?"

"There's another one."

"Another what?"

"Dead body."

SEVEN

FRED TIGHTENED HIS grip on his phone, tried to get his mind to interpret what his ears had heard. Dead body. That doesn't necessarily mean a violent death or even a suspicious death. Some tourist might have keeled over with a sun stroke or a heart attack. But if that were the case, then why was Tuck calling him?

As he was trying to come up with some kind of response, he realized Tuck was still talking. "Looks like suicide this time. But it's ugly. The elderly woman at the rental agency. Shot herself in the head. Still warm. Gun on the floor beside her."

The words cascaded through Fred's brain. Elderly woman? Rental Agency? The woman Allison had a row with yesterday? Before he could go further with that line of thought, Tuck's other words grabbed his attention. Suicide?

He started shaking his head from side to side as if the officer at the other end of the phone could pick up his vibes. The detective in him couldn't readily accept what Tuck had suggested. Something didn't seem right with the scenario.

Before Fred had a chance to ask any questions, Tuck went on. "The manager found her when he came in to open up, a little before ten. He said she'd been depressed, that she carried a gun for protection."

"Protection?"

"He said she lived alone, had worked at the agency for years and knew everybody in town, but didn't seem to have many friends."

The last sentence slid by Fred as his mind went back to the weapon. "He recognized the gun?"

"No. Had never seen it, but she told him she had one and that she knew how to use it." Tuck paused. "I've secured the premises, called in Ed, and Jack is taking the manager's statement."

Fred heard him take two quick breaths, then he added, "I know we just wait for Ed and his crew. And I guess there's not much we need to do for a suicide. Right?"

"Tuck, listen to me. This really doesn't strike me as a suicide."

"You sound pretty sure."

"Of course I'm not sure, but I do know old ladies seldom shoot themselves, even depressed ones. Bottle of pills maybe, or a walk off the end of the pier, but not usually a gun—and especially not in the head. I think you might have another murder on your hands."

Tuck's voice dropped to a near whisper. "That's kind of what I figured, but was hoping I was wrong. I'll talk to you later. Got to go."

The police officer hung up before Fred could ask him for permission to view the scene. Shucks, he didn't need permission. He was still a lawman, not in this jurisdiction, and he was officially retired, but they were minor points.

He hurried back to the pink house. He'd gotten quite fond of the color in the past couple of days since it was nice not to worry about remembering the house number.

But as he went in the back door, he did have a big

worry. How was he going tell Allison about the second death? And how would she react? In his gut, Fred knew this death would probably be ruled a homicide, and he didn't want Allison getting into another murder investigation. He knew instantly, she would regard that thought as sexist, since he had no hesitation about getting involved in it himself. But that was different; he was a professional.

When he came into the living room and saw Allison asleep on the couch, he realized he had a slight reprieve from telling her about the latest event. He dropped the newspapers on the nearest chair, quickly scribbled a note and propped it on the kitchen counter. She'll see it when she got up and it would give him time to come up with a way to tell her about the death without making her think it had anything to do with her or that she had to get involved. *Hon, I've got the van, gone to talk to Tuck. Be back later.*

The downtown area was only a few blocks away. Nothing nor anyone was very far apart in this little beach town. Including, he thought, the killer—a killer who might be watching to see who drives up. Turning abruptly down a side street, Fred parked in front of an ice cream parlor whose sign announced the opening time as two on Sundays. Before exiting the car, he dialed Tuck's cell, told his location, and asked, "Okay if I come up there?"

Tuck hesitated. "I just got off the phone with Ed. He's on his way, said not to let anyone else in."

Fred hid his disappointment, rallied quickly. "And he's right. Can't be too careful. I'll head back to the house. Talk to you later." Before disconnecting, though, the word, "but," slid out of his mouth.

Tuck caught it. "But?"

"But Ed might want someone to talk to my wife. Unless there's more than one elderly woman working there, I assume the victim is the one Allison had a slight run-in with yesterday. Probably not germane, but then…"

"It's Naomi Platt, and she's the only elderly employee there. In fact, there are only two others, Clyde Johansen, the manager who found her, and Meg Freeman, who works part-time. They go by their first names, but Mrs. Platt always insists on being called Mrs.—never Miss or Ms.—and certainly not Naomi. She's been a widow for probably thirty years and apparently had no intention of changing her status. But as to your wife's encounter with her, I'll pass on the information. You never can tell what might be helpful. I'll let you know."

From the way he'd rattled on about the victim's name and marriage status, Fred could tell the young officer was nervous. And he had every right to be—two violent deaths in this quiet beach community were enough to shake anybody up. He shoved the phone in his pocket, closed his eyes. He couldn't believe what he'd just done in telling Tuck about Allison's little set-to with the deceased. Instead of protecting her, he'd open her up for questioning by the detectives. Not that she would mind, but it would be that much harder to keep her from getting involved in the investigation.

Feeling the need for time alone to think about the situation, he started the car, drove to the public parking lot on the other side of Mammy's Pier from where the church service had been. He could see only a few swimmers and waders and castle builders on the beach. It was still too early for serious sunbathers and the waves weren't high enough for surfers.

Kicking off his sandals, Fred moseyed across the sand, his feet slow, but his brain in high gear. If only he'd asked more questions, gotten a better picture of the crime scene. Shot in the head…exactly where? Gun on floor close to body…dropped by victim or thrown by killer?

Other questions with no immediate answers flooded his brain. If the manager was going to open up the agency that morning, what was Mrs. Platt doing there? If she knew everyone in town, did she let the killer in thinking he was harmless? Was the gun she carried for general protection or against a known enemy? Why had she been depressed—illness, financial problems, threats?

He shook his head to clear out the needless speculation—the county investigators would ask all of that, plus much more. They would determine bullet trajectory, gun powder residue, forced entry or not, trace her phone calls—all the minutia of crime investigation. It was of no concern to him. He'd gotten out of the detective business a year ago. All that was behind him. So what if at times he missed the challenge of outwitting a criminal, the thrill of the chase, the sense of satisfaction when the culprit was brought to justice? He was living a quiet, uneventful life now—just the way he liked it. He had to admit it was an ego boost when Tuck asked for his input, but that was going to be the extent on his involvement. After all, he was on vacation.

Still he continued to walk along the beach, hesitant about going back to inform Allison of what had happened. Since he hadn't put on his watch this morning, he pulled out his phone to check the time. It was nearing noon. He headed to his car—time to get back.

HEARING FRED'S CAR drive up, Allison glanced up from the table where she sat with Connie and Trina. The two girls had awakened her when they'd come in earlier and immediately started snatching food from the refrigerator as if they hadn't eaten in days. Now with their hunger assuaged, they were cramming tote bags with towels, sunscreen lotion, bottles of water, and romance novels. Their plan was to roast in the sun and hopefully, to get acquainted with the lifeguard hunks.

"Just don't fall asleep," Allison warned, "or you really will get roasted. Remember, you got up pretty early this morning."

Trina grinned. "Don't worry. I'll poke her every once in a while—or read her a hot love scene from my book. That'll keep her awake."

Before Allison could contemplate the possible contents of a hot love scene, Fred came in the back door. She thought she detected a wary look on his face when he came in, greeted them all with a wave of his hand and then asked her, "Have a good nap?"

"It was dreamy until these two cookie monsters came in looking for something to devour."

"Cookies!" Connie said, dropping her tote bag. "I knew we were forgetting something. "Trina, any of your chocolate chips left from last night?"

"Only if your brother didn't find where I'd hidden them." Trina dug into the dishtowel drawer and came out with a plastic bag. "Hallelujah. Enough to go around."

She handed the bag to Connie who offered a cookie to Fred. He declined with a shake of his head. "Okay, all the more for us. Mom?"

Allison averted her puzzled eyes from Fred long

enough to reach in and grab two luscious cookies. "You girls finish them up. I'm sure the boys have found something to eat."

"And someone to eat it with," Connie said with a smirk.

Munching a cookie, Allison's eyes followed Fred as he picked up part of a newspaper, flopped down on the recliner and pretended to read the headlines. She sat on the arm of his chair, nudged his shoulder. "Something bothering you?"

Before he could answer, heavy footsteps pounded up to the porch, the front screen door burst open, and Dave shouted, "Hey, did you guys hear about the other murder?"

Allison gaped at her excited son and the breathless lad right behind him. Was this a joke? She wouldn't put it pass Dave to come out with something like this and then reveal that they'd found a dead fish on the beach that'd been murdered by a malicious hook.

But Neil's wide eyes seemed to confirm what Dave had said, and when Allison glanced over to Fred and noted his stricken face, she knew it was true. There had been another death.

Fred must have been talking to Vince Tucker and been told the news. That's why he'd come in with a guarded look—a look that said he was either hiding a guilty secret or that he knew something he didn't want to share with her. With Dave's announcement, though, Fred would have no alternative but to tell the story to the whole crowd.

Allison's attention turned to Connie as her daughter gasped and dropped the cookie she'd been nibbling on. Connie's voice wavered as she asked, "Where did you hear that?"

Neil pushed Dave aside, let the screen door slam. "The news is all around. I guess someone saw the police car and got the scoop. Said it probably happened during the church service."

"Yeah," Dave said, "and this time it was some old lady."

Trina gasped. "Who would be mean enough to hit an old lady?"

Dave shook his head. "She wasn't clobbered. She was shot."

Allison slid off the arm of the recliner. Her mind and her guts in turmoil. How could this happen in a sleepy little beach town? It didn't make sense. Was her family safe? Was anyone safe?

Glancing over to Fred, she noted his grim expression, his slumped shoulders. She motioned for the young people to be quiet. "Let's all sit down. I think Fred may have something to tell us."

FRED NODDED. AS UGLY as the truth might be, he knew it was better the wild speculations that seem to circle around the room.

Dave stopped halfway to the couch, stared at the ex-cop, "You already know about the murder?"

"I know about another death." He waited until all his charges were settled before saying anything else. Looking at the four young people in front of him, Fred realized he did think of them as his charges—his responsibilities. *Legally they were all adults, but,* he thought, *they're novices at coping with the evil that can so easily invade our lives.* Now, though, was not the time to get philosophical. He quickly donned his law enforcement personality he'd worn for thirty years and opened the discussion.

"So," Fred said to the boys, "where did you hear about another death?"

When Dave answered, his voice was subdued. "At the Soda Shack. Some kid came in saying some old gal had been shot—murdered."

Neil nodded. "Cindy and her friends got scared, said they were going home. They weren't going to stick around with a killer on the loose."

"All right," Fred said, "let's get a few things straight. One, you do not refer to an elderly woman as an old gal." He stared at Dave until he got the required nod of the head and went on. "Two, there has been another death, but, at this point, it hasn't been ruled a homicide. So, whoever is spreading that rumor doesn't have all the facts." He paused. "And I don't want any of you repeating the rumor, since it may have been a suicide. Understand?"

As ALLISON WATCHED the proceedings, she couldn't help but smile as four heads bobbed up and down—five including her own. The master detective had spoken.

"As reported, the unfortunate person was an elderly lady." Fred went on, "She worked at the rental agency."

Allison gasped. "Naomi Platt?"

"You knew her, Mom?" Connie asked.

Allison covered her mouth, tried to still the panic that seemed to engulf her as she took several quick breaths. It was one thing to find a body on the beach that had no connection to her, but quite another to have had a recent unpleasant encounter with the dead person. Feeling a pang of guilt, Allison reminded herself that Mrs. Platt had only been doing her job in trying to account for the number of keys in circulation. The fact the woman had become rude was merely a lapse of courtesy and could have nothing to do with her death later—or could it? Surely, Allison reasoned, Mrs. Platt couldn't have become so despondent over the incident to have killed herself.

Trying to still the turmoil in her brain, Allison turned to answer Connie's question. "Knew her? No, I didn't actually know her. That is…"

Fred interrupted her and answered Connie's question himself. "We both met Mrs. Platt when we picked up keys for this house, as did probably every other beach house renter in town. That was our only contact with her. So again, the death shouldn't concern this family."

Pausing only long enough to glance over at Allison, he went on, "And keep in mind that this latest death may have nothing to do with the other gentleman who was found dead. The police will be questioning a lot of people, including us—since we did meet the woman. It's what has to be done to gather information. Nothing to worry about."

Allison suspected Fred of knowing a lot more than he was reporting, but was okay with it for the time being. His job now was to calm down the young people, but she wasn't sure how well that was going. The girls still looked pretty upset.

"Sir?" Trina looked at Fred apparently seeking permission to speak. He nodded.

"When we drove into town and you went in to get the keys, I noticed we weren't far from a pier." She took a quick breath, went on. "That was Mammy's Pier and if she was shot, and if it happened during the church service, I would think we would have heard it."

"Not necessarily," Dave said, "especially if it was during the time the saints were marching in."

Fred nodded his head. Allison recalled how much of the congregation had joined in when the band struck up the rousing gospel song, not only singing but clapping as well. She doubted if a cannon volley could have been heard over the racket. Maybe that was exactly what the murderer had hoped—might even have planned it that way. Or if Mrs. Platt had, indeed, committed suicide, it might have been that she didn't want the shot heard at the time. But why? That brought out a whole new batch of questions. Not only why would she kill herself, but why the timing?

She knew her questions would be the same ones the sheriff department investigators would be asking. There was absolutely no reason for her or Fred to speculate about the death. Fred's next statement proved he agreed.

"Now all of us should just try to forget about it," Fred said. "The police will do their investigation and find the answers."

He walked over to the counter, grabbed an apple, and started chomping on it. "Right now I'm ready for some lunch."

The boys joined him in the kitchen. Dave hauled out sandwich makings from the fridge and Neil claimed some sodas. Allison could tell Connie and Trina were trying to mask their concerns as they nibbled on carrot sticks, spread crunchy peanut butter on saltines, and sipped glasses of skim milk.

Allison finally concocted a ham and pickle sandwich and ate it in slow motion while a deep sense of sadness swept over her—for her family whose fun vacation had been tainted by evil, for the untimely deaths of a young man and an elderly woman, for the town of Beacon Beach that had lost its innocence and tranquility.

The sadness, though, was immediately replaced by a sense of foreboding. It was easy to say the deaths had nothing to do with their family, but Allison couldn't quite make herself believe it. After all, she and Fred had been the ones who first noticed the dead man under the pier and reported it to the police. Then the second death had occurred only a day after Allison had an unpleasant encounter with the victim. Probably most people would chalk up the time proximity of the two events as merely a coincidence and let it go at that. Allison wasn't so sure. Could there be a connection? The first death was definitely murder but, as far as she knew, the second one was being considered a possible suicide.

No amount of speculation on her part, though, was a bit helpful. She had to get her mind off the crimes and simply enjoy this precious time with her kids and their friends. All too soon, summer will be over and the young people will scatter in different directions.

She and Fred would be empty nesters again. She smiled as she pictured their quiet evenings together. And quiet evenings sounded really good to her right about now.

EIGHT

BOTH CONNIE AND TRINA were subdued when they picked
up their tote bags. "We'll stay in the beach area right out
front, Mom. You'll be able to see us from the porch."

Allison blinked back tears as she nodded at the two
young women. Both had learned at an early age that
the world could be a cold and dangerous place. Trina
had lost her father in Iraq and a brother to drugs, but
could still see the beauty of life. Connie had suffered
through abandonment by her father and murderous attempts on her mother, but instead of becoming cynical,
she wanted only to help others with their problems. Allison breathed a prayer for their futures.

Turning her attention back to the table where the
boys were devouring their king-size sandwiches and
chugging their colas, she was suddenly very thankful that nothing could interfere with their appetites.
It seemed to signify that life goes on no matter what
happens.

She slipped back on the couch, picked up her book,
pretended to read. It wasn't long before Dave and Neil
came up for air and claimed they were stuffed.

Fred had finished his sandwich and was sipping a
cup of instant coffee when Dave asked, "Want anything else before we clear the table?" Smiling, Fred
shook his head.

Allison could tell Fred was pleased that Dave had

asked and that the boys were cleaning up without being reminded about it. It was short work for them to put everything from the table either in the fridge, in the dishwasher, or in the trash, and then they were ready to go.

Neil headed for the door. "Looks like the surf's coming up. Let's get our boards."

"Great," Dave said. They darted out, and the screen door slammed behind them.

From her vantage point, Allison could see them sprint down the steps, then she saw Dave hesitate, come back up and call through the screen, "Don't worry, we'll stay in view of the lifeguards while we're surfing." She knew it was a rule Fred had established when they'd first arrived, but thought it was sweet of her son to reassure them.

Now that they were alone, Allison beckoned Fred to her side. There was more to the story than he'd told the kids, and as scary as it might be, she needed to get all the details. From the look on his face, he knew the inquisition was coming.

He held up his coffee cup. "Can I fix you some before we get started?"

"No thanks. Might need something later, though—depending on what you have to say." She willed herself to be objective as Fred began.

He started with the call from Tuck, told her verbatim as much as he could remember of what the policeman had said and his own response.

Allison didn't actually interrupt but did supply comments of her own from time to time. "You're right. She probably wouldn't shoot herself in the head—too messy. Possibly in the chest—through the heart if she could position the gun just right, but it would be tricky."

Fred frowned. "You've thought about how women kill themselves?"

"Not specifically. I was just thinking of how I might do it if I were old, lonely, and depressed. Shooting yourself in the heart could be symbolic of all three conditions." Allison shrugged. "But don't pay any attention to me. Go on with your story."

Fred went on about Tuck telling him of Mrs. Platt being widowed for thirty years but still insisting on being called Mrs.

And then Fred mentioned how he'd told Tuck about Allison's run-in with the victim the day before. She noticed his pause, how he searched for face as if she was going to object to the police knowing about her little skirmish with the realtor. But instead, she just kept nodding as he went along.

When Fred paused to catch his breath, she took advantage of the break. "I think I understand Mrs. Platt quite well. She was following the norm for her generation, but she was also using her married name as a shield."

"Shield? Against what?"

"Against a lack of respect that a first name basis might engender, against unwanted advances from the opposite sex. It also gave her a sense of worth since at one time, she'd been loved, had been precious to another person."

Fred shook his head. "You don't know that. The marriage might have been a lousy one, and maybe she wanted advances from the opposite sex and just never got any."

"True. But I like my version better. However, enough of that. Let's talk about when you put my name into the equation. I would hardly have described my short encounter with Mrs. Platt as a run-in. She was rude to me, but I did not respond in kind. I hope you made that clear to Tuck. I certainly would not wish to become one of his prime suspects."

"Not much chance of that when you have dozens of witnesses to place you at the beach at the time— marching in with the saints."

"Good. And when can we expect Ed and Sheila to be here to interrogate me?"

"They're not going to interrogate you. However, they may want you to go over your encounter with Mrs. Platt. An any rate it probably won't be any time soon. Maybe not even until tomorrow."

"In that case, I'm going to go buy some fresh peaches."

Fred handed over the keys to the van without a single question. Allison knew that he knew what was on her mind, and it wasn't peach cobbler. She was going to scout out the grocery lady, introduce herself properly, and have a down-home gossip session, not only about dead men on the beach, but also about widows, about loneliness, and maybe even about guns and suicide.

Allison took her time going down Shoreline Drive as she tried to figure out her approach. Finding the peaches would be no problem; finding the person she wanted to talk to might not be so easy. She doubted that Ms. Purple Pants would be working the checkout counter. The fact the grocery lady had said she'd be at the store this afternoon didn't mean she would be in plain sight.

However, when Allison got to the end of the street, she sighted the warehouse type building with a sign announcing *Shubert's Grocery and Produce* and figured her problem was solved. She had merely to seek out Mrs. Shubert.

Upon entering, she looked around for her target. Not seeing Mrs. Shubert, Allison picked up a basket and started down the aisles. She was pleasantly surprised at the amount and variety of the products displayed and found several items she decided she absolutely had to have: a loaf of rye bread, chamomile tea, and a bag of fun-size Snickers. Her basket was filling up and she hadn't even made it to the fruit and vegetable section yet.

When she did get to that section, Allison ignored the luscious-looking grapes and the pink grapefruit to home in on her original excuse for coming to the store. She picked out six firm, fuzzy peaches and could almost taste their juicy sweetness.

Finishing her selection, she looked up and saw Mrs. Shubert smiling at her. "Glad you made it in. They're going fast."

"They look delicious. Thank you for the heads up." Allison shifted the basket to a more comfortable position. "I didn't introduce myself this morning, but I'm Allison Sawyer, here for a week's vacation."

"And I'm Lottie Shubert. Hope you're enjoying our little town."

Now that's a lead-in line if I ever heard one, Allison thought, and quickly answered, "It's a lovely town, but I've got to admit things are getting a little scary around here. First that young man killed under the pier and now that poor Mrs. Platt. I assume you've heard about her death."

"Oh, yes. We open at noon on Sundays and the first customers were already talking about it. Of course, Harry, that's my husband, and I heard the police siren earlier, but thought it was probably a little fender bender or some such thing. I never imagined anything like a suicide—but that's what's being said. And to think it was someone I knew."

"She was a friend of yours?"

"Not really, but everyone in town knew Naomi Platt. She was rather a fixture."

"A fixture. I don't understand. I only met her once when I picked up an extra key, so I don't know anything about her, but I can't imagine the woman actually shooting herself."

A gleam appeared in her new friend's eyes—the look that says she knows all about the victim and that she would love to share her knowledge with a stranger. Allison obliged her. "My husband claims that I'm nosy, but actually, I'm just interested in people. What was she like?"

Lottie looked around, took Allison's elbow. "Do you have a few minutes? We could talk in my office. I'm supposed to be working on the books."

Allison smiled. "I'm in no hurry."

NINE

LEFT ON HIS OWN, Fred paced, exchanged his tepid coffee for a cold soda, flipped through the Raleigh paper without interest, while all the time his mind mulled over what little he knew of the latest crime scene. There had been plenty of time for the county troops to have arrived, surveyed the situation, and come to some conclusion. He wanted to call Tuck and ask for the latest information but knew that would be overstepping the bounds of their budding friendship.

For lack of anything better to do, Fred started the crossword puzzle in the newspaper. The Sunday puzzle was intended for Mensa members and closet geniuses and since he didn't fit either group, he fumbled through the three-letter words and the giveaways. When he tried the harder ones, he immediately got stumped on an eleven-letter word for venal.

It was late afternoon when his ringing phone rescued him from the puzzle and from his boredom. He grinned when he recognized the number. "Hey, Tuck. What's up?"

Tuck came straight to the point. "Ed's here and he wants to talk to you."

Fred took a moment to savor the sweet words before asking, "They want me to join the party?"

"Something like that. Thought you could look at the pictures—give your opinion as a seasoned veteran."

He was more than glad to offer his assistance, but he tried not to sound too eager. "Well, I guess I could postpone my afternoon nap for a bit. Where should I meet you?"

"At the station. We have the mandatory coffee and donuts; you bring your Sherlock credentials."

"Right." Fred disconnected with a satisfied smile. It was nice to be asked to share his supposed wisdom. He just hoped he didn't fall flat on his face.

Grabbing the piece of paper that held his first message, he crossed through it and wrote another, *Gone for a walk.* No need to be specific. The kids wouldn't care where he'd gone, and he would fill Allison in on the details later. He'd learned it was better to do it voluntarily than for her to squeeze the facts out of him.

The afternoon sun was at its brightest and hottest. By the time Fred had walked the few blocks to the police station he was sweating and thirsty. When he came in the door, he gave a half wave to the assembled group, and made a beeline to the water cooler. He gulped down one cupful of the cold water, carried a refill over to the desk, and made a brilliant observation, "Man, it's hot out there today."

No one disagreed with him.

Four folding chairs flanked a scruffy, spindly-legged card table. The office wasn't big enough for a conference table, but the size of the office or of the table had nothing to do with the determination on the faces of those in the room. Fred immediately sensed the difference between the scene at the pier Friday and today. Then, it had been a stranger whose life had been cut short—now it was one of their own. She may not have been the best-liked person in town, but she was local. That made it personal.

With a nod of his head, Ed motioned Fred to the one empty chair. Sheila sat across from him, welcomed him with the same dignified smile of most southern women that said, *"You may come into my parlor but you'd better behave yourself."* Tuck pulled up his office chair to the table, reached over and shook Fred's hand while Jack, the youngster of the group, gave him a wave. To complete the social amenities, Ed muttered, "Appreciate you joining us."

"Thanks for the invite."

Without any other preliminaries, Ed said, "Now, what we have here is an apparent suicide, but Tuck tells me you don't buy it. Why?"

Nothing like being put on the spot, Fred thought. "Just a gut reaction. In my experience, elderly ladies are particular with appearance, even in death. Looking back at the one time that I met Mrs. Platt, which was Friday afternoon when I picked up the keys to the beach house, she was neatly dressed, subtle makeup, gray hair with soft curls—probably a recent perm. Now, I admit, this is an assumption, but I think that's the way she would have liked to be seen in her casket—not with her head half blown off."

"Hmm." Ed's hum was accompanied by a slight nod.

Sheila's nod was more emphatic. "My grandmother even left instructions about what dress she wanted to be buried in and said that the obituary should read, *died peacefully surrounded by her loving family.*"

"Yeah," Jack said, "but Mrs. Platt didn't have a loving family—or any kind of family, so who would care what she looked like?"

"The thing is," Ed said, "gut feelings can't surpass forensic evidence."

Fred sighed as he waited for the county detective's next words. He knew he wasn't going to like them.

"We got the preliminary findings from the scene. Mrs. Platt did pull the trigger. Her prints were on the gun. Gun powder was on her hand. Gun was lying on the floor just inches from her outstretched hand. Doesn't get much more conclusive than that." Ed paused. "And, the gun was registered in her name."

Ed motioned to the pictures neatly arranged on the card table along with various written reports.

He'd noticed the pictures when he came in, but Fred knew he had to wait for an invitation to view them. Now that invitation had been given, he pulled his chair closer to the card table, quickly scanned the various shots. Then he went back and started picking them up one by one—taking his time to examine each separate scene.

Out of the corner of one eye, Fred noticed Tuck refilling the others' coffee cups and passing around the donuts. Good, he thought, they weren't going to hurry him. He turned his complete attention to the scenario on the table. It wasn't pretty. There was nothing neat about the woman on the floor. Blood covered what was left of her face, matted in her hair, and discolored her white blouse. She was mostly on her back, tilted to her left side, glasses askew, and part of the metal frame above her ear seemed to be embedded into her skull. Her legs, clad in navy blue slacks, twisted under her, feet invisible. Her left hand was entangled in the rungs of a toppled chair, her right hand open, relaxed. Her small, black purse could be seen under the over-turned chair, a piece of tissue peeking out.

The close-up views were interspersed with wide-angle views of the room and its furnishings. After a bit, he voiced his conclusions. "She was sitting in the chair, her purse in her lap, gun neatly tucked away, probably thinking about something. Then, for some reason: a thought, a fear, a sudden depth of depression— she opened the purse, took out the gun. She stood up, placed the gun to the right side of her head, and fired. She fell, dropping the gun, knocking over the chair. She was probably dead by the time she hit the floor. For an older woman, obviously upset, her hand seemed to have been pretty steady."

Four pairs of eyes stared at the ex-homicide detective. Jack was the first to speak. "That's the way it had to be. It was her gun and she pulled the trigger herself."

"I know," Fred said. "We have to go with the evidence. Apparently, my theory that women don't shoot themselves in the head is wrong."

He turned to Tuck. "Any of that coffee left?"

ALLISON HEFTED HER grocery basket, gleefully followed Lottie to her office, and thanked the gossip gods for smiling on her today. It turned out that the office was only a few feet away. The door was open and anyone sitting at the desk would have a clear view of the fruit and vegetable shoppers. Allison quickly realized that Lottie's appearance had been no accident; the woman had apparently been waiting for her. How sweet was that?

When they entered the office, Lottie carefully shut the door and motioned to two easy chairs on the far side of the room. "Just put your basket down and make yourself comfortable. Pretty warm out this afternoon. Care for a glass of iced tea?"

Allison nodded in agreement to all the comments. Since she'd been known to forget things when her mind was elsewhere, she placed her precious peaches at the side of her chair and within her sight. It wouldn't do to return from the grocery store with no groceries. Then she proceeded to the next step Lottie had mentioned and tried to get comfortable in the chair that was too big and too high. Feeling behind her, Allison found a firm pillow and crammed it behind her back—not perfect but it would do for at least an hour. By the time she'd stopped wiggling Lottie was ready with a frosted glass of sweet tea. Allison knew without tasting, it would be as sweet as honey. Only Yankees took their tea straight from the bag. Although many of her friends had started using artificial sweeteners in their tea, Allison doubted the full-figured, happy grocery lady would go that route.

Lottie folded herself into the other chair and both women took a few sips of tea as if they had nothing on their minds but a lazy afternoon of chit-chat. Since Lottie was the hostess today, Allison waited patiently through talk of the weather, the coming end of summer, and the joy of homemade peach ice cream. Only then did Lottie turn the conversation around to poor Mrs. Naomi Platt.

"Actually, I didn't know Mrs. Platt very well. I doubt if anyone did. She seemed to be a loner by choice. But what I meant by her being in a fixture in town was that she had her routine—same places every week at the same time. Thursday was her one day off during the week except for alternate Sundays. She and Clyde Johansen, the manager, traded working on Sundays."

Allison interrupted, "The way I heard it, Clyde found her when he came into the office this morning, so it must have been his day to work."

"Right. So, that leaves me wondering why Mrs. Platt

was there. On her off Sundays, she attended the Presbyterian Church on the other side of the bridge, then lunched alone at The Wagon Wheel—always at the buffet."

Lottie must have noticed Allison's puzzled glance, as she hastened to explain. "And the reason I know all this is because some friends of mine go to that church and also eat at the same restaurant. In the past they've invited Mrs. Platt to join them, but she always refused. Like I said, she was a loner, and she had her routines." Before Allison could comment, Lottie went on, "Her Thursday routine was to get her hair done at Harriet's Hair Salon and then come here for her groceries. Thursday evenings she played bingo at the VFW hall. To my knowledge, she never varied her schedule."

Lottie leaned back, sipped her iced tea, gave Allison a chance to absorb the information.

It didn't take long for Allison to come up with a question. "So what was so compelling to make her miss church and go into the office on her day off? And did she go there with the intention of killing herself?" Allison was thinking out loud and didn't really expect an answer, but Lottie surprised her.

"Unless it was a statement."

"Statement?"

"Against the company—against her co-workers. Maybe she didn't think she was getting the respect she deserved."

"Why would she think that?"

"Because Meg Freeman only works mornings on weekdays and some Saturdays. She's only been there less than a year and has her eyes set on bigger things. She's taking some college business courses in the afternoons and goes off often on weekends to conventions or whatever. She's only using this job as a stepping-stone.

"Clyde, on the other hand, has no ambition at all. He takes off on slow afternoons to play poker with his cronies. At least that's what he wants his daddy to believe. His father, Ben Johansen, who owns the fishing store next door, also owns the realty business and pretty much lets Clyde run it the way he wants, but Ben wouldn't be happy to know little Clyde was spending a lot of time with a certain married woman on the other side of the bridge."

"It sounds like Mrs. Platt was left with most of the work to do at the agency."

"Pretty much. And I doubt if either of the others showed much appreciation—or respect—for all she did."

Allison's thoughts immediately went to her visit to the realty office the day before. Meg Freeman certainly hadn't shown the older woman much respect when she'd taken over the duty of handing out Allison's key. How would Mrs. Platt, who had worked there several years, feel about having her duties usurped by a fairly new part-time employee? And what had Clyde Johansen said to Mrs. Platt about her rude behavior toward a customer? Had she felt humiliated, snubbed? The woman was certainly angry when she went to the back room and slammed the door. But do angry people kill themselves?

Since Lottie seemed to be waiting for some kind of response, Allison voiced what she'd been thinking, "Committing suicide is a drastic way to gain respect."

"I know, and I can't believe she did that. She would never leave Sidney all alone."

Allison sat up straighter. "Wait a minute. I thought Mrs. Platt didn't have any family."

"No family here. She does have a nephew, lives in Chicago. He and his wife visited a few years ago. I don't think Mrs. Platt was very hospitable and they never came back. He's probably her heir unless she made a will and left everything to some charity—not that she had much."

Lottie's voice drifted off as apparently had her thoughts. Allison tried to get her back on track. "But then who is Sidney?"

"Oh, Sidney is her pet canary. She has me order special food for the bird. I keep a supply on hand although one bag lasts for weeks. Birds don't eat much, you know." Lottie let out a little laugh. "Not like Buster, my terrier. I swear that dog is always hungry."

But Allison wasn't concerned about Buster; her thoughts were on the orphaned canary. "But who will take care of Sidney? The poor thing."

"That's the question. Do they take birds at the animal shelter?"

A sharp rap on the door stopped Allison's next comment. The door opened and a young blonde cashier stuck her head in. "Sorry. But Elsie needs your help with a customer."

Lottie immediately set her tea down and rose from her chair. Allison got up also, grabbed her shopping basket, and headed toward the door. They shrugged at each other acknowledging the end of their gossip time. Lottie went to Elsie's cashier line while Allison went to the other one, paid for her purchases, and left the store with her mind spinning. Neither she nor Lottie believed Mrs. Platt's death was suicide. But if not, that meant there was another murderer loose in Beacon Beach. Or was it the same one? And, she wondered, what would happen to poor Sidney?

TEN

FRED LOOKED AROUND the room. Not one of the four cops looked pleased that they didn't have another murder on their hands to solve. Was it because they knew the suicide victim and it hurt to realize an elderly, lonely woman was so desperate she'd taken her own life? Did they feel guilty because they knew other elderly, lonely men and women in the community and did nothing to ease their pain?

Or were they, like himself, not completely convinced that the evidence pointed to the truth?

He knew Ed and Sheila would continue to investigate. They would talk to people who knew Mrs. Platt, follow her movements on the previous days, ask about her mood, her health, her finances, how she came to own a gun, where and when she learned to shoot it. And at the end of all the questionings, they would end up with the same conclusion: for whatever reason, she had pulled the trigger herself.

It was time to change the subject for now. Fred got up, refilled his coffee cup, reached for a glazed donut, and directing his attention to Ed, asked, "Any movement on the other front?"

Ed blinked, thought a moment, said, "Oh, yeah. We found his car. Didn't Tuck tell you?"

Tuck shook his head, finished swallowing the swig of coffee he'd just taken, and said to the room at large,

"As much as I like Fred and value his opinion, I didn't know I was supposed to keep him in the loop about every development."

Throwing up his hands, Ed laughed. "That's not what I meant, but I don't see any harm in it, and his observations have been helpful. What do you think, Sheila?"

"I think we ought to give him a temporary badge and swear him in. Of course, with our budget restraints, he would have to work pro bono."

"Whoa, there. I'm on vacation and I'm supposed to be spending time with my lovely wife." Fred paused just long enough to let his audience suspect he would absolutely love to work pro bono for them, but had to appear to be hesitant. In case they didn't figure it out, he went on to explain, "But since she's an amateur detective, she wouldn't begrudge me the opportunity to assist the local authorities—as long as I report back to her."

Studying the smiles around him, Fred knew he'd made his point. "So, where did you find the car? What shape was it in? Any ID?"

It was Jack who spoke up. "I found it by my supreme deductive ability. I just asked myself, *If I were here on nefarious business and wanted to be inconspicuous, where would I park my vehicle?*"

Sheila let out a whoop and waved a hand in front of her face. "Where did that sentence come from? Nefarious? Inconspicuous? Vehicle? Are you planning on sending this story to The New Detective Magazine?"

Jack sat up straighter, favored her with a slight smirk, and went on, "As I was saying before I was so rudely interrupted, I deduced our John Doe would park his car in a secluded spot. Thus, I searched all the private and public lanes that run down to the beach usually used by fisherman who want quiet and privacy. On my fourth or fifth try, I found a car parked to the side of the lane but no fishermen in sight. South Carolina tag. I called it in and learned the car had been stolen from a bar parking lot in Charleston sometime Thursday evening."

Fred glanced over to Sheila who looked as if she wanted to hassle Jack some more, but a small shake of Ed's head stopped her. After thirty years in law enforcement, Fred was accustomed to friendly bantering between personnel. He could tell both Sheila and Jack enjoyed their give-and-take and neither took it seriously. Ed, though, perhaps because of his position as chief detective, wanted to keep everything on a professional level.

Going on with his story, Jack told them about the car's owner in Charleston fingering the guy on the next bar stool as the thief, saying he must have somehow gotten the car keys. "The car owner's description of the guy pretty much matches our John Doe," Jack said, "including the clothes he was wearing. But no one in the bar claimed to have seen him before the night the car went missing.

"From Charleston, he must have driven straight up Highway 17, through Myrtle Beach and then on to our little town, less than a two-hour drive. Once here, he met up with…someone—a friend, an enemy, a partner in crime. Whoever it was, we know the meeting didn't end on a friendly note."

"Nothing personal found in the car?" Fred asked.

"Nope," Ed said. "If he had any luggage, the killer must have taken it. We didn't find a candy wrapper, a cigarette butt, gas receipt, nothing except various fingerprints that are being checked out. But I'm betting whoever cleaned out the car wore gloves. And since John Doe's prints aren't in the system we're no closer to an ID."

Silence filled the room—a silence of frustration. Fred knew there wasn't much else that could be said. With no ID of the victim, it lowered the chances of finding his killer.

The silence was broken with a slamming door and a tall redhead's shrill voice. "What happened, Tuck? I just got back to town from the outlet stores for their sales and stopped to get gas. Zeke told me Mrs. Platt was dead. That she killed herself. How horrible. That true?"

Fred recognized Mrs. Platt's coworker from the realty office but couldn't recall her name. Tuck supplied it as he quickly rose and hurried to her side. "I'm afraid it's true, Meg. Clyde found her body this morning when he opened up."

"But what was she doing there? It wasn't her Sunday to work? Unless she traded with Clyde. They do that sometimes. What was it? A break-in? A robbery? We don't keep any money there except for some petty cash—nothing worth stealing."

Tuck guided Meg around the table, motioned for her to sit in his desk chair. "Nothing like that." Fred could tell the young cop was uncertain what to say. He looked at Ed, his eyes begged for help.

The county detective nodded, rose. With one hand, he swept the stark pictures of Mrs. Platt, which still lay on the card table, in a pile and flipped them over. He extended his other hand to the newcomer and introduced himself. "Ed Tuttle, detective on the case. Did you know Mrs. Platt?"

"Of course, I knew her. I worked with her. What happened?"

Tuck stepped forward. "Ed, this is Meg Freeman. She works part-time at the realty office." He swallowed hard and continued, "She was a friend of the deceased."

"Which is why I demand to know what happened." Meg stared at the detective. "Have you found her killer yet?"

Ed hesitated. Fred sympathized with him. If the detective said the evidence pointed to suicide, then the news would soon be all over town. If he didn't, the public would think there was another killer on the loose and that could lead to panic. If he refused to make any comment, the people in town would assume the worst.

With a sigh, Ed made his decision. "It appears that Mrs. Platt took her own life."

Meg Freeman's eyes opened wide as she put a hand over her mouth and gave what sounded like a wail. The wail was followed by a torrent of words. "How terrible. I knew she was upset when Clyde sent her home yesterday, but I never imagined she would go that far. I followed her out and tried to calm her down, but she was afraid she'd lose her job and she said she didn't know what she would do then. Oh, the poor thing."

When the woman stopped to catch her breath, Ed started his questioning. "Why did Clyde send her home? Was she not feeling well? Had there been an argument?"

"Clyde didn't tell you?"

"Suppose you tell us what led up to it."

Fred shivered a little when he realized Meg was going to describe Allison's encounter with Mrs. Platt. Thank goodness, he'd already mentioned it to Tuck so he couldn't be accused of withholding any pertinent information.

Ms. Freeman told the story much the same way as Allison had, including the part of Clyde Johansen giving the renter a voucher for free lunches as a form of apology for rude behavior on part of an employee.

Allison's name wasn't mentioned, so Ed had no idea the woman involved was Fred's wife. Even though it had no bearing on the case, Fred knew that part of the story had to come out. And he knew Ed would be following up with Clyde as to why he hadn't mentioned the episode when his statement was first taken.

After getting Meg Freeman's contact info, Ed excused her, said he might be in touch later. Fred watched as Tuck assisted Meg from her chair, escorted her outside and the two of them stood on the sidewalk for a few minutes and talked. Tuck had one arm around the woman's shoulders and it looked as if he were trying to calm her down. It crossed Fred's mind that perhaps Tuck and Meg had a relationship that went beyond city cop and local employee. And why not? Meg Freeman was a very attractive woman and Tuck was a handsome young man. So, what if the woman seemed to have a few years on him? She looked to be in her thirties and Tuck was maybe twenty-five or six. It wasn't unusual for a man to be attracted to an older woman.

When Tuck came back into the office he gave the others a thin smile. "She's pretty upset. The news was quite a shock to her."

Ed nodded. "Understandable."

Leaning back in his chair, Jack stared at the ceiling a long moment before turning around to Tuck and said with a grin, "Maybe you'd better check on her when you get off duty. Make sure she's doing all right."

"Yeah. I guess I'd better."

In the uncomfortable silence that followed, Fred glanced at his watch. "Well, it's getting late. Allison's probably at the house now and wondering where I am."

Ed had started a conversation with Sheila, so Fred said his goodbyes to Tuck and Jack. He asked Tuck to explain to Ed about Allison's part in the episode with Mrs. Platt and to let them know if Ed wanted to talk to her.

He made the walk back to the pink house in record time.

ALLISON LOOKED UP from the counter where she sat peeling and slicing peaches and greeted Fred with a soft smile and an even softer, "Hi, Hon."

He came around to the kitchen area, gave her swift kiss. "Hey, yourself, Hon, but what are you doing in the mess hall? I thought we agreed the adults in the family were not to do any cooking this week."

"Mom's just peeling, not cooking," Dave said as he stirred a pot on the stove. "Neil and I have everything else covered. I'm making my famous spaghetti sauce while my buddy will be doing the garlic toast and baking a succulent peach cobbler."

"Sounds good," Fred said as he snatched a cola from the fridge. He walked over to where Neil had divided a blob of white dough into two blobs and had spread out one in a baking dish.

"Didn't know you were a bakery chef, Neil. I take it that's the beginning of the peach cobbler."

"Sure is—a lesson I learned from my big sister. Just start with some biscuit mix and you can transform it into a myriad of tempting dishes. In this case, I'll spread the peaches out, smother them with melted butter, brown sugar, a variety of spices and cover it with the rest of the dough. You get a taste of this, Mr. S., and you'll want to remember me in your will."

Allison grinned as she heard Fred mutter, "Always did like a self-confident kid."

Rinsing her hands of peach juice, she followed him to the living room. When he plopped down on the couch, she followed suit, scrunched up next to him, and whispered into his ear, "That was a mighty long walk you went on."

"What you do you mean?"

"The note. It just said you were going for a walk."

"Oh, yeah. Well, as a matter of fact, I did go for a walk—and ended up at the police station."

"By chance?"

"Not exactly." He leaned closer to her. "Let's go upstairs and I'll tell you all about my afternoon."

Taking her by the hand, he pulled Allison up and called out to Dave, "Off to take a quick shower and a short nap. Holler when supper is on the table."

"Will do."

As they climbed the stairs, he asked, "Are the girls around?"

"In their room—probably napping. I think the early morning church service and all that sun has gotten to them."

Allison had carried the crossword puzzle she'd been working on with her and when they got to their room, she climbed on the bed, propped pillows behind her back. "I'll try to finish this blasted puzzle while you're showering. It's a tough one."

"I know. Only got about six words myself." At the

bathroom door, he stopped and asked, "By the way, did you find the word for *venal*?"

"Oh, sure—*corruptible*. That one was easy."

Allison tried not to laugh as he shook his head, but she savored her little victory.

After a bit, she tossed the puzzle aside and waited impatiently for Fred to finish his shower and fill her in on his afternoon at the police station.

While he was getting dressed, Fred started with the case of the body on the beach: how they found the car, that it had been stolen from a bar in Charleston, no personal effects of victim in car.

"That's very interesting," she said, "but what I'm really waiting for is the case about poor Mrs. Platt."

Her wait was rewarded with a full account: the pictures, the evidence of suicide, the unexpected visit from Meg Freeman. She took it all in, not commenting at all, but allowing herself to nod in agreement at times during the narrative and shaking her head in disbelief at other times.

A dozen questions flashed through her head, but she asked only one. "What did she buy?"

Fred stared at her as if she'd just flown in from another planet. "What? Who?"

"Meg Freeman, of course. She said she'd been shopping at the outlet stores. Didn't any of you smart detectives ask her what stores, what time she got there, what she bought, and did she have receipts?"

"No. Why would we?"

"Because it sounds to me like she was trying to establish an alibi."

Fred leaned forward, took both of Allison's hands in his, looked very concerned. "Didn't you hear me say

Mrs. Platt's death had to be a suicide—her gun, her prints, powder burns on her hands?"

"I heard, but that doesn't mean I believe it. And you didn't either a few hours ago."

"That was before I heard all the evidence. You can't get around it."

"I admit it sounds damning, but my brain won't accept it. You told me this morning when Tuck first called you, that he said that Clyde, the manager, told him Mrs. Platt had been depressed. Well, if she was, it came on mighty quickly because she certainly wasn't depressed Thursday when she got her hair fixed, bought groceries, and played bingo."

"How do you know all that?"

Then it was Allison's turn to tell her mate about the visit with Lottie Shubert. "And I bet," she went on, "if you inquire about her day on Friday, you'll find nothing out of the ordinary. That only leaves the incident with me and Ms. Freeman on Saturday and her behavior then was one of anger—not depression. She slammed her chair against the water cooler and slammed the door as she went into another room. That doesn't sound like depression to me."

At that moment, Dave's voice floated up the stairs. "Come and get it!"

Allison could see the relief on Fred's face as he jumped up from the bed. But she wasn't quite through with him. "And why didn't Clyde tell Tuck about sending her home on Saturday and maybe threatening her with losing her job? I think you guys better check out his alibi, too."

ELEVEN

FRED WAS PUZZLED by Allison's sudden outburst. Why was she so in denial of accepting the verdict of suicide? After a year of marriage, one would think he would understand everything about his bride, but this development didn't fit the Allison he knew. She would never let personal feelings get in the way of forensic evidence. Was it possible she was feeling guilty? Could she be taking some sort of responsibility about what happened to Mrs. Platt?

When they reached the bottom of the stairs, the sight of four happy, healthy, and apparently carefree young people plus the tantalizing aromas from the kitchen made Fred forget his worries. He grabbed Allison's hand, led her to the table as he called out, "And let the feast begin."

Afterward, as the girls cleaned up the kitchen, Dave challenged the others to a friendly poker game. Neil and Fred quickly accepted while Allison demurred.

"Come on, Mom," Dave urged. "I promise we'll let you win at least one hand."

Just as Fred expected, the offer riled her. "Let me win?" she countered. "Do I have to remind you that I was playing poker when you were still in diapers?"

"No." Dave grinned. "I recall you said you put yourself through college on your winnings. However," he went on, "I think you may have lost some of your edge."

At that point, Connie came around the corner and snapped Dave with her dish towel. "You'll have to wait your turn, little brother, because tonight's my chance to whip her at Scrabble."

Allison fanned herself as if overcome with praise. "It's so nice to be popular."

The rest of the evening went just as Fred had hoped— fierce competition at two tables and no mention of murder or suicide or cops.

SLINK SPENT THE evening sipping beer, going over the day's events—and putting away the unused revolver. It couldn't have worked out any better. When Mrs. Platt had pulled out her gun, it was as if she were offering her own method of execution. It had been no problem to overpower the old woman and force her to aim the gun at her own head.

And the cops had bought the suicide bit without a second thought. It couldn't get any better. Raising the beer can, Slink gave a toast. *Here's to a perfect day.*

WHEN FRED OPENED his eyes Monday morning, he hoped the family could put all thoughts of murder and suicide and detectives aside and just enjoy their vacation. Of course, it was not to be. The real world wasted no time before intruding. It started with a phone call from one of the investigating detectives. Sheila asked if it would be convenient for her and Ed to come by. Fred understood the request to be merely a courtesy since they had the right to interview anyone with possible knowledge regarding Mrs. Platt's death. Although the verdict of suicide was apparent, they still had the obligation to get a complete picture of what might have led up to the event.

When asked, Allison nodded her head, and suggested they come as soon as possible. "Might as well get it over with," she said, then added, "I'll make another pot of coffee."

Fred wondered briefly if any crimes would be solved without the impetus of caffeine.

All four of the young people had plans for the morning that didn't include being interrogated, and since none of them had ever seen the victim, they were free to go their merry way. As he was going out the door, Dave called back. "Hey, Mom, what time do you want us here to go to that freebie lunch?"

Allison let out a small sigh, hesitated before answering. "Maybe we shouldn't go. Somehow, it doesn't seem fitting to benefit from another's misfortune."

"Don't be silly, Hon," Fred said. "The fact that we have a chit for a free lunch has nothing to do with Mrs. Platt's death. We'll all go, and we'll enjoy it." He turned to Dave and the others. "Be back here by one."

The kids clattered down the front steps as a county patrol car drove up in back. Fred went out the kitchen door and motioned for Ed and Sheila to come in. Allison had on her best hostess smile and appeared completely relaxed. No reason for her not to be relaxed, he thought, since detectives and interrogations were old stuff to her.

After the pleasantries, and with everybody seated comfortably with full coffee cups, Ed started the proceedings. "So, Allison, I understand you had an encounter with Mrs. Platt Saturday morning. Since it might have a bearing on her state of mind, I'd like to hear about it."

"Of course, I'll tell you exactly what occurred." And she did—in minute detail: Mrs. Platt's rudeness, Meg

Freeman's intervention, the older woman's response with the chair colliding into the water cooler and the slamming door. "Needless to say," Allison added, "Mrs. Platt was not a happy camper. In fact, she was enraged."

Ed and Sheila had both been taking notes and nodding. At the end of the recitation, it was Sheila who made the first comment. "Enraged? Not depressed?"

Allison shook her head. "Definitely not depressed. In fact, it would be my guess, that she sat in the back room, fuming, and thinking of ways to get even with the little snipe who had usurped her authority. And," she added quickly, "committing suicide would not be one of the ways."

Fred bit his lip to keep from making any comment and studied Ed's reaction. Outwardly, there wasn't any, but Fred knew the detectives mind was digesting everything he'd heard.

He took a sip of coffee, leaned forward a little, "Allison, did Fred tell you about the forensic evidence?"

"Of course. Her fingerprints were on the gun, on the trigger, and there was gun powder residue on her hand."

"And it was her gun. But you still don't think it was suicide?"

"No."

"Why? Just because she didn't exhibit any signs of depression in the short period of time you observed her?"

"I'll explain, but may I ask you a question first?"

"Yes."

"Where were her glasses?"

The question took Fred by surprise and, judging from their faces, the two detectives were also puzzled by it. He tried to remember what he may have reported to Allison about her glasses, but couldn't come up with anything.

Sheila was the first one to respond to the question. "Hanging from one ear—as I recall." She placed an envelope on the coffee table, poured out the pictures, found the correct one showing Mrs. Platt's glasses still on her face but dangling in a skewed position. The detective handed it to Allison.

Allison nodded. "Just as I thought. That proves it."

"Proves what?" Ed demanded. "The bullet hit the glasses, knocked them sideways. What's wrong with that?"

Allison leaned back in her armchair, crossed her legs, rested her chin on her left hand, and smiled sweetly at the perplexed detective. Fred had no idea what was going on in her head, but he was enjoying the show.

She reached over to the end table where she'd placed her reading glasses and held them up for inspection. "Let me illustrate. These glasses have the same type of frame as those of Mrs. Platt. I noticed them the day we met. The frame is sturdy, solid. I estimate it to be at least one-eighth of an inch thick." Fred saw Ed give a slight nod.

Reaching one hand across the coffee table to Ed, Allison asked, "May I borrow your gun?"

Ed reeled backward and a resounding "NO!" echoed around the room.

She shrugged. "Okay, then we'll improvise." Picking up the pencil she'd used to do the crossword puzzle, she put the glasses on, turned the right side of her face toward the detectives, tried to place the eraser end of the pencil above the ear and slightly to the front. Ed and Sheila stared at the profile in front of them while Fred moved his chair closer to get a better view.

"Please note, Lady and Gentlemen, that I'm having a very difficult time positioning my gun barrel to get an optimum shot. The frame of these blasted glasses keeps getting in the way. Therefore, if I'm really determined to kill myself, I would take the glasses off." Allison removed the glasses, dropped them on the table and repositioned the pencil eraser. "Now, I have no problem. The bullet will go through the temporal bone and directly into my brain."

Silence hovered over the group for a few seconds. Fred had comments he wanted to make, but hoped one of the others would do so first.

"Interesting scenario," Ed said, "but someone else holding the gun would have the same problem."

"True. And that person would be unlikely to pause long enough to remove Mrs. Platt's glasses. My theory is that someone taller and stronger grabbed the victim, held her tightly and, ignoring the obstacle, fired through the frames and into her head."

Fred beamed at his bride. She was one savvy lady. Too bad her story was full of holes because she had completely overlooked the hard evidence.

Sheila voiced what he was thinking. "But the fingerprints? The powder burns?"

To his astonishment, the objections didn't faze Allison a bit. "I'm glad you asked. I was coming to that."

All three of her listeners sat back in their seats. Fred figured they were all thinking the same thing, "What in the world is she going to come up with next?"

ALLISON TOOK A deep breath. So far, so good. No one in her audience had called her crazy yet—although one or both of the detectives may be thinking it.

Instead of sleeping much the night before, her mind had gone over and over the dilemma of the forensic evidence as opposed to her gut feeling. Her guts had won the match. Now she had, at the very least, to plant some doubts in Ed's and Sheila's brains so they would consider her theories.

"The fingerprints," she said, "are easy to explain. It was her gun. She carried it in her purse. She probably practiced at the firing range. Her prints would be all over the gun, including the trigger. And the reason why the prints of the actual shooter aren't on the gun is because the perpetrator wore gloves—probably thin surgical gloves. Again, I would like to illustrate how I think the act went down, but to do so, I really need an actual gun." Ignoring Ed, she smiled at Sheila. "Would you trust me with your weapon, Sheila, if I promise not to point it at anybody?"

Without so much as a glance at her superior officer, Sheila unsheathed the gun, took the bullets out, and handed it to Allison. "Sure—why not?"

"Thank you. Now, I'm going to ask you to do some role-playing. You get to be the killer, Sheila, while I'm the victim." Allison put on her reading glasses, got up from her chair being careful to keep the gun pointed toward the floor, moved over to the side of the room, and motioned for Sheila to approach her.

Looking at the two seated men, Allison spoke in a melodramatic tone of voice. "It's some after eight o'clock Sunday morning in Beacon Beach. By Mammy's Pier, most of the town is clapping and singing, but in the realty office Mrs. Platt, who should be home getting ready to go to church, uses her key to let herself into the office. She's alone there as she knows Clyde won't be in to open up until ten. That gives her an hour or so to snoop, or to hide something, or to look for something that's hidden. She has her purse with her and in the purse, is her gun. She hears a noise. Someone else is coming in. Mrs. Platt knows or senses she's in danger. She opens her purse, pulls out her gun—probably for self-defense or maybe to scare the intruder."

Allison raised the gun, turned toward Sheila, but even though now the gun wasn't loaded, she kept it pointed at the floor. Continuing her monologue, Allison said. "Keep in mind Mrs. Platt is short like me. The intruder is probably stronger and taller—like Sheila. In a flash, the intruder grabs Mrs. Platt's right hand…"

Picking up on her cue, Sheila grabbed Allison's gun hand and wrapped her other arm around the victim. With no further instructions, Sheila placed her trigger finger over the finger already on the trigger, and keeping the gun pointing down, she forced the weapon to Allison's temple—and said, "Bang!"

Sheila loosened her grip on the victim and the gun. Allison collapsed on the floor, the gun dropped beside her. The detective retrieved her weapon and reloaded it. Then sliding down in the nearest chair, and in a near whisper, Sheila said, "It could have happened that way. It really could have."

"Amazing," Fred said. "And that would account for the powder burns on the woman's hands, too."

After scrambling to her feet, Allison stood directly in front of Ed. "Sorry about the theatrics, but did I get my point across?"

"You did. Not that I'm buying it entirely, but it's certainly given me something to think about. One problem

I see is that both people would have to have awfully skinny fingers to get both of them in the trigger space."

"Well, we know Mrs. Platt was rather petite. Now you just have to look for a tall bloke with thin fingers."

Ed nodded. "And then charge him with two murders."

"Two?" Sheila said. "I don't follow."

"Think about it," the lead detective said. "How probable is it that we would have two different murderers in the same week in this little town? I've figured all along the two cases were connected. Even if Mrs. Platt's case is eventually ruled a suicide, it still has to be connected to our John Doe death."

Fred had been nodding his head all the time during Ed's last comments. "Right. The lady saw something or knew something. So, either she posed a danger to the killer and had to be eliminated, or she had a sudden sense of remorse over something she did or didn't do about her knowledge."

"I vote for the danger part," Sheila said. "From what I've learned about Mrs. Platt, she wasn't a woman given to bouts of remorse."

TWELVE

AFTER WAVING GOODBYE to the two detectives, Allison flopped on the couch, and fanned herself with a magazine. "Remind me to never try out for our Little Theater plays. Being on stage is exhausting."

Fred leaned over, kissed her cheek. "I'm proud of you."

"Why? I just made a fool of myself."

"No you didn't. You made us detectives think a little deeper. And it's important for law enforcement officers to examine all angles—not settle for the easy solution. Even though I'm retired from the business, I should have remembered that. I'm sure Ed and Sheila feel the same way."

"Now what?"

He pulled her to her feet. "Now we'll take a peaceful stroll on the beach, let the waves roll over all our anxieties. Then we'll put on some decent clothes and the whole family will enjoy a free lunch."

Just the sound of her lover's calm voice was enough to start her anxieties packing. She felt blessed, protected. No matter what might happen, he would always be there for her and the kids.

Neil was on a winning streak and was in no hurry to leave the arcade. Dave snatched the Atlanta Braves cap off his head and swatted his friend's arm. "Either come with me right this minute or you miss a free meal and you're on dishwasher duty the rest of the week."

"Okay. Okay. You don't have to get bent out of shape about it. Sometimes you're a mite overbearing."

Only the fact that Neil ended his last sentence with a wide grin saved him from another beating with Dave's cap. The way the two teased each other, a bystander might take them for brothers in spite of them not looking anything alike. On the rare occasions when Dave became philosophical, he figured the reason Neil and he were such good friends was because they agreed on all the important things in life and disagreed on everything else. It kept their relationship from being boring.

On the way to their beach house, the sight of an ice cream vendor sparked a debate about which kind of receptacles were best. "With a cone," Dave said, "you have to lick as fast you can to keep the ice cream from melting down the sides. But with a cup and spoon you can take your time to really savor it."

Neil came back with, "Then you spend the next ten minutes looking for a trash can to dump your empty cup and spoon in. In the meantime, I'm enjoying the remnants of my crispy cone."

As with most of their discussions, there was no right or wrong—only a sharing of opinions.

Approaching the porch, Dave slowed down, put a hand on Neil's arm. "Let's do our best to keep everything upbeat at lunch. I'm a little worried about Mom. The dead guy under the pier followed by the weird death of that lady at the realty office has her shook up a little. Remember: no arguments, no shenanigans, and definitely no mention of murder and mayhem. Understand?"

"Yep. Except for one thing."

"And that would be…?"

"Your definition of shenanigans."

Dave answered by whipping his cap off his head and swatting Neil's ear. "That's an example of shenanigans, and you'll get more if you don't behave."

THEY DECIDED TO drive two cars because Allison wanted to explore the stores in Beacon Heights after lunch while the young people were anxious to get back to the beach.

"Can't waste the rays," Connie explained. "I've got to get a tan that will last at least until Christmas. Once school starts back, I'll be lucky to see daylight again."

"And for some strange reason," Dave said, "bikinis aren't approved campus wear, so Neil and I have to store up all the memories we can."

Allison nodded. "I understand. And while you people are basking and gawking, Fred and I will be buying some mementos to enjoy in our declining years."

Fred shook his head. "Hey, speak for yourself, lady. I'm buying a metal detector and going treasure hunting in the sand this afternoon."

"Whatever. But for now, let's have a nice, pleasant lunch."

And they did. The service was impeccable, the cuisine superb, and the conversation varied from anecdotes of past vacations to looking forward to the upcoming school year. There was no mention of the recent unpleasant happenings.

Dave brought them back to the present with their plans for Wednesday—fishing for the boys and shopping for the girls.

Allison had no problem with joining the girl category since shopping knew no age boundaries. And apparently, the prospect of throwing dead bait into the water and bringing out a slimy, wiggling fish appealed to males of all ages.

After nearly two hours, the luncheon food had run out as had the talk. They parted ways in the parking lot. The young people headed back to the beach while the older generation hit the sidewalks.

WHILE THE SAWYER party was enjoying their free lunch, Slink cased out the houses on Shoreline Drive. Ambling past the green house, past the pink house, past the cocoa brown house next in line, Slink noticed all the cars at all the houses were gone. *Perfect. Now I can search that other bedroom upstairs. If I don't find it there, I guess I'll have to start all over again.*

Using the back door as before, Slink inserted the key, quickly entered, headed for the stairs, took them two at a time. The far bedroom door was open. The intruder stepped in and noted immediately the hairbrushes and various bottles on the dresser top, a robe thrown over a chair, and pillows propped up on the bed. *Damn. I'll have to be careful not to disturb anything that could be noticed. That's going to take more time.* Starting in the bathroom and working around to the bedroom, Slink searched the same areas as had been done in the rest of the house—behind and under drawers, behind furniture and pictures, in corners and cracks, removing screws over electrical outlets and then carefully replacing them. One of the dresser drawers stuck a little while being put back in and needed to be tipped a little before finally sliding into place.

Nearly an hour and I haven't found a thing. Why in the world did I ever agree to let him take care of the

*money? I went along with him when he said it would
be too risky to start spending it immediately. He said
money from banks was often marked in some way—and
he should have known since he'd worked in a bank. So,
he comes up with the big idea to hit the liquor store to
get some spending money and hide the bank loot for a
few months. But how stupid was it to hide it in the house
he was renting at the time? Then when he decided it
was safe to start spending it, he'd gotten greedy and
said he wanted more than just half. And I thought he
was my friend! Some friend!*

*Nothing's gone right with this job. How many more
people will I have to kill before I get my money?*

Checking the time again, Slink knew the search
would have to be continued later. Putting away the
screwdriver and looking around to be sure nothing had
been disturbed, the intruder hurried down the stairs and
left the pink house with the vow, *I'll be back.*

ALLISON HAD BEEN planning on taking a nap when they
got back to the beach house, but then decided it was
too nice an afternoon to waste sleeping. The heat had
abated, a soft breeze was stirring, and the waves seemed
to be calling to her. Fred hadn't been able to find the
metal detector he wanted and he suggested heading for
the water. She agreed.

After putting on her swimsuit, she pulled out the
drawer that contained her tee shirts and shorts. Thinking she might want to put a shirt on later, she reached
in to grab one and paused. Something was wrong with
this picture. All the contents were on one side of the
drawer as if someone had shoved them over. "Fred, were
you looking for something in this drawer?"

Fred finished pulling up his trunks before answering and frowned, "Why would I do that? I doubt anything would fit me."

"Well, somebody's been in here. I certainly don't leave my clothes bunched together like this. Look."

Fred looked, shrugged his shoulders. "Maybe Connie wanted to borrow a shirt or something."

"Yeah, that must be it. I don't mind, but I don't like her leaving a messy drawer. I'll talk to her later about it."

"Fine. But for now, grab a towel and let's stroll along the beach."

"I don't feel much like strolling," she said. "I fancy a quick dip and then a little lazing."

"Fine. Then we'll take our chairs and umbrella and watch others as they stroll."

They put their claim on a few square feet of sand far enough back to offer a panoramic view of those who were sunning, strolling, and swimming. After playing like otters in the water for several minutes, they headed back to their patch of beach.

Stretching out in her chair, Allison enjoyed watching the volleyball throwers, the kite flyers, the castle builders. An added bonus was a gaggle of lively sea gulls. She knew that *flock* was the correct name for a group of gulls but the term *gaggle* seemed to fit better. They cawed; they shrieked; they scolded. Along with the sound bites, they put on an air show as they swooped and swirled above the heads of their many admirers. But it was the way they walked that really fascinated Allison. Their dull gray tail feathers waved back and forth as they waddled around on their toothpick legs, stopping in mid-stride to pluck a breadcrumb or a speck of cheese or a crushed potato chip from the sand. Then for no apparent reason, one of the tribe would change direction and walk sideways as if he were starting to line dance. She half-expected him to segue into a Texas Tango or the Electric Slide just as she'd done on many Saturday nights.

She continued to stare at the birds until the soft breeze gently closed her eyes and Allison morphed into a vegetative state becoming like a grain of sand in a world of peace.

She didn't know how long the peace had lasted, but she knew immediately when it was broken. Someone walking by had brushed against the umbrella, tilting it just enough to let a sliver of sunlight creep under her eyelids. But before she could get too riled up about the intrusion, a familiar voice calling her hubby's name brought a smile to her face. Tuck was here and that might mean more information regarding the investigations of two deaths in Beacon Beach. All thoughts of laziness fled from her mind and were replaced with avid curiosity.

Fred swiveled his head around to the voice. "Hey, Tuck. Help yourself to a towel and have a seat. Wouldn't want you to get that pretty uniform messed up."

Tuck grinned. "A lot of people would get up and offer their own chair to an officer of the law."

"I guess you're right about that. Too bad I'm not one of them."

Allison had no patience with the male sparring match. She tossed a beach towel at Tuck and demanded, "Sit. Talk. Anything new?"

Tuck sat and told the news. "Ed has a new theory he's batting around—something about Mrs. Platt didn't shoot herself because she didn't take her glasses off ahead of time."

Fred roared.

Smothering a laugh, Allison said, "So the detectives shared my theatrics with you?"

"It was mostly Sheila doing the acting, but she got the idea across, and she seems pretty sold on it. Ed's not committing one way or the other. I'm still trying to get my head around it."

"And Jack?"

"He wasn't in the office when they came by. I'll fill him in later and get his take." Tuck's face became sober. "Ed did make one important decision, though, as a result of your little playacting."

Allison didn't like the term *playacting* but she let it go so she could hear about the important decision.

Apparently, Fred was intrigued, too, as he leaned forward, and asked, "What decision?"

"He ordered a full autopsy on Mrs. Platt."

Sitting straight up in her chair, Allison blurted out, "You mean, one hadn't already been done? Why not?"

"Because it was thought to be suicide by gun. A couple of years ago, all North Carolina law enforcement agencies were instructed not to do autopsies on certain categories of death."

That wasn't enough of an answer for Allison. "What categories?"

Tuck looked to Fred for help. "Your office got the memo, didn't you?"

"Yeah. I remember it. Mostly it made sense, but we still kept the option to do one if there was any question."

Allison repeated, "What categories?" No way was she going to let information like this pass her by.

Nodding, the young officer conceded to the demand. "One: people over forty who appeared to have died from natural causes. Two: victims of alcohol or cocaine poisoning. Three: people who committed suicide by gun or hanging."

It was a few moments before Allison found her voice, and then she blasted out a loud, "Why?"

Fred answered while Tuck was catching his breath. "Financial reasons. The state pathology department is under-funded, and complete autopsies are expensive."

"Well, that's ridiculous," Allison said. "Don't those Raleigh bigwigs care about how our citizens are dying?"

Tuck jumped back into the conversation. "It's not as bad as it sounds, Allison. Like Fred said, we still have the option to order one if we have doubts."

"And where were your doubts before I jumped into the arena? Fred told me the forensic evidence indicated suicide—and all of you believed it."

Fred reached over and patted her hand. "And it might still be ruled a suicide, Hon. Remember, your idea is only a theory—a theory that could be disproved by further evidence."

Allison leaned back in her chair. "I know. Sorry I made such a fuss. We have to believe the evidence." Then shaking her head, she muttered loud enough for both men to hear her, "But I hate for people to get away with murder."

Silence surrounded the trio for a few minutes as each seemed to be in deep thought. Allison surfaced first with a question for Tuck. "Who's taking care of Sidney?"

Tuck blinked, frowned, shot a questioning look at Fred. Fred responded with a shake of the head. Both men stared at the questioner and almost simultaneously asked, "Who's Sidney?"

"Mrs. Platt's canary. Didn't you know she had a pet canary?" Without waiting for an answer Allison went on, "Lottie Shubert told me about the bird. Mrs. Platt buys a certain brand of food for her pet. Lottie said she has to special order it." Leaning forward in her chair, Allison looked the young police officer in the eyes. "Can you explain to me why a person who loved a pet enough to order special, expensive bird feed, give him an old-fashioned name like Sidney, and would then go off and commit suicide without making arrangement for his continuing care?"

When Tuck didn't answer immediately, Allison flopped back, nodded her head. "I think you cops better add that little tidbit to your forensic evidence."

It took a few seconds, but Tuck regained his composure and his cop persona. "I'll check with Ed about that little matter. He and Sheila went through the house, looked for any clues as to her state of mind. As far as I know he didn't find any, and he didn't mention a canary. He also notified the next of kin, a nephew in Chicago. It might be the bird was mentioned then. At any rate, the nephew and his wife are scheduled to fly into Wilmington this morning and then come here to make funeral arrangements and settle up her affairs. He may want to take Sidney back with him."

"Well, if he doesn't, let me know. I always kind of wanted to have a canary." As she said it, Allison turned her eyes enough to catch Fred's expression. She interpreted it to read something like, *Oh, yeah. Our cat and dog are going to love having a bird in the house.* To his credit, though, he didn't say a word.

Fred thought it best to change the subject from Mrs. Platt to John Doe, so he asked Tuck, "Anything new on the other case?" He paused, then added, "Or as Ed would put it, 'the first part of the case'? He made it pretty clear this morning that the two deaths are related—and I agree."

"No doubt about it. We just have to figure out how."

Before Tuck could say anything else, Allison spoke up. "Fred told me about the car being stolen from a bar in Charleston and the dead guy's picture matched a man who'd been at the bar. But it doesn't make much sense to me. A man dressed in expensive sports clothes like he was surely has a pretty decent car. Why steal one?"

"Probably," Tuck said, "because he didn't want his own car to be spotted in the area. Maybe it was a car that would attract attention and be remembered."

Allison's mouth opened again, but Tuck raised his hand to forestall her next comment. "And before you ask—yes, the Charleston police are checking to see if any abandoned car is parked in the area of the bar. So far they haven't found any."

Sliding back in her chair, Allison shrugged.

Noticing the slight flash of irritation from Tuck, Fred instantly empathized with the officer. When he'd first met Allison, there were several times her blunt comments about his murder investigation really ticked him off.

As Tuck rose to leave, Fred stood up also. "Glad you dropped by. Just so you'll know, we'll be gone much of the day Wednesday. The girls are going shopping while the boys and I will be fishing."

"Exactly what people on vacation should do. Have fun. What do you have planned for tomorrow?"

"Nothing special. More sun and sand I guess."

Allison sat up straight, gave Tuck a sweet smile. "But I'll tell you what I would like to do."

Oh, oh, Fred thought. *Now what's on her mind?*

As if Tuck had the same thought, the officer raised his eyebrows. "Why do I have the feeling I'm not going to like it?"

"There's no reason why you shouldn't like it. I just want to meet Mrs. Platt's Chicago family—to offer them my condolences. That's all. Oh, and to tell them I would love to take Sidney if they don't want the canary."

"Well," Tuck said slowly. "I could mention it to them."

"Good. Just give us a call."

Tuck quickly shook hands with Fred, nodded to Allison, but before he could make his escape, two bronzed, muscular bodies blocked his exit route. The tallest one grinned, said, "Saw the uniform over here, and wondered if my mom was being arrested again."

The uniformed officer stared at the speaker, frowned, turned and looked question marks at Allison.

She nodded. "As you may have guessed, Tuck, this is my son. He may be a foot taller than I am, but we share the same big mouth and nosy nature." Turning to the boys, she made the introductions. "Meet Dave Aldridge and his friend, Neil Stone." She waved a hand back at Tuck. "Boys, this gentleman in the uniform is Officer Vince Tucker of the Beacon Beach Police Department. You step out of line this week, and he's the one you'll have to answer to."

Fred had been watching the boys rather warily but smiled when Dave put on his best manners to shake the officer's hand and said the usual, "Pleased to meet you, Sir." Neil quickly followed suit.

Before either boy had a chance to mention the recent crimes, Fred stepped up, slapped Tuck on the back. "Nice of you to drop by. See you later."

With a wave of one hand, the officer smiled and bounded up the steps over the sand dune.

"Didn't mean to butt in," Dave said. "We were just going to get a snack and then try our luck with the surf boards." He hesitated a bit, and then blurted out, "Well, anything new on the crime front?"

Fred shook his head. "Afraid not." Even though both he and Allison had told the young people the killings did not involve them, Fred knew Dave just couldn't step away. The boy had his mother's genes and couldn't help but be intrigued by a mystery.

"Well, then, we're off." Dave and Neil headed toward the pink house while Fred and Allison leaned back in their chairs. For the rest of the day, Fred was determined to think of nothing except the sun, the sand, the ocean, and his lovely bride.

At the table that evening, the subject of the next day's activities came up again. The girls had heard of a carnival in a town a few miles away, asked the boys if they would like to go.

"Sounds great if they have decent rides," Neil said.

Connie gave Neil her innocent smile as she asked, "By decent, do you mean terrifying, bloodcurdling, and hair-raising?"

Nodding his head and grinning, Neil said, "Oh yeah, and petrifying to boot."

"Then the infamous Octopus ought to do the trick."

"And the first one that turns green," Trina said, "buys pizza for the rest of us."

Allison shuddered as she pictured the wild ride, the piercing screams, the resultant nausea. The idea of any kind of carnival ride was enough to set her stomach churning without following it with a pizza.

"Not to change the subject," Allison said, "but, Connie, the next time you look for something in one of my dresser drawers, don't leave everything lopsided."

"What are you talking about? I haven't been in your drawers. In fact, I haven't even been in your room since Trina and I helped you move in."

Trina held up her hands. "Me either. Why would I want something from your drawers? Not to be frivolous, but I'm several inches taller than you and a little thinner around the waist. Nothing you have would fit either of us."

Dave grinned, gave Neil a poke in his arm. "The same thing could be said about us guys—not that we're into cross-dressing."

"Okay. That's enough. I guess I messed up the drawer myself when I had my mind of something else—just forget I said anything."

But Allison couldn't forget it. She wasn't exactly a neat-freak, but she'd always kept her dresser drawers tidy.

THIRTEEN

TUESDAY MORNING ALLISON was on her second cup of coffee when the boys slammed out of their room. Dave came up to her, brushed his hair out of his eyes and slobbered a kiss on her cheek. "Morning, Ma, how art thou this day?"

"I art fine, which is more than I can say for that mop of hair of yours. You definitely need a haircut before classes start."

"Actually, I was thinking of going shoulder length this year."

Allison smiled. She never could beat her son at the silly repartee game, but she kept trying. "In that case, I'll buy you a pink ribbon for your ponytail."

"Better make that blue. I don't want to confuse anyone."

Picking up a magazine, she swatted him on the behind. "Better get in the kitchen before Neil eats all the Crunchy Critters."

For just a moment, tears welled up in her eyes as Allison marveled at how normal everything seemed right now, right here. If only there wasn't the specter of a murderer in their midst.

And why, she wondered, was she so sure the culprit was still in Beacon Beach? She thought about her self-posed question a little and came up with the answer. The murderer has to be someone local—someone who knew

Mrs. Platt, someone who must have known John Doe, someone who had a secret to hide, and someone who would look very suspicious if he suddenly left town.

Surely Tuck and Jack as well as the county detectives have been batting around names of possible suspects. Every town has certain people known to skirt the law or who are prone to violence or who have some shady areas in their lives. Checking alibis would probably prove futile though. Anyone could swear they were home sleeping when John Doe met his demise, and it would be hard to dispute a claim of being in the crowd at the beachside worship service when Mrs. Platt was shot.

All those thoughts led Allison back to the same conclusion—there was an unknown murderer in their midst. And it made her wish she could wrap her arms around all four of the young people to keep them safe.

Fred came whistling down the stairs at the same time the girls came out of their room, but from the scowls on their faces Allison could tell they didn't share his good mood.

Trina's voice, usually soft and pleasant, came out loud and shrill. "But I would like at least one real date during this vacation instead of being chaperoned by your kid brother and his sidekick."

The words floated across the room, caught Allison's attention, and set off alarm bells. She didn't need any internal discord to add to her anxiety. And from the surprised looks on the male faces, they also had heard the peevish comment.

Dave was the first to react. "If you're referring to that gorilla of a lifeguard who shaves his chest, has more tattoos than a drunken sailor, and the brains of a flea, as the real date, then go for it. Just don't come to me for sympathy when you find out he's more than you can handle."

Jumping up from the table, Neil was about to join the fray when Fred stepped into the center of the room, put his hands on his waist and said, "Everybody shut up and sit down."

Allison couldn't help but grin. Old cops never die, nor do they fade away. She was just thankful she was already sitting and hadn't opened her mouth to say a word.

The boys sat back down at the table and stared at the man-in-charge. The girls slid down on the couch and stared at the floor.

Taking a deep breath, Fred paced back and forth a few times, looked to Allison as if asking her permission to continue. Nodding, she smiled at him. She knew he took his job as father to her kids very seriously, and she appreciated it.

He continued to stand as if he were the professor and they his students. At his first words, all their eyes were focused on the teacher. His voice was soft, conciliatory. "Living in close quarters is bound to raise some tensions. And I understand, Trina, both you and Connie are adults and under ordinary circumstances are able to take care of yourselves. But these are not ordinary circumstances we find ourselves in. There have been two violent deaths and therefore we should all be cautious."

Allison nodded her encouragement and he went on. "Your mother and I want you to have a good time, but we also want you safe. And there is safety in numbers. I agree the carnival tonight would probably be a good date place, but it might also be dangerous. And, Connie, you know how your mother can be a worrier. So how about humoring her, and all stick together? If you all have dates, you can take the van. It might be a little crowded, but that's part of the fun. Right?"

"Right," Connie said. "Now can we go and line up those dates for tonight if we promise to behave ourselves?"

Fred waved a dismissive hand. "Go. Have fun."

As the quartet did their disappearing act, Allison whispered to the room, "And be safe."

"Whew," Fred said as he slipped down beside Allison. "This fatherhood bit can get sticky."

"But you handled it magnificently. And on an empty stomach, too. I'm proud of you."

"Proud enough to fix me cheese omelet?"

"Absolutely."

He leaned back and watched as Allison cracked the eggs, shredded the cheese, poured a little milk and put in a drop of vanilla. He was perfectly capable of making a superb omelet on his own, but it was nice to be waited on occasionally. During the school year when they both worked, they alternated cooking and housekeeping chores. It'd been their understanding from the beginning. Although he still thought her quick acceptance of his proposal was, at least in part, due to the fact he could make a marvelous beef stew.

They'd finished eating and were clearing the table together when his phone rang. It was Tuck, who without any preliminaries said, "Tell Allison she got her wish."

Fred mind was blank. *What wish?* He repeated out loud what he'd just asked himself, "What wish?"

"To meet Jeremy Green and his wife, Teresa."

The names didn't mean a thing to Fred who blurted out, "Who are they?"

Tuck sighed. "They're Naomi Platt's nephew and his wife. Remember, they came in yesterday, and Allison said she would like to meet them and ask if she could have Sidney if they didn't want the canary?"

"Oh, yeah. I remember now. So, does that mean they're agreeable to meeting her and/or to giving away the bird?"

"Both."

Fred thought Tuck sounded awfully tired for it being early in the morning. "Are you okay? Are they giving you a hard time? You want us to come over there?"

"No. Yes. Yes."

It took Fred a few seconds to translate the answers. No, Tuck wasn't okay. Yes, the relatives were giving him a hard time, and yes, they should come. "Fine. Give me the address and we'll be there shortly."

When he ended the call, Fred explained it to Allison as he fed the address into his phone and got the directions.

As Fred backed out into the street, she asked, "Why do you suppose the Chicago kin are giving Tuck a hard time?"

"Don't know, but guess we'll find out."

MRS. PLATT'S HOUSE was much as Allison had expected: one story, probably three bedrooms, small porch with a rocking chair, a minuscule yard that was well kept but had no flowers. It was only a few blocks from the beach, but the waterfront hotels, condos, and elevated beach houses blocked any view of the ocean. From the outside, it appeared to have been well maintained. It wasn't prime property but might sell for a family vacation home or for an investment property to rent out at reasonable rates.

A vintage Camry was parked in the narrow driveway and Allison assumed the car had belonged to Mrs. Platt. In Allison's mind, the car seemed to fit the elderly woman: plain and dependable. A shiny, new rental car was parked directly behind it while Tuck's police cruiser was pulled up in front of the house. Fred pulled off the street and parked in behind Tuck. Nobody was in sight, but the front door was open and as she and Fred exited the van, Allison heard low voices coming through the screen door.

"It's all right, Dear," a pleasant feminine voice said, "We can stay a few days. The police have to do their work, and delaying the funeral won't be a problem."

"That's not it. I just hate the thought of an autopsy. Aunt Naomi was such a private person."

Tuck must have heard them come up the steps because in a moment the screen door opened and he motioned them in. The officer turned to the couple in the room, "Mr. and Mrs. Green, I'd like you to meet Fred and Allison Sawyer." He paused as if not sure where to go from there.

Allison took advantage of the silence, stepped forward and reached out her hand to Mr. Green. "I'm so sorry for your loss, Mr. Green. I know this has been a shock to you."

The man shook her hand, nodded. "I'm glad to meet you. It was nice of you and your husband to come. The few times we visited, we never met many of my aunt's friends."

Fred reached around Allison to shake the nephew's hand and explained, "We weren't actually friends since we'd just met her, but…she seemed like such a nice lady."

Mentally shaking her head, Allison thought, not for

the first time, that Fred wasn't a very good liar. She turned to the woman. "Like my husband said, Mrs. Green, we hadn't had time to get to know her well, but I did learn she liked to play bingo, loved her canary, and was a sharp shooter." Allison pretended to fan herself. "I hate guns myself so I had to admire her for being so independent."

Mrs. Green gave a low chuckle. "She was that. She lived alone for thirty years and wanted it that way. We knew she liked to walk to work and around town and carried the gun for protection. Although, I never understood who she thought she had to be protected from in this sleepy little town." The woman shrugged. "As a matter of fact, I never really got to know her. I'm glad you and your husband had gotten acquainted with her. If fact, you seem to know as much about her as we did. And please, call us Teresa and Jeremy."

Allison took the cue and ran with it. "When was the last time you visited here, Teresa?"

Turning to her husband, Teresa asked, "Was it four years ago, Jeremy? Or five?"

"Close to five. Remember, we stopped on our way to that convention in Miami, spent the night?"

"Oh, yes, but I'm afraid Aunt Naomi wasn't much for company. As far as I know, her job and her few pastimes were her life and that was enough for her. You can imagine the shock when we got a call from the police saying she'd committed suicide."

Jeremy came closer, slid his arm around his wife's waist. "And it was even a bigger jolt when the next phone call said it might be murder." He shook his head. "Why would anyone want to murder my aunt? It doesn't make sense."

Before either Allison or Fred could comment, Tuck stepped forward. "And that is what the county detectives are trying to figure out and I think it better not to speculate."

Staring at Tuck as if he were an alien being, Allison bit her tongue to keep from saying anything wrong. Why was Tuck being so touchy?

Fred must have picked up on the hostile vibes between the officer and the nephew, and rushed to Tuck's defense. "Well, I know the splendid police force here will get to the bottom of the matter. We're simply here to ask if you would allow us to adopt the canary if you don't want him. My wife is a real animal lover—both the furry and feathery kind and you can be assured Sidney will have a good home."

Teresa Green beamed at him. "Oh, that would be such a relief. We had no idea what to do about the bird. Pets aren't allowed in our apartment complex—not that we would have time to care for him anyway—plus the expense of flying the bird to Chicago."

All the time they'd been in the room, Allison had tried to locate the birdcage and its occupant, but hadn't found it. That was explained when Jeremy headed to the back of the house. "Aunt Naomi kept him at her bedside. I'll get him."

Glancing at Fred, she had no problem reading his mind. He was thinking something like: *No bird is going to be living in my bedroom, and he better not do any singing during the night, either.*

Jeremy carried the bird, the cage, and its stand from the bedroom, kept on going through the living room, straight through the door, and down the steps. He had no intention to give them a chance to change their minds.

Fred had no choice but to follow him. Allison felt sorry for the slightly dazed canary swinging back and forth wildly and uttering something that sounded like bird talk for, *Help, I'm getting dizzy.*

At the same time, Teresa handed Allison a box filled with bird feed, a cover for the cage, and various toys. "Again I want to thank you for your interest in Aunt Naomi and for taking the canary. I know you'll give him a good home."

Allison wanted to continue her conversation with the Greens in hopes of learning a little more about Naomi Platt's history, but Teresa had already opened the screen door so Allison could carry her load out. Both of them stopped at the top of the steps, though, when another car drove up and a tall redhead sashayed out. Teresa backed away and hovered close to the screen door.

The newcomer eyed the two men by Fred's car, but zeroed in on the younger man who had just deposited the canary in the back seat. "You must be dear Naomi's nephew. I know this must be so hard for you, and I just want to extend my condolences."

Jeremy straightened up, nodded. "Thank you. I appreciate it." He reached out to shake her hand. "Were you a friend of hers?"

"Oh, I was much more than a friend. We worked together at the realty office. She never mentioned Meg Freeman to you?"

"Afraid not. She never talked much about her work."

"That's understandable. She wasn't much for chatter."

Staring at her, Allison tried to come up with the real reason why Mrs. Platt's co-worker would be here, and what did she mean by "dear Naomi"? From what she'd observed, neither Meg nor Naomi cared much for each other, and Meg didn't strike Allison as a woman who cared about amenities.

Tuck came out on the porch, shielded his eyes from the sun, and asked what Allison had been thinking. "What are you doing here, Meg?"

She gave him a wide-eyed mischievous look as she climbed the steps. "Since when do I need an invitation to extend my sympathy to a bereaved family?"

Before Tuck could respond, Teresa spoke up, her back to the door. "It was kind of you to come. I'm Teresa Green."

"And I'm Meg Freeman. As I told your husband, Naomi and I worked together. She's going to be greatly missed at the office as well in the community."

"It was nice of you to come. We haven't met many of Aunt Naomi's friends."

"Well, you can be sure there will be quite a few at her funeral. Do you know yet when that will be?"

Teresa shook her head, looked over at the policeman by her side. Tuck answered for her. "It's not been decided yet. I'll let Clyde know, as he may want to close the office."

Meg turned back to Teresa. "Actually, there's one other reason I came today."

"Oh?"

"Yes, you see, I loaned Naomi a book last week and I would like to get it back if that's all right with you. But I don't want to bother you to look for it. It's probably on her desk. I could just go in and get it."

Meg started toward the door but Teresa blocked her way. "Well, we had started packing a few things we were going to give to Goodwill. The book may be in there. What's the name of the book?"

Allison noticed Meg hesitate then smiled as she said, "'The Pirate and the Lady.'"

"Sounds like a romance."

"It is. A spicy one. That's one of the things Naomi and I had in common. We both loved romantic novels."

It was all Allison could do not to protest. She couldn't even imagine the proper Mrs. Platt reading a spicy book. But then what did she know?

Teresa must have felt the same way. "I didn't know Aunt Naomi read romances."

"Well, we all have our little secrets, don't we?"

Teresa shrugged. "Anyway, If I find it, I'll send it over to the office."

"Thanks. And if there's anything I can do for you while you're here, please let me know."

Meg trotted down to the sidewalk, waved to Tuck and the other men and drove away.

Allison realized she'd been standing in the same spot for quite a few minutes blatantly eavesdropping on the conversation. Turning to Teresa, she said, "I'll be on my way, too."

When she got to the car, she deposited her load in the back seat next to Sidney's cage, and spoke to Fred, "Sorry, it took me so long."

The men exchanged waves and goodbyes while Allison leaned over her seat to reassure her new pet. "It's all right, Sidney. I know you're a little confused right now, but you're going to love your new home."

"Sure," Fred said, "and you're going to love having a cat for a roommate."

FOURTEEN

As THEY DROVE AWAY, Fred noticed Allison flopped back in her seat and took a couple of deep breaths before fastening her seat belt. His bride was definitely not happy and he knew he was about to find out why.

"Well," she sputtered. "That didn't go quite like I had wanted."

"What do you mean?" he asked. "You got the bird. That's what we came after."

"Yes, but a friendly little chat with the Greens would have been nice. Instead, Meg Freeman showed up."

"A chat about what?" Fred knew exactly what Allison was leading up to, but he tried to maintain his apparent innocent manner.

"A chat about dear Aunt Naomi—about why she carried a gun for one thing, about why they didn't visit her more often, about…oh, I don't know…just about things."

"Well, the nephew said that his aunt was a private person, and it seems that he's the same. And since Tuck probably got all the pertinent information he could out of them we'll just leave it at that and forget about the Greens."

When Allison didn't answer immediately, Fred figured she wasn't content to leave it up to Tuck and was hatching up some kind of scheme on her own. After a minute or two, he noticed her nodding her head a bit.

"Let me guess," he said. "You have an idea on how to get Teresa Green off by herself and get her talking."

Allison stared at him in apparent surprise. "Of course not. You said to forget about the Greens and that's just what I intend to do. We'll go back to our pink house, get Sidney settled down, and then go for some more waves and sun. Okay?"

"Sure. Okay," he said. "No problem."

As EXPECTED NONE of the young people were at the house, and Allison took her time trying to find the perfect place for the birdcage. She wondered if Sidney had a private personality like his previous owner or if he might enjoy being the center of attention. Did he prefer to be in the sunlight or the shadows? Fred had already ruled out the bedroom for his abode and since the kitchen was often pretty crowded, that left the living room or the hallway.

She hadn't made up her mind yet when Fred headed for the staircase. "I thought you wanted to get some more waves and sun. Just put the crazy bird by the front window and let's change into our suits."

Allison jerked her head up. Fred has sounded irritated, and that didn't sit well with her. What had happened to her easygoing, agreeable husband? If he hadn't wanted her to adopt Sidney, he should have said something earlier.

"What do you mean, 'crazy bird'? He hasn't made a bit of noise since we picked him up. He's depressed, and the least you could do is be nice to him."

"I know. I know. I'm sorry I sounded so grouchy. It's just that this vacation isn't going the way I'd envisioned it. I just wanted to have a nice, quiet time at the beach with the woman I love—not flitting around meeting strangers and picking up strays."

Feeling contrite, Allison knew Fred was right. Their vacation was half over and they hadn't built up many good memories yet. She gave him her brightest smile. "I'll beat you upstairs, into my swimsuit, and into the water." Before he could make a comeback, she was dashing up the steps.

At the top of the staircase, she stopped, looked back, grinned, and motioned him onward with her forefinger.

"Just wait, Hon," he said. "That's going to cost you a dunking."

"Only if you can catch me."

The quick clothes changings and the even quicker sunscreen applications were followed by a race to the water. Allison darted between sunbathers and beach chairs and sandcastles. With each stride her cares and her years dropped further away. As he'd promised, when Fred caught up with her, she was soundly dunked. She came up spitting and coughing and reveling in the moment. This was what a vacation should be.

For the next several minutes, the two of them cavorted like dolphins: jumping, diving, splashing. Allison was the first to call for a time-out. She crawled out on the sand and collapsed in a heap.

Fred soon joined her. He lay prostrated on the sand, his face turned to one side and both hands above his head. He croaked out two words, "I surrender."

She wiggled over to him, dropped her head on his back and said, "Me too."

When they both recovered enough to sit up, Allison noted the fact they had no towels with them. "The next time you challenge me to a water fight," she said, "make sure we have some towels."

"Will do, and the next time you expect me to exercise like this, better pack a lunch. I'm starved."

"Then I guess we'd better head back. I'm first in the shower."

Fred grinned. "Fine by me. That means you can be getting out the sandwich stuff while I'm getting the sand off."

FRED WAITED ON the front porch while Allison occupied the shower. He knew he had a silly grin on his face as he relived their playful antics in the water. This was going to be a vacation to remember fondly in spite of the intrusions of dead bodies. His wife, his kids, and the kids' friends were safe—and that's all that really mattered.

As if his thoughts conjured them up, all four of the kids trouped up from the beach. Dave's long legs took the steps two at a time and the moment he came to a stop his mouth took over. "Hey, Pops. Did Mom ban you from the house?"

"No. But she might ban you, if you don't lower your volume. I don't think the lifeguards want to hear what goes on in the pink house."

Connie skittered up the steps and over to Fred's chair. "Oh, is there something going on in the pink house we should know about?"

Not to be outdone, Neil leaned over Connie's shoulder and grinned at Fred. "Just be assured, Sir, if you need any advice, I aced my Advanced Psychology exam."

Trina let out a cackle that reminded Fred of the yard chickens his grandmother used to raise, but before he could get started down that particular memory lane, Trina went on, "All you know about psychology, Neil, you learned from 'Annie's Mailbox' column."

Fred had heard enough of this nonsense. He stood up and announced, "I will now go upstairs for my shower. When I return, I hope your mouths are crammed with food and all I hear is happy munching."

As much as he enjoyed the kids' silly palaver, sometimes it got to be a little too much.

He met Allison coming down the stairs as he was going up and gave her fair warning, "I think they all reverted to the seventh grade, so be prepared."

"Don't worry. Seventh graders are my specialty."

THE YOUNG PEOPLE were still on the porch, so Allison went out to join them. "One word of caution to you before you go in," she said.

"But, Mom," Connie said, "Fred knew we were just teasing him, didn't he?"

Allison frowned. "This has nothing to do with Fred. I'm sure whatever nonsense you laid on him went in one ear and out the other. This is about Sidney."

The four faces in front of her went blank. Finally, Dave said, "Who in the world is Sidney?"

Allison stared at them, bit her bottom lip, and asked, "I didn't tell you about Sidney?"

"No, Mom," Connie said. "I'm sure I would have remembered a name like that. What about him?"

"Oh. Well, in that case, let's go inside and I'll introduce you, but keep your voices down. He might be a little sensitive for a bit."

Allison couldn't help but notice the question marks that flitted back and forth between the foursome. It would have been funny if she hadn't been having second thoughts about the wisdom of adopting a canary. What would happen when they got home? Would the bird be safe alone with a cat in the house while she and Fred were at work? Lancelot didn't take well to strangers, and she had no idea that he would welcome the new adoptee.

Motioning the young people into the living room, Allison walked over to the window at the foot of the staircase where the birdcage hung. The canary sat huddled on the floor under his swing as if afraid to venture out into the rest of the cage.

"This is Sidney. He belonged to Mrs. Platt from the realty office who died recently." Allison couldn't bring herself to mention how Mrs. Platt died, but the kids knew the stories going around town. "Since her family didn't want the bird, I offered to give him a home. It may take him a while to become accustomed to us, so be gentle around him."

Connie was the first to respond. "Oh, the poor thing. He's scared. I bet he misses his owner. But isn't he beautiful? His feathers are as yellow as butter and so smooth. You can tell he's been well fed—and well loved."

Allison noticed Dave putting on his skeptical face and wasn't surprised when he came out with, "Wow, Connie, one look and you know all about him. Way to go."

For perhaps the first time in their history, Connie didn't come back with a caustic retort to Dave's sarcasm.

Allison could sense something was happening between the girl and the canary and she motioned for the others to step back and be quiet. They instantly obeyed.

They watched in fascination as Connie slid one slim

finger into the cage, carefully plucked up a small seed that had fallen out of the feeding dish, and held it up as an offering. At the same time, she kept up a soft, almost cooing monologue. "I know we just met, Sidney, but you and I are going to become best friends. Maybe I can take you back to school with me and when I come in after classes you can sing to me and I'll tell you all about the hard test I had or the body I had to dissect or the obnoxious interns. How about it? Think we'll make a great team?"

Allison anticipated Connie's question as her daughter pivoted around. "Can I, Mom? Can I have Sidney? My apartment could use a little cheering up."

Swallowing a lump in her throat, Allison nodded. "Sounds like a good idea. I have all the pets I can handle for right now."

Connie grinned, turned back to the cage, and moved her finger holding the seed a little closer. Sidney cocked his head on one side. Allison thought he looked as if he were waiting for the next chapter in the story his new friend had been telling him, and Connie obliged. "You'll have a wonderful view out my window. It overlooks a parking lot and you'll get to watch people coming and going all day long."

She wiggled her finger again. "You'll have to come get this food because I can't move my hand any closer."

Everyone in the room seemed to hold their breath, as Sidney hopped up to Connie's finger and snatched the seed. There were several seeds on the floor of the cage, so Connie flicked some in Sidney's direction, and then pulled her hand away.

With a triumphant smile, she shooed the assembled crowd back. "Let's leave him alone to enjoy his lunch."

As they headed toward the kitchen area for their own lunch, Dave slipped his arm around Connie's shoulders. "You were fantastic, Sis. You're going to make a terrific doctor with that bedside manner."

Allison was dabbing at her eyes as Fred came down the stairs. He looked over to the young people and they all appeared to have secret little smiles. "What's going on?"

Dave took a deep breath, put a little swagger in his voice, "You've heard of the Horse Whisperer haven't you, Fred?"

"Sure."

"Well, Connie just became a Canary Whisperer. Mom can tell you all about it later. Right now, it's chow time."

Sandwich making at the pink house had become so routine that soon everyone was munching on his/her creation. Allison glanced up from her cheese and tomato to take a peek over at Sidney. He seemed to be enjoying his own lunch.

FIFTEEN

His APPETITE SATED, Fred rose, stretched, and asked, "Well, what's on everybody's agenda this afternoon?"

Allison headed for the couch. "I've got a book I need to finish, and I'm staying right here until I find out what happened to poor little Mary Beth."

Trina slouched into the living room and picked up a paperback. "Guess I might as well finish this book, too. Nothing else to do."

Fred saw Allison lift her head, give Trina a quizzical look, "I thought you kids were out finding dates to go to the carnival."

Dave came in and slipped down beside his mother. "We thought so, too. But it turns out none of the local gals go to the carnival during the week. It's way cooler to go on Friday night."

"Our lifeguards go Friday, also," Trina joined in, "as it's the end of their rotation and they have the night off."

Neil grabbed a cookie on his way out of the kitchen and between bites stated what they all knew, "But we'll be long gone come Friday night."

Fred stared at the dejected foursome. "So what's keeping you from going anyway?"

Connie gave Fred one of those looks he'd learned to interpret as: *You've got to be kidding.*

Her next words proved him right. "Go to a carnival with my kid brother and his sidekick? I don't think so."

Neil apparently didn't care for Connie's attitude. He squared his shoulders, put his hands on his hips, and declared, "I'll have you know this sidekick can be a lot of fun. I can out-scream you on The Octopus and out-eat you at the deep-fried Twinkie stand."

Connie burst into laughter. "How can I turn down a date like that?" She turned to Trina, "Do I hear a second to the motion?"

Trina nodded her head slightly. "Might as well."

Dave held up a hand. "I'm in," he said, "just so the word doesn't get back to campus that I went to the local carnival with my sister and…her sidekick."

With a gleam in her eyes, Trina stuck her right forefinger in the middle of Dave's tie-dyed tee shirt and, in a voice that she'd perfected as a museum curator, said, "And no selfies with me in your pictures. I have my reputation to consider, too."

So, it was decided. The young people changed from beach dress to carny dress. Allison assured them the old folks could manage to make a dinner on their own, and Fred pulled out several bills from his wallet. "The rides are on me. Who's going to be the treasurer?" Since Dave was the closest, he snatched the money and dashed out the back door followed closely by Neil and Trina. Connie made a detour to the birdcage to assure Sidney she'd be back later so they could have a good talk.

When the noise of laughter and of the car dissipated, Fred snuggled close to Allison, whispered in her ear, "And what are we going to do the rest of the afternoon?"

Allison lay down her book, pulled Fred closer, gave him a soft kiss—then slowly shoved him away. "There's no 'we' for now. I want to finish this book."

Sitting straight up, Fred said, "Well, if you're going to act that way, I'm taking a walk."

"Fine. Tell Tuck 'hey' for me."

As he went down the back steps and turned right, Fred muttered, "It's just not fair. She can read my mind a whole lot better than I can read hers."

Approaching the Beacon Beach Police Station, Fred noticed the county sheriff department car there as well as the local vehicles. He hesitated. As friendly as all of the officers had been to him, he still knew he was an outsider. He certainly didn't have the right to intrude on their meeting. Since he had no new information to contribute, his visit here was merely out of curiosity.

But as he turned to leave, Jack flung open the door and called to him, "Hey, Fred. Thought I saw you through the window. Come on in. Got some news you should hear."

Fred gave the young cop a wave and a big smile as he trotted up the sidewalk. His detective genes started dancing around and his heart started pounding harder. Had he been a little hasty in retiring? It felt good to be in the middle of another investigation. Maybe when he got back home he could offer his services as a consultant to the sheriff department there. Shoving the idea to the back of his head, he greeted the assembled team.

"Did I hear something about news?"

"Sure did," Sheila said as she slid her chair over to make room for him.

Tuck set a cup of coffee in front on him and added, "Big news."

Taking a sip of the coffee, Fred glanced around the table. "Well, what do I have to do? Beg?"

Ed shook his head. "No. I was just wondering why Allison wasn't with you."

"She's taking a break, but if I promise to relay the information as soon as I get back to her, will you, please, tell me?"

Fred could tell from the grin on Tuck's face that Ed was messing with him, and he really didn't mind. That's what fellow detectives do when they're working on a case together—which meant he and Allison were now considered members of the team.

"Sure. You don't have to get testy about it." Ed took another sip of his coffee and came out with the announcement. "Our John Doe is actually George Yates from Pennix, South Carolina—a small town not far from Charleston. His stepsister, who lives on the outskirts of Charleston, recognized the sketch in the Sunday paper, but since she'd been out of town for a few days, didn't see it until last night. She called her police station this morning and they called us. According to her, she wasn't close to George, hadn't seen him in several years and had no idea why he was in this area."

Fred pondered the new information while Ed worked on his coffee. "Therefore, knowing his ID isn't much help in finding his killer."

"Not yet," Tuck said. "The stepsister gave permission to search his apartment, but she doesn't appear to have legal rights so the local police are getting a warrant. They might find something pertinent."

"Like a name of somebody he might have visited in Beacon Beach?"

"I doubt if we'll get that lucky, but we'll wait and see."

Ed took up where he'd left off. "The PDs in both Pennix and in Charleston are looking into his past: employment, friends, travels, finances, the whole gamut.

We'll find something that ties him to Beacon Beach and in some way to Naomi Platt. I've still no doubt the two cases are related."

Silence hung heavy in the small office as everyone was wrapped in their own thoughts. After a bit, Jack broke the stillness with a question to Ed. "When do you expect to get the autopsy report on her?"

"Probably not until tomorrow unless I can hurry them up."

Fred rose to his feet. "I'd better be getting home to my better half and fill her in."

Sheila gave him a big smile. "Tell her we missed her."

"Will do."

Fred hurried back to the pink house, anxious to tell Allison the latest development.

He slipped down beside her on the couch, pushed her book out of the way, and before she had a chance to get irritated with him, he asked, "Want to know who John Doe is?"

Punching him lightly on his arm, she said, "That's like asking me if I want a cup of coffee in the morning. Tell me. Who is our mysterious corpse?"

"His name is George Yates from Pennix, South Carolina. Picture identified by a sister."

Allison seemed to ponder the news of John Doe's identity and his residence in her own deliberate way. He could imagine her brain digesting the information but had no idea what she might make of it. He waited patiently.

After a bit, she came up with a question. "How far is the town of Pennix from here?"

"Well, it's about a hundred miles from here to Charleston, so add maybe another twenty to it."

"So probably a two-hour drive?"

"Something like that—depending on traffic."

Just so he would have something to do while waiting for Allison's next comment or question, Fred zapped a cup of water in the microwave, stirred in some instant coffee and added a pack of artificial sweetener. Taking a sip, he nodded in satisfaction. It wasn't as good as the station house brew but it'd do in a pinch. When he wandered back into the living room, she was ready for him.

"When we were in Mrs. Platt's house, I noticed she had a landline phone and the realty office also have landlines."

"And your question is…?"

"I was wondering if it's possible to find out if George Yates called the realty office and spoke to Mrs. Platt or called her at home." She paused for a quick breath and then went on, "Because if, as Ed says, the two cases are related, it's likely they knew each other and were in contact."

It took a few moments for Fred to process the question, but his answer was short. "Probably."

"Probably what?"

"Probably it is possible to ascertain if he called the realty office since his sister would know his phone number, although I doubt they could find out who he talked to—unless one of the other two in the office remembers a call from him. And secondly, probably because they could find out if he called her home, but…"

Fred stopped talking as a sudden thought flitted through his brain. "On the other hand, Mrs. Platt may not have known him personally, but she might have recognized his name if and when John Doe was identified."

"How?"

"Because she usually gave out the keys to the rental units and he may have rented a house from them in the past."

Fred could tell by Allison's scowl that she didn't think much of that idea. "And you think she would remember the names of hundreds of renters that go through that office? I don't think so."

"Yeah, you're right. That's quite a stretch. So, how about we forget Mr. Yates and Mrs. Platt for now and see what we can find for supper."

"Good idea."

They raided the fridge for leftovers and finished up the strawberry ice cream. While Allison sipped on chamomile tea, Fred had another cup of instant coffee. The rest of the evening was quiet as they played a few boring games of rummy, and watched the late news. Not knowing when the kids would come in, Allison wished Sidney a good night, and put the cover over his cage.

They were about to call it a day when the young people came drooping in. The boys collapsed on the sofa, Trina sipped a glass of soda water while Connie asked if there was any Pepto Bismo available. From their appearances Allison concluded each one of the quartet had had all the food and rides a body could take for one day.

It wasn't until Fred mentioned the next day's activities that they perked up a little. "We better turn in," he said. "The boys and I have to be at the marina at eight, and I'm sure you girls will want to get an early start on your shopping."

Dave nodded. "I hope you've got a good supply of Dramamine, Fred. I'm not sure I can take a rocking boat in the morning."

"Not to worry—got it covered."

Connie let out a groan. "I'm not sure I can face a mob of shoppers in the morning. My stomach is still on a whirly-gig."

Allison gave her daughter a quick hug. "You'll be fine in the morning. All you need is a good night's rest."

ACROSS TOWN, SLINK was also making plans for the next morning. *I've got to get back into the pink house. I know the money is there. It has to be. He told me earlier he'd found the perfect hiding place when he was renting there, and had left it since he planned on returning later to retrieve it—when it was safe to start spending it. Why in the world had I agreed to that crazy plan? And why hadn't he had sense enough to reserve a rental on the place? Nothing to do now except search until I find it.*

SIXTEEN

Morning came, but Connie knew she was far from being fine. She'd spent most of the night in the bathroom. Her stomach was determined to rid itself of whatever spoiled concoction she'd eaten at the carnival. She couldn't imagine how Trina could sleep through all the retching and belching and moaning, but her roommate seemed to be in dreamland the entire night.

"Good thing I'm not dying in here," Connie muttered between upchucks, "Trina wouldn't wake up long enough to call 911."

When dawn slithered its way through the closed blinds, Connie finally was able to doze off. It wasn't long, though, before she was roused back to consciousness by the refrigerator door slamming, followed by Dave and Neil bickering over something. She plopped a pillow over her head, but it wasn't enough to keep out the sickening odor of frying bacon. Thank goodness she didn't have anything else in her stomach that could come up. Burrowing deeper under the covers, Connie shut down all her senses and slid back into a deep slumber.

The next thing she knew, someone was shaking her, shouting at her. "Wake up, Sleeping Beauty. We've got to hit the outlets."

"Go away. Let me sleep."

"How can you sleep on such a beautiful day? Think

of the End-of-Summer sales and huge discounts—a day shoppers dream of."

Trina's bubbling voice, usually so welcomed, bored into Connie's brain like a dental drill. She edged out from under her covers, blinked a couple of times and glared at her friend. "And how could you have slept all night when I was upchucking my guts? It was probably that last Patty Melt you shoved down my throat that poisoned me."

Connie was immediately sorry for her outburst when Trina leaned over, brushed the hair out of her eyes and patted her on the cheek.

"Why didn't you wake me up? I could have…" Trina's voice trailed off as she ended the sentence with a shrug.

"I know. You couldn't have done anything to help, and the old saying that 'misery loves company' is absolutely not true. I want privacy in my misery, so I'm glad you had a good night's sleep. But now I have to catch up. You and Mom go shopping without me."

"You do look pretty wrung out. But I know your size; I'll bring you back some goodies."

"Don't bother. I don't need many clothes. I'll be wearing scrubs much of the time."

"You can't wear scrubs on dates."

"What dates? I'll be too busy to have a social life."

Trina gave her their "don't try to fool me" look they'd perfected through the years. "On the other hand," she said, "scrubs can look pretty sexy."

Connie shooed her away. "Go tell Mom I'm taking a sick day from this vacation."

Knowing she wouldn't be allowed to go back to sleep until she'd been examined and quizzed by her mother aka the family physician and confessor, Connie propped up on her pillow and waited.

It took longer than she expected and her eyes were beginning to droop when the door opened and her mother came in carrying a tray with food on it. The last thing Connie wanted was to see, to smell, and especially to taste was any kind of food.

"Sorry you had a rough night," her mother said, "and you're absolutely right about staying home and sleeping."

Connie had a hard time believing what she'd heard. She'd expected something like: *What on earth did you eat? How many rides did you go on?* What had happened to her mother—the gym/health teacher who had hounded her for years to eat right and play sensibly?

The answer came in her next sentence. "Of course, I would think someone who had completed a year in med school would know better to eat all that junk food from open-air food vendors, but maybe you haven't had that course yet."

Well, Connie thought, two could play this game. "I appreciate your concern, Mom. But you can take your oatmeal and sarcasm away. I'm not swallowing either one."

Her mother laughed. "Of course not. And it's not oatmeal. Just a piece of dry toast and a cup of warm milk."

"Yuck!"

"Sure, it's yuck, but it's what you need and what will stay down. Now Trina and I are going shopping, and you can sleep the day away since there'll be no one around."

"Thanks, Mom. Sorry I was so snarky. I'll try to eat some. Will you check on Sidney's food and give him fresh water?"

"Sure will. 'Bye, Hon."

"Be sure his door snaps shut when you finish. I noticed yesterday it was bent a little."

"Don't worry about Sidney. Just get some rest."

FRED AND THE BOYS walked to the marina and arrived a little before eight. Ben wasn't in sight, but Fred spotted a younger version of their skipper strolling along the waterfront. Although the two hadn't been formerly introduced, they each stopped and nodded. Fred reached out his hand. "You must be Clyde from the realty. Want to thank you for the complimentary lunch our family had. Excellent food."

"Glad you enjoyed it. I heard that you fellows were planning on going out today. Hope you have a good catch."

"Thanks." Fred turned to his companions. "Boys, this is Clyde Johansen, Ben's son."

Dave stuck out his hand. "Pleased to meet you, Sir. I met your father yesterday, and I'm really looking forward to our trip."

"Me, too," Neil said as he shook Clyde's hand. "And thank you for the lunch."

When Clyde made no comment, Fred said, "I didn't know you and your dad worked together."

"We don't. We may look alike, but that's where the resemblance ends. I just like to walk along the water before being holed up in my office all day. Dad practically lives on his boat."

"But he must tell you about his clients since you knew we'd booked him."

"Nope. He didn't tell me, but you know small towns—everybody keeps up with everybody else."

There was something about Clyde that Fred didn't much like, but he tried to hide his irritation. "I didn't know that included the tourists."

Clyde chuckled. "But you're not just an ordinary tourist. Tuck seems to think a lot of you."

"So Tuck told you I was going fishing today?"

"Not really. He told Meg and Meg told me."

Now Fred was really irked. He liked the young officer and hadn't expected him to be a blabbermouth. He recalled Meg was the pretty redhead who worked at the realty office and who'd rushed into the police station Sunday demanding what had happened to Mrs. Platt. He also remembered how Tuck had put his arm around her as he escorted her out. "So, Tuck and Meg are close?"

"No one gets close with Meg. Believe me, I've tried. But she and Tuck do date on occasions, which is further than I ever got. But hey, I get to enjoy her company in the office even if she does just work part-time."

Fred considered his next words carefully as his detective mind whirled around. "And now that Mrs. Platt is gone, I guess you'll be seeing more of the lovely Meg. That is, I assume she'll be working full-time now."

"No such luck. I offered her the position, but she brushed it off—said she had plans to move back to Atlanta as soon as the summer season is over. That means I have to break in a new assistant." He checked his watch. "Which means I have to get to the office now. Got an applicant coming in." Nodding down toward the boats, he added, "And I see Zack coming to get you. Must be he's taking you out instead of my dad. Anyway, have a good day."

"Yeah, you too."

Zack came up, introduced himself, welcomed them

aboard, explained that Ben had other plans for the day. Fred was a little miffed that it wasn't Ben who was commanding the boat, but then decided it didn't make any difference. Ben had said they were partners and alternated working both the store and the boats.

When they boarded the boat, Fred was amused as both Dave and Neil seem to immediately revert back to being eager teenagers on a new adventure. They explored everything in sight, asked if they could go below deck to check out it out, and bombarded Zack with questions.

Fred tried to match the boys' enthusiasm as the boat roared out to sea, but he'd been a fisherman all his life, and this was old stuff to him. Besides, his mind was still on Clyde.

What was it Allison had said when he told her about Meg Freeman coming into the police station? Something about checking her alibi and then adding, *Better check Clyde's alibi, too.*

He knew Ed and Sheila had questioned both Clyde and Meg, but that had been when the death was considered a suicide. Of course, officially it still was death by a self-inflicted gunshot wound, but maybe it *was* time to start checking alibis.

In his prior murder investigations, the whereabouts of the victim's family members at the time of death were always carefully noted. And in this case, the people in the realty office were the closest Mrs. Platt came to having a family here in Beacon Beach. Maybe he should talk with Ed later about it. The lead detective had seemed to welcome input from both him and Allison, so it wouldn't be as if he were being pushy.

As Fred thought further of the situation and the possible suspects, he became troubled about the fact that Tuck might be dating a possible person of interest— and perhaps filling her in on the investigation. Was it possible that Tuck was telling Meg what was going on in the police department and Meg was passing it on to Clyde, and possibly to many other people in the small town? If so, it certainly wasn't a good way to run an investigation.

Maybe he'd better do some inquiries on his own, and since Ben wasn't around, he would sound out Zack a little. The skipper had slowed the motor as they neared their fishing spot so one could converse now without shouting.

The next several minutes were spent in getting their poles ready, along with instructions and safety tips from Zack. Dave and Neil were eager students, and Fred hoped the boys would catch something they could brag about in the coming months.

The father figure in Fred was pleased that Zack stayed close to the boys, always on the ready to give help with any problems, encouraging them, and seem-ing to have a good time himself. When the kids seemed pretty settled and the captain leaned back on the railing to light a cigarette, Fred decided it was a good time to start a conversation.

"I was talking to Clyde Johansen this morning," Fred said. "He sounded like he didn't have much liking for being a seaman."

Zack shook his head, smiled. "Let me put it this way…he would rather ride a mule across the desert than to take a spin in a boat. That's why Ben bought the rental realty—to give him a job and keep him out of trouble. Don't get me wrong. Clyde's a good boy, but he's not overly ambitious. He tends to skip out of the office whenever he gets a chance. But he and his daddy get along fine—as long as they don't try to change each other."

"Sounds sensible. Does Clyde's mother agree with that philosophy?"

"His mother is long gone. She left both of them a good many years ago, but don't waste your sympathy on them. They're not one bit lonely."

"I see," Fred said. And he did see. Two healthy, care-free bachelors in a tourist town wouldn't have any trouble finding companionship. But he was getting away from the purpose of his investigation, so he tried again. "I guess Clyde was pretty upset, though, about Mrs. Platt's death—losing a long-time employee like that."

Zack studied some of the dials on the panel and slowed the motor a bit more before answering. "He wasn't so upset about losing her as he was about the way it happened."

"Yeah, and finding her dead in the office must have been mighty hard to take." When Zack made no comment, Fred continued, "But I heard that Clyde planned to let her go anyway. That true?"

"Guess so. All I really know is that Clyde called Ben Saturday afternoon, and then Ben filled me in on it when I hauled in that evening."

That statement startled Fred, and he asked, "So you and Ben are partners in the realty office, too?"

"Oh, no. That's strictly in the Johansen family. But, you see, Ben and I are so used to discussing things that he blurts out anything that's on his mind, and I do pretty much the same."

"I know how that works. I used to have a buddy like

that." Fred wiggled his pole a little just to make the fish think he was serious about this fishing gig, and glanced over to the boys. They were staring at the slow-moving water as intently as if they were watching an action movie, and their voices were muted to a low rumble. Fred turned his attention back to Zack wanting to hear the rest of the story.

"So why did Clyde call Ben on Saturday?"

"To ask what to do about Mrs. Platt. It seems she'd been getting more and more irritable with clients, and then the incident with your missus really teed Clyde off." Zack took several puffs on his smoke before going on. "Now, you've got to understand. Ben's a nice enough fella, but he always has his eye on the bottom line. I wasn't surprised that he told Clyde if Mrs. Platt was bad for business, he'd have to get rid of her."

Zack paused, stomped out his cigarette and rubbed a hand through what was left of his hair. "I felt bad for her, but I never imagined she'd take it so hard that she'd kill herself."

Their conversation was interrupted by a yell from Dave. "Hey, Zack, I've got something. What do you think it is?"

IT WAS LATE MORNING and the sidewalks along Shoreline Drive were empty except for one casual stroller. The garage of the pink house contained a red convertible, but it didn't worry Slink. The Beacon Beach grapevine passed the news of the men walking down to the dock for a day of fishing and of the ladies going shopping. Knowing the occupants would be gone most of the day, Slink was in no hurry. The intruder was also quite optimistic that this time the search would be successful.

I don't know why I hadn't thought of it before. He once told me, when he was a kid, he would hide his contraband in the recess at the top on the venetian blind in his room. He could squeeze in cigarettes, a little coke, even porn if the picture was folded just right. Why not money? One of the recesses might not hold all the bills, but he could have used several. All I need is a small screwdriver to pry open the front of the blind and a plastic bag to put the loot in—and my surgical gloves, of course. Can't leave any fingerprints behind. I'll start with the empty bedroom upstairs.

Slink unlocked the back door as usual, marched across the room and stopped abruptly at the foot of the stairs. *What on earth is that bird doing here?*

The intruder tried to come up with some explanation, couldn't, decided it didn't matter, and hurried up the stairs. Dragging the desk chair over to the window of the empty bedroom, Slink got to work.

CONNIE STIRRED IN her sleep. Something had interrupted her dream. Blinking, she tried to recapture the feel of waves lapping at her feet, the sun on her shoulders, the handsome lifeguard smiling at her. It was no use—the pretty picture was gone and was replaced with the feel of sand in her throat. Fully awake now, she scrambled out of bed, lunged for the bathroom, and gulped a glass of water. She refilled the glass and this time sipped its contents slowly. Just as slowly her brain came alive. Had she heard someone come in? Back in the bedroom she glanced at the bedside clock. Ten after eleven. Were Trina and her mom back from shopping already? Must be the sales hadn't been so great after all.

Thinking they may have come back to check on her,

Connie did a quick inspection of herself. Her stomach was no longer rebelling; she was well rested and just a little lightheaded. Apparently, her body had won over the ptomaine poisoning with no serious complications. And, as strange as it seemed to her, she was hungry. Opening the bedroom door, she headed for the kitchen and called softly, "Mom? Trina? You here?"

The only answer was a shuffling sound that seemed to come from upstairs. Had the two of them gone up there so they wouldn't disturb her? Her mind danced around that notion for a few seconds before dismissing it. Her mother would have sidled into the room to check the patient for a fever, or Trina would have burst in anxious to display her purchases. Neither one would have simply ignored her.

That left Connie with the frightening thought that maybe someone else was in the house—someone who didn't belong here. Had Trina or Mom, in their hurry to hit the summer sales, forgotten to lock the doors, and a beach bum had decided to look for cash laying around or for something to pawn?

Holding her breath, she very quietly slipped back into the bedroom to get her phone. She had to call 911, report a burglar. But the phone wasn't there—not on the nightstand—not on the dresser. Fumbling for the jeans she'd had on the night before, she searched all the pockets—nothing but wadded tissues and ticket stubs. Edging her way to the bathroom, her eyes flitted over the sink, the back of the commode, the stand that held her make-up and hairbrush, but her phone wasn't there.

Where could she have left it? She'd been feeling so sick when she came in, all she'd wanted was to curl up and forget her misery. Now as panic whirled around in her brain, the nausea made a comeback. She felt her stomach twist into a knot and knew her pulse was racing.

She took several deep breaths like she always did before a crucial exam and tried to still her runaway brain. The first thing she had to do was to get dressed. She couldn't go prowling around the house in just her panties and tank top. Not wanting to waste time getting clean clothes, she slipped on the jeans and tee shirt she'd worn the day before.

Edging her bare feet into the hallway, she noted the door to the boys' room was open. Remembering past days when Dave usually kept his bedroom door shut so their mother couldn't see his chaos, she tiptoed in that direction, peeked in. The room was empty, the beds were unmade, clothes were on the floor, cookie crumbs covered the bedside stands. Everything here was normal.

Going back into the living room, she looked around. Nothing seemed to be disturbed. Sidney was in his cage close to the end of the stairway, pecking away at his breakfast as if nothing unusual had happened. She relaxed a little. If there was an intruder, he must be upstairs, looking for something to steal, but since he thought the house was empty, he would have no intention of hurting anyone. Who the person might be tantalized her mind for a bit. Maybe someone who kept an eye on the beach houses and watched who came and went and who was proficient at picking locks?

Trying to keep her fear of spooks and shadows under control, she debated what to do next. Run to the beach, grab the first person she saw and ask him to call the police? But what if she were mistaken? Maybe the noise she heard was the air conditioner blowing some papers around or swishing the drapes. She didn't want to make a fool of herself. Maybe she should check it out.

Starting toward the stairway, Connie steeled her nerves, bit her bottom lip and tried to control her breathing. She took a step up—hesitated. Glancing over the stair railing, she glimpsed the pair of heavy horseshoe bookends she'd gotten on Saturday. Remembering Madame de Hoya's story about them being lucky horseshoes, she leaned over and grabbed one in case she needed a weapon.

She was halfway up when her common sense kicked in. *What on earth was she doing? If there was really was an intruder, she needed to get out of the house fast.*

As she started to make a U-turn, a tall figure appeared at the top of the stairs and charged toward her. Before she had time to react, Connie was bulldozed backward and rammed against the stair banister. A powerful hand shoved her head back while its mate grasped her throat.

SEVENTEEN

IN TERROR, CONNIE gasped for breath. She clawed at the attacker's hands with her right hand while she grasped her feeble weapon in her left hand. Twisting, turning, and gyrating her head and body as much as possible, Connie tried to loosen the hands that were strangling her. But her attacker's grip tightened—and tightened some more. She made a feeble attempt at kicking the intruder, but the vise-like pressure didn't let up.

She couldn't breathe. She couldn't fight back. She felt her body growing numb, her brain getting foggy.

As she started going limp, she felt the weight of the lucky horseshoe in her left hand. Willing her body to respond one more time, she drew back her arm and slammed the heavy bookend into the side of her assailant's head.

An incensed howl echoed through the room as the hands around her throat loosened a bit. It was enough for Connie to grab some quick breaths and feel the blessed air seep into her lungs for a few seconds. Making use of the respite, she raised her weapon again and, with a savagery she didn't know she possessed, pounded the sharp edges against her enemy's head.

But it wasn't enough.

The intruder was taller and stronger and with one sweep of a powerful arm, Connie's lucky horseshoe was knocked out of her hand and plummeted down the stairs.

Seconds later Connie felt herself reeling backward. Unable to stop her precipitous plunge, her head struck each riser as she passed and then crashed into the stand of Sidney's birdcage. The cage fell over; the door snapped open; Sidney flew out to investigate.

Connie came to rest near the corner of the living room bookcase just behind the recliner. A long pair of legs kicked at her as a blurred figure ran past. And she heard a string of curses just before the blackness overtook her.

BY NOON ALLISON'S ENERGY, as well as a big part of her budget, had evaporated among the clothes racks. She now had a lovely print tunic draped over her arm along with a couple of lightweight pantsuits that would do for the classroom until the weather turned colder. But as much as she usually enjoyed shopping and trying on outfits, today one part of her mind hovered around the pink house and her daughter. *Maybe I shouldn't have left her all alone. She looked so pale when we left. What if she wakes up and needs something? We really should go back and check on her.*

Allison's brain told her worrying about Connie was foolishness and that it wouldn't be fair to Trina to cut their shopping day short. Her gut told her otherwise.

She was about to mention going back when Trina beat her to it. "I'm a little worried about Connie. Maybe we should check on her. We can always go shopping another day."

"Right," Allison said. "Let's pay up and get back over the bridge."

Allison forced herself to drive within the speed limit, although, for some crazy reason, she felt an urgency to get back to her daughter. Being a pragmatic person, she didn't put much stock in metaphysics, but she did trust her maternal instincts. She had to be sure Connie was all right.

When they pulled in under the pink house Trina jumped out and grabbed her packages. "I can't wait to show Connie the matching beach loungers I bought for us. One is Passion Purple and the other is Salsa Red. I'll let her choose."

Allison shuddered and hoped the loungers didn't live up to their names. Balancing her bags in one hand, she inserted the key into the back door.

Trina zipped in, hurried to their bedroom, opened the door, and called, "Hey, Con…." Turning slowly around, she said, "She's not there."

Allison did a quick check of the kitchen and living room. "Not out here. How about the bathroom?"

She watched as Trina dumped her goodies on the unmade bed and knocked on the slightly ajar bathroom door. "Connie?" When no answer bounced back, she threw open the door and scoured the room. Coming back out to the hallway, Trina shrugged her shoulders. "Maybe she got to feeling better and went to the beach."

Allison placed her bags on the couch, turned to the counter to look for a note her daughter might have left. As she rotated around, she saw the stair railing and wondered briefly if Connie might have gone upstairs. Then an object near the foot of the stairs caught her attention. *What was Connie's horseshoe doing on the floor?*

At about the same moment, she saw the toppled birdcage. Fear caught at her throat, her lungs. She couldn't breathe. She couldn't make any sense of what she was seeing. *What had happened here?*

Frantically, Allison eyes darted around the room. The recliner seemed to have been moved a bit. She pushed it aside—and saw one bare foot. "Oh no! Connie!" Dropping to her knees, Allison patted Connie's pallid cheek, noted her shallow breathing, felt a faint pulse. "Trina," Allison yelled. "Call 911. Now!"

Trina darted over, gasped as she saw her friend on the floor, but immediately pulled her out her phone and punched the numbers. Allison could hear the sob in her voice as she tried to explain the emergency. "My friend must have fallen down the stairs. She's unconscious." Trina paused as the person at the other end apparently asked a question. "Yes," Trina said. "She's breathing."

"Tell them her pulse is weak," Allison added.

Trina's manner became more controlled as she went on, "Her name is Connie Aldridge. Age twenty-three. We're at a beach house on Shoreline Drive." She stopped and whispered to Allison, "What's the house number?"

"Three something. Just tell them it's the pink house—and to hurry."

Ending the call, Trina slipped down beside Allison. "The woman said not to move her."

"I know."

Allison pushed back Connie's hair from her forehead, leaned forward, kissed her cheek. "My poor baby. What happened to you?" As she straightened back up, she saw red streaks among the strands of hair. It was then Allison's tears began to cascade.

At the same time, she heard Sidney give a short chirp, glanced over to where the bird was balanced on the edge of the bookcase.

Allison got her emotions under control long enough to instruct Trina to set the birdcage upright and put Sidney back in. "Connie fell in love with that bird the minute she saw him. We've got to take good care of him."

With the canary safely tucked in, Trina whispered, "I'm going outside to watch for the ambulance."

Allison nodded, then her brain shut down and her heart took over. *You're going to be all right, Baby. You're strong. You're determined. Remember when you were learning to ride your two-wheeler? You ran into the fence, hit your head and blood dribbled down you face. But it didn't stop you. Nothing can stop you. You have a marvelous future. I'm going to see you graduate from med school, see you start your practice as a pediatrician. Fred and I will brag on you to all my friends.*

Fred! Her mind did a quick U-turn to the other members of her family. She had to let Fred and Dave know. But how? Could she call a fishing boat miles out to sea on her cell phone? And once she reached them how long would it take for them to get here? She needed her men by her side now—wanted to hear their reassurances that Connie was going to be fine—wanted Dave to crack a joke about his sister's hard head—wanted to cry on Fred's shoulder.

She heard a siren wail to a stop. She heard the door open and Trina directing the EMTs to the staircase. It was only when she saw the young man and woman approach with a gurney that she realized she would have to move and leave her daughter to their expertise. But she didn't go far. Keeping her eyes trained on Connie, Allison slid up to the arm of the recliner and watched while the professionals examined their patient.

They checked Connie's vital signs, her reflexes, her

head, her response to stimuli. Connie did not react to any of it. As they worked the man kept asking questions and Allison responded as best she could.

"What happened?"

"I don't know. We came home and found her like this."

"Has she been sick, had dizzy spells?"

"She was vomiting during the night—something she ate at the carnival made her sick, but she was better this morning—just tired. Wanted to sleep in rather than go shopping."

"She on any medication?"

"No."

"She was alone here?"

"Yes."

Carefully aligning her body and protecting her head, the two slid her onto the gurney and covered her with a sheet. The girl took over the questioning getting all the legal information. "We're taking her to St. Vincent's Hospital. You can follow us in your car."

"I can't ride with her?"

"No."

Trina reached out and took Allison by the hand. "Come on. I'll drive."

Allison gave Trina a grateful smile, pointed to the car keys on the counter.

The ride across the bridge and across the town was a quiet one. Allison willed her mind to shut out everything except good thoughts. *The hospital might be small but they must be equipped to handle all kinds of emergencies. Connie would receive the care she needed. She would wake up and laugh over a silly thing like fainting and hitting her head. Somehow word would be gotten to Fred and Dave and they would soon be here.*

When Trina drove into the emergency room parking lot, Allison was relieved to note the heliport just to the right of the hospital. If need be, Connie could be transported to a large medical center.

By the time Allison and Trina reached the waiting room, Connie had disappeared into one of the treatment cubicles. The desk clerk informed them a doctor would be out to speak to them as soon as possible. In the meantime, Allison answered all the necessary questions and signed her name in whatever place the clerk indicated. It didn't matter to Allison what she was agreeing to—she just wanted to get the paperwork out of the way and be with her daughter.

When the clerk was satisfied, Allison posed the problem of getting hold of Fred. "My husband and son are deep-sea fishing on Ben Johansen's boat. Is there any way I can get a message to them? They need to be here."

"We don't have that capacity, but the police can contact the boat."

"Then would you call Vince Tucker and ask him to do that?"

"Oh, you know Tuck?"

"Yes. We're friends." Allison didn't mention that they had only met him a few days earlier, but in that short time, he'd become like a friend.

"Sure, I'll give him a call."

After that there was nothing to do but wait—and pray. She and Trina found seats close to the swinging doors labeled *Staff Only* and waited.

As the minutes plodded by, Allison alternated between staring at the door and with pacing in circles while Trina made frequent trips to the vending machines. Even though they'd missed lunch, Allison couldn't make herself eat any of the candy bars or potato chips Trina offered. She sipped on a cup of coffee until it had lost all its warmth and flavor, but she continued to hold the cup with both hands because it helped control her trembling.

She was in the middle of her pacing cycle when the door opened and two men approached. The doctor in green scrubs was youngish and robust and had worried eyes. The face of the young officer with him was furrowed in what seemed a cross between fury and pity. Putting aside her puzzlement as to why Tuck was here, she focused on the doctor and asked the only question that mattered, "She's going to be okay?"

Instead of answering, the doctor slid down in a chair and nodded for her to sit. "You're her mother?"

She felt Trina's arm around her as the young girl pulled out a chair and helped her in it. Allison nodded and held out her hand. "Allison Sawyer."

A strong hand clasped hers. "Dr. Bridger. I'm afraid your daughter has suffered a rather severe injury and it's going to take a while before we can predict the outcome."

It took a few moments for Allison's brain to decipher the words. They didn't make sense. "But she only fainted. I know she bumped her head, but it didn't look too bad. You mean she might have a concussion—something like that."

"I'm sorry, Mrs. Sawyer. But there's no easy way to tell you this. Your daughter didn't faint, someone tried to strangle her."

Somewhere in the back of her brain, Allison heard

Trina whimper like a hurt puppy, and Tuck seemed to be saying something about calling in the detectives, and the doctor's strong hands were holding her. None of it made any sense.

She closed her eyes, blocked out everything except Connie's lovely face, her laughter, her determination. *I've got to be strong for her. I've got to listen. I have to hear all the doctor has to say.*

She took a deep breath, brought herself back from the edge. Shaking her head, she stared at the doctor. "I'm sorry. I guess I lost it for a minute. You said someone tried to strangle Connie. Someone broke into the house and assaulted her? That's why she was unconscious?"

"Yes. She might have a mild concussion from the fall. But the real problem is that we don't know if the compression on her throat cut off oxygen to her brain for any length of time or if there will be any lasting effects."

"When will you know—about lasting effects?"

"I can't say. I've contacted a neurologist in Wilmington. She's coming as soon as possible and will make the treatment decisions—whether to transport or not. Keep in mind, Mrs. Sawyer, your daughter could wake up at any time and be fine. If not, we'll do a brain scan... and go from there."

The words *strangle* and *neurologist* and *brain scan* raced around in Allison's head like a tornado. Connie had been attacked—she was unconscious—she might have brain damage.

Her thoughts veered to the men in her life. Dave and Fred needed to be here. She needed them. Connie needed them. Turning to Tuck, Allison sniffed, wiped at her tears, and asked, "Did you contact the boat?"

"Yes. They're on the way back. Should be here within an hour."

"What did you tell them?"

"Only that Connie had fallen and was in the hospital."

"Good." Allison's whimpers ceased as she morphed into an avenging mode. "Now, what's your plan to catch the brute who did this? It had to be somebody she met at the beach. Some jerk who tried to get too friendly, who wouldn't take no for an answer. Somebody who knew she was alone in the house." Allison paused, dropped her head. "I'm sorry. I know I'm rattling. It doesn't matter. When she wakes up, she can tell you who did it."

Tuck didn't respond to Allison's last statement. He only patted her on the back and said, "Ed and Sheila are on the way to the beach house. If you'll give me your key, I'll meet them there. Since the house is a crime scene, we'll make arrangements for you and your family to stay at a hotel tonight."

Allison swiped at a tear. "That's thoughtful of you, but I'm staying right here until Connie wakes up—and I'm sure the others will, too." Swiveling back to the doctor, she asked, "May I see her?"

"Not right now. They're moving her to the ICU. Once they get her settled, you can go in for a few minutes."

Nodding, Allison blinked back more tears as she searched her purse for the house key.

Tuck took the key, started to leave, turned back. "Was either door unlocked when you arrived home—like, maybe, Connie had let someone in?"

Allison thought a moment, then shook her head. "No. We went in the back door but I had to unlock it. And then before we came to the hospital, I checked the front door and it was already locked."

She turned and stared at Trina. "Would Connie have let someone in she'd met on the beach and then lock the door after him?"

"No way. She's much too savvy for that. If someone knocked, she would have answered the door and possibly gone out on the porch to chat, but she would never have invited him in with no one else there."

"That's my opinion, too, but I'm glad you agree, Trina." Swerving her head back to Tuck, Allison said, "That means someone either forced their way in or the person had a key." Several terrible scenarios raced through her head before she could speak again. "Either way, some monster hurt my daughter, and you've got to find him."

"That's just what I intend to do."

Allison watched Tuck march down the hallway and slam out the door of the emergency room.

EIGHTEEN

DAVE WAS HAVING a blast. He hadn't hauled in any catch yet, but he'd had a couple of thrilling tugs-of-war with what he imagined were mammoth marlins or sailfish. The fact that whatever had been on his hook managed to escape didn't dampen his spirits. Both Neil and Fred had pulled in small to middling catches, but nothing to brag about.

Glancing over to Fred, who was in the process of rebaiting his hook, Dave saw Zack come up and say something to him in a low voice. The quick change of expression on his stepdad's face alerted Dave to the fact that this was not good news.

His apprehension was proved valid when Fred strolled over and, in a very controlled voice, said, "I guess we'll have to cut this gig short, boys. That was a message from Tuck saying Connie had taken a fall and was in the hospital and he thought we ought to come in."

Red flags flew up in every corner of Dave's brain. The biggest one let him know that his sister was in serious condition. No way would his mother have interrupted their fishing trip for a sprained ankle or a bruised shin. And if Connie were conscious, she wouldn't have let her mother call them. And the most frightening of all was the thought of Tuck being involved. Lawmen didn't investigate falls or minor injuries.

Like most siblings, he and Connie squabbled, teased,

and aggravated each other. But they also had a close bond. Having been reared by a single mom who was often overworked and stressed out, they had depended on one another for comfort, for companionship, for supplying unspoken needs.

And Dave knew Connie needed him now.

As the boat was turning around, Neil came up to him, put a hand on his shoulder. His friend didn't have to say a word, but Dave could see the message in his eyes. *I'm here for you.*

Pulling in his line, Dave started to put away his gear—and said a silent prayer.

SLINK STARED INTO the mirror, dabbed antibiotic cream on the forehead laceration, glad that the Band-Aid would be hidden by hair. At the same time, Slink damned the wildcat who'd inflicted the injury. *What in the hell was she doing there anyway? They were all supposed to be gone. And why didn't I make sure she was dead before I left? The word on the street is that she's unconscious, but what if she wakes up? Could she give a description to the police? Somehow, I've got to make sure she doesn't talk. I've got too much at stake for that little snipe to mess me up.*

AS THEY PULLED up to the dock, Fred heard Zack say the expected things. He hoped Fred's daughter was going to be all right; let him know if there was anything he could do, blah, blah, blah. Fred knew the captain meant well, but the words were like so much static in the air. The only voice he wanted to hear now was Allison's assuring him that Connie was going to be fine. The lovely, vibrant, determined young woman was the daughter he'd never had, just as Dave was his son. He'd been blessed with a ready-made family, and he couldn't stand the thought of losing any one of them.

Since they'd walked to the dock, Zack offered to drive them back to their beach house where they could get their car to go to the hospital. Fred accepted the offer.

As they approached the pink house, a shudder went through Fred's body. Something was terribly wrong here. Why were two different police cars parked in the street behind the house? The moment Zack stopped the car, Fred jumped out, gave the captain a quick wave, headed for the back stairs. He was followed closely by Dave and Neil. They were met by a stone-faced young cop standing in the doorway.

Jack Hendrick, Tuck's partner, blocked their entry. "Sorry, Sir," he said to Fred. "I can't let you come in."

Fred's heart tumbled. His voice failed. His brain couldn't make sense of the situation. While he was trying to come up with an intelligent question, Dave stepped forward.

In a calm, sure voice, Fred heard his son state the obvious. "You mean this is a crime scene?"

The deputy nodded.

"So Connie didn't just fall?"

Again, Jack bobbed his head and then found his voice. "She was found unconscious at the foot of the stairs. There's evidence of a struggle."

"What do you mean *found unconscious*? She was alone? Where was my mother—and Trina?"

Fred could tell Jack didn't much like answering questions, but faced with Dave's determined glare, he complied. "According to Mrs. Sawyer, her daughter didn't feel like shopping so she and the other young lady went to the outlets for a while, but then returned…and that's when they found…" Jack's voice trailed off momentarily, then his cop voice returned. "Tuck said he would meet you at the hospital and fill you in on the details. In the meantime, we'll continue our investigation here."

Figuring the other part of the "we" had to be the county cops, probably Ed and Sheila, Fred knew the family would learn nothing more until the police had completed their work. At that time the officers would give out only the information that wouldn't compromise the investigation. He knew how that worked. And although he certainly intended to be in on the investigation later on, at the present time he couldn't even think clearly.

But Dave wasn't ready to move on yet. "Let me get this straight. Connie was alone here when some varmint attacked her?"

"I really can't tell you anything else," the deputy said.

Fred held his breath as the two young men glared at each other: the deputy was determined not to give out our more information and the brother was desperate to learn the details.

Neil stepped up, touched Dave's arm. "Come on, we better go." Holding up his phone, Neil said, "I've got the directions to the hospital—it's on the other side of the bridge."

Dave took a deep breath, stepped back from the steps. "I understand," he said to the deputy. "Then we'll be on our way to the hospital and leave you to your work." He turned to Fred. "Come on. Let's check on Connie."

Almost in a daze, Fred slid into the front passenger

side as Dave started the car. What had started off as a glorious vacation day, with the girls shopping and the boys fishing, had turned into a nightmare. And Allison was in the midst of the ordeal. He should be at her side, needed to be at her side.

As Dave backed out of the garage, Fred stared at the young man by his side. How could he seem to be so calm? His sister had been attacked; she was unconscious; her condition could be serious. It was almost as if Dave had anticipated bad news and had steeled himself to bear it.

Fred marveled at Dave's self-control while he, the seasoned detective, was nearly going to pieces thinking of what might have happened to Connie. He was learning what every law enforcement officer realizes when crime hits close to home—*it's different when it's your own family.*

DESPITE HIS OUTWARD APPEARANCE, Dave was not calm. His gut was tied in a knot. His brain was caught up in a whirlwind. And his heart was being squeezed by fear. Somehow he knew Connie's situation was grave. She might be permanently injured, maybe become an invalid, be unable to fulfil her dream.

In the midst of his internal chaos, Dave recalled the time he'd fallen out of a tree and broken some ribs. He'd been six at the time and should have been too old to be a crybaby, but while their mother had run into the house to call the ambulance, he'd sobbed for Connie not to leave him.

She'd put her arms around him and whispered. "Don't worry, little brother, I'll always be right here for you."

As the car crossed over the bridge to the mainland and headed toward the hospital, he responded to that memory. *And I'll always be there for you, Sis. No matter what.*

The hospital was small; only a few cars in the parking lot, but Dave noticed a beach police cruiser was one of them. He'd only met Officer Tucker briefly, and at the time, the cop had been sitting on the sand, looking more like a tourist than a peace officer—not a picture that inspired much confidence.

And Dave's first glimpse of the ICU waiting room did nothing to instill any confidence in him either. There were only a scattering of uncomfortable looking chairs and one lumpy sofa. When Dave glimpsed his mother's and Trina's anguished faces, he hoped to high heaven the doctors here were of a better caliber than the surroundings indicated.

Fred rushed over to the two women and Dave heard him whisper, "Is it bad?"

His mother nodded while a tear crept down her cheek. Dave's spine stiffened. Someone had hurt his sister and he was going to find the one who'd done it. The resolve didn't make sense. He was no cop. He didn't know the town. He didn't know the circumstances. He didn't even know what friends she'd made on the beach who might be suspects. Most days he and Neil had gone their way while Connie and Trina had gone theirs. But what he lacked in knowledge and experience, he could make up for in determination.

The local and county police would do their investigation, but how much time could they spend on a home invasion and attack when they had murders to solve? *Unless this turns out to be another murder.* The hor-

rible thought flashed through his brain and was immediately and deliberately banished. No way was Connie
going to die.

He glanced over to where his mother and Fred were
huddled together. She apparently was telling him all
she knew of the attack and of Connie's condition. Neil
had gravitated to Trina to get his information. Dave
joined them.

He kept his voice low. "Can you start over, Trina, and
tell me everything you know about what happened?"

She nodded, swiped back her tears. "Well, as you
know Connie got sick at the carnival. When she woke
up this morning, she still wasn't feeling well and didn't
want to go shopping. You fellows had already gone and
your mother didn't want to leave her alone, but Connie
insisted. Said she just wanted to sleep." Trina shrugged,
blinked back more tears. "So we left. But I made sure
the front door was locked, and when we went out the
back, we locked that one, too."

"So," Neil put in, "she either let someone in or he
broke in or he had a key."

"The police officer told us there was no sign of a
break-in and," Trina went on, "I know Connie wouldn't
have invited a man in the house when she there all
alone."

"Are you sure?" Dave asked. "Neither one of us has
been around her much this past year. Maybe she's gotten little lax on safety precautions that Mom drilled
into her and me both."

Trina shook her head. "Not Connie. In fact, she's
been lecturing me about getting a chain on my apartment door. She says locks aren't enough these days."

Neil voiced just what Dave was thinking. "That

means the perp had a key—but how?" Then Neil went on to answer his own question. "Could be a previous tenant didn't turn in his key—maybe said he lost it. Probably happens a lot."

"Let's skip that part," Dave said. "The cops have to be looking into it. What I want to know is what happened to Connie. You found her unconscious?"

Trina's eyes started to water again and Dave slipped an arm around her shoulders. "I know this is hard for you. Just take your time."

Closing her eyes momentarily, Trina took a couple of quick breaths before she went on. "She was crumpled at the foot of the stairs. The birdcage was tipped over. It looked as if she had fallen down the stairs."

Neil interrupted. "But why would she had gone up the stairs?"

"I don't know unless she was looking for something—or heard something." Trina paused. "But you know the strange thing was that one of her bookends was on the floor next to her."

Dave shook his head. "Bookend?"

"Yes. She'd bought a set of horseshoe bookends the day we went antiquing. She said they were lucky and, since they were heavy, they would be able to hold her mammoth textbooks."

"Oh, yeah," Dave said. "I remember seeing them. They were on the bookcase next to the stairs. Maybe it got accidentally knocked down."

Neil shook his head. "I think maybe she grabbed it for a weapon. Connie's the type of girl who would fight back with anything she could get her hands on."

Dave nodded. "You're right. But the attacker was bigger, stronger and pushed her down the stairs."

"That's not all he did," Trina's voice became a whimper. Both boys stared at her as she went on. "The doctor said she was choked—deliberately strangled."

"Omigawd!" Dave fell back into a chair, dropped his head. "What kind of devil would do that?"

All kinds of weird thoughts swirled through Dave's head as he tried to make sense of what had happened to Connie. Somebody had tried to kill her. Why? There had to be a reason. As hard as it was to think about, he had to ask. He turned to Trina. "Any sign of her being sexually assaulted?"

Trina shook her head. "I don't think so." She closed her eyes as she was trying to picture the scene again. As she opened her eyes, she shook her head again. "Connie had her jeans on, and her clothes weren't ripped or opened or anything."

Neil voiced what Dave had just been thinking. "That means that whoever attacked her, meant to kill her— so she couldn't identify him." The three of them stared at each other a few moments before Neil went on. "So maybe she knew him."

"Maybe," Dave said, "or maybe could give a good description."

Slapping Dave on the back, Neil smiled. "And that's just what she'll do when she wakes up."

"I can't wait until she wakes up. I've got to do something now."

"But what can you do?" Trina asked. "The police are doing all they can."

Dave stood up, grabbed his cell out of his pocket, and walked away from them.

Neil skidded after him. "Where are you going?"

"Out in the hall. Have to call someone." Dave couldn't

explain to himself, let alone his friends, why he had a sudden urge to call Sally Sawyer. She was Fred's sister and she'd embraced his new family but didn't want to be called Aunt Sally. In the year since his mom and Fred had been married, Sally had become, not only a friend to both him and Connie, but a mentor, an advisor, and a sounding board. He had to let her know what had happened, but more importantly, he needed to solicit her help in finding the louse who'd hurt her.

Sally had the most analytical mind of anyone he'd ever met—and that included all of his college professors. Last year when Fred had been shot and nearly died, she compiled all the information available that ultimately led to the unveiling of the culprit. Maybe she could do it again. At least, he was going to ask her to try.

Fred had said his sister was a genius. Dave believed him, and they needed a genius right now to figure out who had attacked Connie and why. Sally was the head of a girl's school in Florida, but her school year didn't start for another two weeks. It shouldn't take her that long to solve the puzzle.

She'd given both him and Connie her cell number, told them to call any time. He took deep breaths as the phone rang once, twice, three times. It was on the fourth ring when she answered with, "Hey, Dave, what can I do for you?"

It was all he could do to choke out, "We need you."

NINETEEN

IT TOOK A WHILE, but Dave finally managed to explain about Connie's condition, how she'd been found, and that they had no idea why anyone would want to hurt her. By the time he'd finished talking, Sally had a game plan ready.

"I'm driving up—be there late tonight. In the meantime, you and your friends have an assignment."

"But what can we do?"

"You have your laptop with you?"

"No. Neil and I drove right down from camp and personal laptops weren't allowed there. It was all nature and outdoor stuff. And I know Mom told Connie and Trina not to bring theirs. This was supposed to be all fun—no studying or research."

"I understand. Then go to the gift shop. Buy three notebooks or tablets to write on. Each of you are to write down a diary of everything that's happened between the time you arrived Friday until now. What you did, all the people you met, any particular impressions you had of anybody, what was said that might be important, what was going on in the town that people were talking about."

As she stopped for breath, Dave butted in, "Like the murders in town?"

Dave heard a brief intake of air before Sally blurted

out, "Murders? There's been murders in that little town?"

"Yeah. One, maybe two—unless the death at the realty office was a suicide. But Fred said it had nothing to do with us—for us not to be concerned, so I haven't paid much attention to the talk."

"Well," Sally said slowly, "he's probably right, but it's possible there could be a connection between those deaths and the attack on Connie. I want you and your friends to write down all you know of the previous events as well as what you've heard other kids say about them. Okay?"

"All right. We can do that."

"But don't bother your mother or Fred with questions. Just tell them I'm on my way. I'll talk to them later."

As he pocketed his phone, Dave understood Sally's plan. She was going to work with him and his friends to get to the bottom of Connie's attack without worrying or involving his parents.

He walked back into the waiting room, went over to where his mother huddled in a straight-backed chair, her head bowed, her hands clenched. Fred must have stepped out for a minute. He touched her shoulder, kissed her on the cheek, "I called Sally, told her about Connie. She's driving up."

"Oh, good. I'm glad you called. It hadn't crossed my mind to even let her know. It'll be so good to see her."

"Yeah, it will. Anyway, I'm going downstairs for a little bit with Neil and Trina."

She looked up at him and nodded. "Fine. I'm sure there's probably some vending machines where you can get a snack."

For probably the first time in his life, the thought of trying to eat anything nearly made him gag, but he didn't correct her. "Be back soon."

He motioned for Neil and Trina to follow him as he headed for the hallway. They did, but Trina balked when Dave said he wanted them to go with him to the gift shop. "I can't leave. Besides," she said, with tears welling in her eyes, "we have to wait until Connie wakes up to buy her flowers."

Dave slid his arms around her. "I know she's your best friend. That's why we've got to try to find out who did this to her. Come on down, and I'll explain."

On the elevator, Dave told them about his Aunt Sally, her amazing intellect, and what she had assigned them to do.

"Makes sense," Neil said. "I'm in."

Sniffing, Trina wiped at her eyes. "Me too, although I don't really understand how it will help, but I guess it can't hurt."

"Now, remember, not a word of our project to Mom or Fred. I told Mom that Sally is coming, but it's supposed to be only for moral support."

ALLISON GLANCED AT the clock in the waiting room. It was only a little after two-thirty. How could that be? It seemed like hours and hours since she and Trina had come back from shopping and found Connie on the floor. A nurse had assured her some time earlier that she would be allowed in to see her daughter soon, but the summons hadn't yet come. What were they doing in there?

She glanced over to her husband. He'd come in from stretching his legs in the hallway and she told him about Dave calling Sally and that she was driving up.

"I'm glad," he said. He slid one arm was around her shoulders, brushed his lips against her cheek. "You and Sally get along so well." He gave a half-grin. "In fact, you seem to tolerate her pushiness better than I do."

"She isn't pushy—just determined. And I like that trait in a person. And," she said, "she'll be some comfort to Dave. I'm afraid I haven't been much support for him. I haven't even explained to him how we found her or what the doctor said."

"It's okay. I found out that Trina filled him and Neil in on everything."

Allison nodded. "Good. I'm so glad he has friends his own age with him. In my condition, I wouldn't be much help to him."

The door to the Intensive Care Unit opened; a young man in blue scrubs stepped out. Was that a slight smile on his face or a trick of the fluorescent lighting? Allison held her breath, nudged Fred.

"You're Connie Aldridge's parents?"

They both nodded. This time he definitely smiled as he held the door open for them. Allison took this as a good sign and asked, "Is she waking up?"

"She's responding to tactile stimuli."

For some reason his usage of medical jargon irritated Allison. "Responds to tactile stimuli? You mean her body jerks in pain when you jab her with needles? Well, I guess that's something to be thankful for."

The nurse's smile disappeared faster than a magician's silver dollar.

Fred squeezed her hand tightly that she interpreted to mean *Don't antagonize Connie's caretakers.*

"I'm sorry," she said to the young man. "Didn't intend to sound so bitchy." Allison's voice dropped a decibel. "But she's my baby girl."

"I understand."

She doubted if he really did understand, but he'd been well trained to deal with distraught family members. Now she had to train herself to deal with whatever lay ahead.

The nurse led them to Connie's cubicle. She was propped slightly on one side so her face was to the entry curtain, almost as if she were expecting company. Her eyes were closed, her hair neatly combed and pulled back, both her very tanned arms lay on top of the sheet—both with needles in place, but only one arm was receiving fluids. Allison assumed the second needle was for back-up or meds. Although she was hooked up to oxygen tubing, her breathing seemed completely normal.

Allison swung her focus momentarily away from her daughter to the overhead monitor. To her untrained eyes, the blips and dips seem to be maintaining a steady rhythm.

Behind her she heard the nurse explain they were allowed only a ten-minute visit.

"Wait a minute," she called out to him as he was leaving the cubicle.

He paused, turned, said, "What?"

"Where's the cut on her head?"

The nurse shook his head. "She doesn't have a scalp laceration."

"But I saw the blood. When I found her unconscious, she had blood on her face. She must have a cut somewhere."

"Well, of course, they cleaned her up in the E.R. so

she may have had some blood on her, but I assure you she has no lacerations." He pulled back the curtain to the hallway. "I'll be back in ten minutes."

Allison gave Fred a puzzled look. "I don't understand."

Fred grinned. "Maybe our little girl got in a lick or two before she passed out."

"You mean the blood may belong to her attacker?"

"Maybe. I'll give Tuck a call when we leave. If there's any spilled blood by the staircase, we might get our culprit's DNA."

But, Allison thought, *DNA is only good if you have a suspect to match it with.*

For the rest of the ten minutes she forgot all about DNA and suspects and spent the precious time whispering to both Connie and God.

When they came back out to the waiting room, Allison was surprised to see Ben Johansen. What was the fishing store owner and boat captain doing here?

He crossed the room to them, gave Fred a quick handshake and patted Allison lightly on her shoulder. "When Zack told me about your daughter I wanted to come and see how she was doing. Sorry about your fishing trip being interrupted, Fred."

Allison stared at the man while Fred gave a slight nod. Neither said anything. Ben seemed embarrassed. "Well," he said, "just wanted to let you know if there's anything I can do..." His voice trailed off, then rallied. "She's going to be all right, isn't she?"

Since Fred didn't respond, Allison knew she had to say something. "We appreciate your concern. She's actually doing very well."

"Then she's awake? That's great."

Allison shook ahead. "Not yet, but the doctor assures us that she'll be fine." She took note of Fred's quizzical look, and couldn't explain even to herself why she'd lied. There was something about Ben she didn't like, and she wasn't about to share her fears with him.

"I'll be off then." He turned to Fred. "And anytime you want to reschedule the trip, let me know."

Fred had a very uneasy feeling as he watched Ben walk away. Could Allison's optimistic prediction of Connie's soon recovery possibly put the girl in more danger? He knew how fast news traveled about the little beach town. Ben would report to Zack and Clyde and probably many of his customers. They in turn would tell their friends and the message would continue to travel. It wouldn't take long for Connie's attacker to hear that his attempt on her life hadn't succeeded. It would be even a shorter time for the culprit to think about finishing the job.

He whispered to Allison about going to the restroom. Instead, he hurried to the end of the hallway and dialed Tuck.

The officer listened politely to what Fred knew was rather a wild premonition about Connie's attacker trying to get at her again.

"I understand," Tuck said, "but what do you want me to do?"

"Call ICU and instruct the nurses there to admit no one except the immediate family or someone accompanied by the immediate family."

"And me," Tuck added.

That demand shook Fred up a bit. "Why you?"

Tuck sounded rather testy when he answered. "Because I'm the cop investigating this whole thing. And

I don't need a family member with me when I'm questioning a victim. You remember the protocol, right?"

"Oh, yeah, sure." Fred paused. "But you'll take care of the other?"

"I will. As soon as I get a chance. Anything else?"

Fred wasn't pleased with Tuck's attitude, but he realized the cop was under a lot of pressure. He thought a moment and then remembered that he had intended to call Tuck anyway about another matter. "Yes, one more thing. There are no lacerations anywhere on Connie which means that any blood on the scene has to belong to the attacker. That could be important."

"Indeed it is, because that means we have a good sample of his blood as well as some tissue. We found what looks like a bookend with both on it. We'll bag it. We're also taking fingerprints from the stair banister, but we'll have to eliminate all of your gang before knowing if we have anything."

The elevator door opened and Fred saw the young people heading his way, but he continued his conversation, "So you need our fingerprints to compare with the ones you've found. I understand."

Dave was at his side in a nanosecond. "They found fingerprints? You talking to the police? What else did they find?"

In the midst of Dave's questions, Fred also heard Tuck's next sentence. "And there's something else."

Fred's first reaction was to shelter Dave from whatever else Tuck was going to say. Dave was wounded enough without knowing a lot of details. But was that the right thing to do? As he stared at the strong young man in front of him, Fred made his decision. "Wait a minute, Tuck, I want to put you on speaker for the kids can hear it, too."

In a moment, Tuck's voice surrounded the foursome in the hallway. Fred made a quick survey to be sure no one else was within earshot.

"Well, it's nothing spectacular, but interesting just the same." The policeman paused, then went on. "When Ed was inspecting all the rooms, he noticed the venetian blind in the empty bedroom upstairs was dangling."

"Dangling? I don't understand."

"The drape was pulled all the way back and screws holding the blind in place had been removed. That must be what the intruder was doing," Tuck said, "when he heard Connie downstairs and started down."

"Or Connie heard him and started up."

"Possibly. But the important thing is now we know Connie wasn't the primary target. He was searching for something. She interrupted him and he tried to kill her so she couldn't give a description."

Fred's voice broke as he asked the question, "But what could be that important?"

"Either money or drugs."

"So a former tenant or guest or cleaning lady or whoever hid something valuable at one time and now wants to retrieve it."

"That's what it looks like. Ed assigned one of his people to take down every blind, every drape, every curtain rod to thoroughly search them."

"Yeah," Fred said, "I guess that would be the next logical step." At a loss of anything else to say, he ended with, "Thanks for keeping us in the loop."

"Sure. And you let me know any change in your daughter's condition."

As Fred pocketed his phone, Neil spoke up, "So, it was just somebody looking for something? Nothing to do with Connie?"

Fred nodded. "Seems that way."

"And then," Dave said, "that eliminates the possibility some jerk was stalking her."

"Thank goodness," Trina said. "I've been going crazy trying to remember all the hunks we'd talked to on the beach and wondering if one of them had attacked her."

Fred turned to the trio. "Come with me while I tell Allison the latest development."

Dave grinned. "And I've got some news for you, too, unless Mom already told you."

"She told me Sally was coming. Glad you called her. I should have done it myself."

Fred had always had mixed feeling about his only sister. He loved her dearly and was proud of her accomplishments, but sometimes she could be a bit overwhelming. "Your mother will be so pleased to see her," he said. "They seem to understand each other."

TWENTY

WHILE SALLY WAS tossing pajamas and jeans and shirts and face creams into her travel bag, her mind was going over the recent bad events Dave had told her had occurred in Beacon Beach. In addition to the attack on Connie, a man had been found dead on the beach—a victim of foul play, and there had been a suspicious death at the realty office. Surely, she thought, the latter two events would have been mentioned in the area papers. She knew Wilmington was the nearest large city to Beacon Beach and by scanning its newspaper's articles on her computer she found mention of both deaths: the unidentified man and Naomi Platt, an elderly employee of the Beacon Beach Realty Office. She also read in a follow-up article that the man had been identified, but there was no further information regarding the investigation into his death. That could mean the police didn't know much, or they weren't giving out what they did know. The article about Naomi Platt's death stated the police regarded it as a possible suicide. The realty office would be closed by the time she got into town, but she might make a visit there in the morning.

After booking a room at a beachside hotel, she was on her way. Her thoughts rambled. Of course, her first order of business was to go to the hospital and check on Connie's condition. Then if she felt she could leave to do some investigation, she would start snooping around. At the hotel, she might act like a curious tourist and get the local take on the recent tragedies; at the realty office, she could give an assumed name and be an obnoxious customer who would insist a Mrs. Platt had reserved a beach house for her. That ploy ought to elicit some pertinent information about the deceased. Even though she knew neither plan might actually work out, she felt better having at least a hazy plan of action.

Traffic on I-95 was typical for late summer: tourists going in both directions either heading for their vacation destination or hurrying back home, locals trying to get to appointments or meeting business clients for lunch, and teens relishing the last few days of freedom before school started back.

Sally let her mind roam back to when she first met Connie and Dave. Fred was in the hospital fighting for his life from a bullet in his chest. She thought the authorities were moving too slowly in finding the assailant, so Sally took it on herself to form her own detective agency and enlisted the Aldridge family. Maybe it was time to reactivate the team with new recruits. From what Dave had told her, Sally figured Trina and Neil would be eager participants.

Somewhere in Georgia she stopped for gas, an energy drink, and an update from Dave on Connie's condition.

He answered on the first ring and his, "Hey, Sally," sounded a little more cheerful than earlier.

Not one to waste words she asked, "What's the latest on Connie, and how is your mother doing?"

"I got in to see Sis for a few minutes. Trina and I went in. They only allow two people in for ten minutes every couple of hours, so it was the first time I'd seen her since..."

Sally could feel Dave's pain as he tried to get control of his voice, but she kept silent as she knew he didn't want any empty platitudes.

After a few moments, he went on. "She didn't look sick at all. Just looked like she was sleeping, except..."

"Except what, Dave?"

"Well, don't ever tell her I said this, but the times when I used to wake her up for school—when we were kids—she was always hugging her pillow and her hair looked pretty punky."

Sally grinned into her phone at Dave's remark. The girls in her school would consider being called "punky" a high compliment, but she knew Connie was well beyond that stage.

Dave paused and Sally heard him take a deep breath.

"But today her head was flat on the pillow as if she was looking at the ceiling even though her eyes were closed. And her hair was combed and pretty—and she looked like an angel."

His voice broke, but before Sally could say anything, he went on and she could tell he was trying to add a bit of humor. "A very tanned angel. You know, Sally, I always thought sick people were supposed to be pale, but she's not a bit pale. How could that be?"

Sally was tempted to explain the difference between being sick and being comatose, but her common sense overruled her teaching habits. Instead she asked, "Has the doctor been back in?"

"Don't know. The nurse didn't say anything about it. Mom said a neurologist was supposed to be coming from Wilmington, but I doubt if the big gun has arrived yet. Mom and Fred are in there now. When they come out I'll see if there's an update. Mom seems to be holding up quite well—at least outwardly. She's pretty good at hiding her feelings."

"I know. Did you tell them I'm on the way there?"

"Oh, sure. They're both glad. But," he added, "as far as they know your role is only for comfort and support."

"That's exactly what I want them to think. We'll keep our detecting off the radar screen for now. Got to go. Tell them I'll be there as soon as possible."

"Oh, wait a minute," Dave said. "Something I forgot to tell you."

"And that is?"

"The local cop here said, it looked as if the intruder was looking for something because one of the drapery rods had been taken apart. It seems that Connie might have simply interrupted the search and that's why she was attacked."

Sally pondered that information for a moment and filed it for closer examination later. "There's something, too, that I forgot to tell you," she said. Before Dave could ask, she went on with more instructions. "I want you and your friends to keep a list of everyone who attempts to see Connie or who asks about her condition. Understand?"

"Sure," Dave said. Sally heard a bitterness in his voice as he went on. "Connie's condition is just as important to her attacker as it is to her family—only we've hoping for opposite outcomes."

ALLISON BLINKED BACK tears as she and Fred returned to the waiting room. This time, though, instead of being tears of despair, they were of relief and cautious optimism. Connie seemed to be showing signs of improvement. Although she hadn't opened her eyes yet, the nurse said she was making random movements in bed and moaning at intervals. He said it may indicate she was coming back to consciousness and was possibly remembering the attack.

Dave, Trina, and Neil were just coming back in from the hallway and she hurried over to give them the latest report. "She's moving some. She's trying to talk. She's going to wake up."

Trina rushed forward, enveloped her in a giant hug. "Of course she is. Connie's not going to sleep her vacation away."

Allison's brain told her that both she and Trina were doing their best to believe their own lies—but it was the only way they could cope.

When Trina stepped back to grope for a tissue, Dave took her place. Allison had to bend her head back so she could look into his eyes. The one good thing both her kids had gotten from their long-gone father was their height, but she credited herself for giving them bulldog tenacity. And that tenacity was going to keep Connie going.

It didn't even surprise her when Dave gave voice to her thought. "You know, Mom, Connie is working overtime right now trying to find a path through the mess that bump on her head caused. But she'll find it. She will."

"I know." She took a breath that went all the way down to her toes and then let it slide out slowly and confidently. Stepping back, Allison smiled and repeated, "I know."

Fred reached out a hand. "Come on," he said. "We

need to get some exercise—been sitting here too long. Let's go down to the coffee shop, get a bite, maybe even walk outside a little. Dave can man the fort here."

Allison nodded. He was right. She had to get out, stretch, get a different view than the closed door that separated her from Connie.

Waiting in the hallway, she could hear the murmuring of voices as Fred was probably instructing Dave to call if there was the slightest change. At the same time, she saw a sign she hadn't noticed before. When Fred came out, she took his hand, motioned to the sign and arrow. "Let's go to the chapel first."

As DAVE WATCHED his mother and stepdad leave, he felt as if he was being smothered—by worry, by inactivity, by the unknown. And he knew the only remedy was to keep his mind busy trying to solve the many puzzles that swirled around in his brain. Who had attacked Connie? Any why? Was there a connection to the earlier deaths? Was the culprit a local, a stranger, a drifter? He glanced over to the notebook he'd purchased at Sally's request. He'd dropped it in one of the chairs, but as yet, he hadn't written the first word in it. Trina and Neil, however, were sitting side by side on the far end of the room and both were busy scribbling away. He grabbed his tablet and slid down beside them.

Trina looked up, gave him a weak smile. "This may not help a bit in solving the mystery of who attacked Connie, but at least it's keeping me busy. Better than simply fretting and going crazy with worry."

"She's right, Dave," Neil agreed, "which I think is what your aunt intended. I'm looking forward to meeting her."

Neil's attention shifted to the hallway. "And there's another gal I wouldn't mind meeting." Recognizing the caveman timbre Neil affected whenever he encountered a particularly attractive female—no matter what age— Dave swiveled around to see the object of his friend's admiration. He had to agree.

The tall and very shapely female entering the waiting room was well worth admiring. Dave's brain skipped back several years to when he'd been enthralled with comic books that featured Amazon queens—and here was one in person. Except for the flaming red hair and the fact that she was dressed in a pink seersucker pant-suit rather than an animal skin, she could have posed for one of the covers. When she started in their direction, he dropped his eyes to the notebook in his lap, but since it was closed and he had no pen in his hand, he couldn't pretend to be writing.

He waited until her flip-flops stopped flopping before looking up and giving her a smile befitting royalty.

Before he could think of anything to say, she opened the conversation. "I'm Meg Freeman. I work in the realty office. We were devastated when we heard one of our renters had been attacked. I assume you're with the Sawyer family."

After bobbing his head up and down a few times, Dave found his voice. "Yes, I'm Dave Aldridge. It's my sister that's here."

Neil closed his notebook, motioned Meg to a chair facing him. "And I'm Neil Stone, friend of the family. And this," he said, signifying the girl next to him, "is Trina Moffat, also a friend."

Meg slipped into the offered chair and crossed her legs. "I can't tell you how sorry we at the office are at what has happened. This is such a safe and nice little town. We've never had any trouble before." Turning back to Dave, she asked, "How is she? Your sister is going to be all right, isn't she?"

It took Dave a few moments to raise his head and answer her question as he'd been fascinated with how the pink polish on her toes exactly matched the pink in her pantsuit and in thinking her long legs were probably as long as his. Then, almost defiantly, he said, "Of course, she's going to be all right. She's a fighter. We're sure she'll be coming around any time now."

"But she's not awake yet?"

He shook his head. "Not yet—but it's only a matter of time."

"I'm so glad. Like I said, we at the realty office were worried. I'll go back and tell them the good news." She rose in one swift, graceful movement, reached down and patted Dave's shoulder. "Keep up the good vibes."

As Meg disappeared down the hall, Trina spoke up, "I don't like her, and I'm certainly going to put her name in my notebook."

A flash of disbelief crossed Neil's face. "For heaven's sakes, why don't you like her?"

"She's too smooth. Too beautiful."

Neil let out a sound somewhere between a snort and a chuckle. "Why is it," he said, "that ordinary women can't stand a perfect body and face on another woman."

"And hair," Dave added. "Don't forget those lovely tresses."

Instead of dodging the question, Trina had her answer ready. "Because that's all they are: body, face, hair. That woman doesn't have a sympathetic bone in her lovely body. She probably lost the coin toss in the office as to who would give the official commiseration to the family."

"Well," Neil said, "I for one thought she commiserated very well. I may even stop by the realty office later and thank her for the visit." Swinging his head around, he asked, "What did you think of her, Dave?"

A quick grin crossed Dave's face, "You know I'm honor-bound to disagree with you, and, in a way, I did suspect her expression of sympathy was too syrupy to be real. And she probably only wanted to know what Connie was doing, because she was expected to bring back the information. It might be the boss is wondering if Mom might sue the company for negligence or something."

"And she should," Trina said.

Before either of the boys could comment, Dave saw a woman in a brown uniform come in and head toward the couple on the other side of the room. Getting quickly to his feet, he grabbed his notebook.

Neil jerked his head up. "Where you going?"

"To be nosy. Sally said we should get all the information we could on everything that's gone on. That uniform has to have some info."

Striding over to where his mother and Fred sat, he slid into a chair near them just as the officer approached. His mother's gaze went from him to the woman and back again. She gave them both weak smiles.

Sitting up taller, she spoke to the officer. "Sheila, this is my son, Dave." Turning to him, she finished the introduction. "Sheila Davidson, with the county police department."

Dave rose, put on his best manners as he shook her hand. "Pleased to meet you, Officer Davidson."

"Likewise."

With the introductions out of the way, Dave wasted no time asking the all-important question. "Any clue as to who did this to my sister?"

The officer shook her head. "Not really. As I'm sure Tuck told you, she must have interrupted an intruder searching for something—probably money or drugs. But in our search, we didn't find either one."

Dave refrained from peppering her with further questions and stepped back out of the way. "I'm sorry. Sometimes I can be a little pushy." He pulled a chair up and placed it catty-corner from his mother. "Won't you have a seat?"

"Thank you—and I understand. I can be a little pushy at times, too." Officer Davidson sat down, reached over and grasped one of his mother's hands. "Any change in her condition?"

A slight shake of her head and a lone tear was the only answer to the officer's question.

"Well," she said, "then we just have to keep praying. But, I do have a little information I can share with you."

Dave quickly slid down in a chair next to Fred and leaned forward so as not to miss a word. Both Fred and his mother gave Officer Davidson their full attention.

"The police who searched George Yates's home found a receipt from Beacon Beach Rental Agency from last March."

Dave frowned. "Who's George Yates?" he said. But no one seemed to hear him as both of the others were intently listening to the officer.

"So he'd been here before," his mother said. "I wonder why no one could identify him—especially someone from the rental agency."

"Maybe someone did," Fred put in. "Maybe that's why Mrs. Platt was killed."

"But who is George Yates?" Dave asked again.

This time Officer Davidson answered. "The former John Doe who was found dead on the beach a few days ago. He lived in a small town near Charleston, but the interesting thing about the receipt was the place he was renting here."

Fred smacked his hands together and a sly grin crept over his face. "If I were to guess, I'd say he rented the pink house on Shoreline Drive."

Swiveling his head from Fred back to the officer, Dave saw her give him a thumbs-up.

His mother's head jerked up and she raised one hand. He recognized the signal. It meant *Hush! I'm thinking.*

Silence hovered over the foursome for several seconds until she finally nodded and explained. "When I went to the agency to get an extra key and before Mrs. Platt became agitated, she told me we were lucky to get that particular beach house because someone had called and asked for it specifically. But since Fred had already made a deposit, she had to turn him down. That someone may have been George Yates."

"But he came to town anyway," Dave said. "Why?"

"My guess would be to recover whatever it was he'd hidden in the pink house." Officer Davidson got up, stretched, pushed back strands of hair. "But he was killed before he had a chance to do any searching, probably by his partner-in-crime."

Dave rubbed his chin, stared at the officer. "What crime?"

"We don't know for sure, but there's a possibility

they may have been involved in a bank robbery and a liquor store robbery in Atlanta."

"Let me get this straight," Dave said. "You think the loot from a bank robbery is hidden in the pink house, and that one person has already been killed over it, and that's the reason Connie was attacked?" Getting to his feet, Dave hovered over the officer. "And you haven't done anything to protect my family?"

Fred took one long stride, came up to Dave's side, put an arm around his shoulders. "Easy now, son. We've got to stay calm. Up until now the police had no reason to suspect any connection to our beach house. They'll get to the bottom of all this. And we just have to keep believing that Connie's going to be all right."

CONNIE BLINKED HER EYES, opened them wide, quickly shut them again. *Who turned on that bright light? Mom knows I don't like bright lights in my bedroom.* On her next attempt to see what was going on, she squinted against the light, turned her head slowly from side to side. Then in twisting her head to locate the slight beeping noise that seemed to come from above, she saw tiny pyramids parading across a TV screen. She studied them for a few seconds, then smiled in relief. She noted that the patient's heart showed a regular rhythm—a little fast but regular. Bringing her head back around, she spied the IV fluids hanging at the head of the bed, noted that the rate of the drip was about equal with her own respirations. That meant there was no urgency to get the fluid or medication into the patient. Another good sign.

But who was this patient? She couldn't bring a face into view. And why was he or she in an Intensive Care Unit since the vital signs seemed to be all right?

Too tired to try to solve the puzzle right then, Connie closed her eyes and drifted back into dreamland.

SLINK HAD NO problem in keeping up with news about the young girl in ICU. It was the street gossip of the hour and appeared to be of the "good news, bad news" variety. To Slink, the good news was Connie Aldridge was still comatose and therefore no threat to identifying her attacker. The bad news was that the girl could wake up at any time and perhaps describe the person who'd tried to choke the life out of her. On the other hand, even if she did come out of the coma, there was a chance the girl wouldn't remember anything. But not willing to depend on chance, Slink mulled over possible ways to keep someone quiet—preferably forever.

IN BETWEEN HER allowed visits to see Connie, Allison alternated pacing and praying with sitting and praying. She greeted well-meaning visitors with a hint of a smile, tried to eat a few bites of whatever Dave or Trina or Fred brought to her, and made periodic visits to the restroom so she could drop her coping façade. She kept repeating to herself and to everyone else that Connie was going to be all right. Most of the time she even believed it.

When the neurologist from Wilmington completed her examination, and spoke to the family, she was cautiously optimistic. However, the doctor did is not attempt to give a time-table regarding the hoped-for recovery.

The afternoon wore on; nurses changed shifts, daylight dimmed in the windows, the automatic streetlights blinked, and Dave reminded her about Sally's imminent arrival.

Allison loved and respected her sister-in-law, but at times had a problem with Sally's full-throttle approach to situations. Sally saw obstacles as hills to climb and disappointments as energizers. She'd overcome heartbreak, prejudice, and penury to break through barriers, and expected others to do the same thing. But she could also be empathetic in times of crisis, and right now, Allison needed the softer side of her in-law.

As she heard the elevator door open and the clap of Sally's sandals, Allison readied herself for the hugs and for the advice that were soon to follow.

With a bulging tote bag hanging from each hand, the newcomer took in the room with one sweep of her eyes. She lifted a bag and wiggled her fingers at the young people in one corner, but marched determinedly over to her brother and his bride.

Rising from her chair, Allison opened her arms and hurried forward. At the same time Sally dropped both bags and lunged across the room. They collided somewhere in the middle. Allison was surprised at the tears that flooded her eyes and realized how glad she was to see her boisterous and bossy sister-in-law. Since Allison had been an only child and Sally's siblings were both boys, the two of them had formed a special bond. "I'm so glad you're here," Allison managed to say between her tears and sniffs.

"Me too. And I'm going to stay here as long as necessary." Sally gave Allison another bear hug, stepped back, grinned at Fred who was waiting his turn. When the two of them parted, Allison wasn't a bit surprised to see Dave next in line.

"You've must have broken every speed limit in three states," Dave said.

"Sure did, but it was worth it to see my handsome nephew." Her gaze went to the twosome behind him. "And to meet his friends I've heard so much about."

Allison was proud of Dave when he politely introduced Sally to Trina and Neil, and said nice things about all three of them. In spite of his outrageous horseplay at times, he really was becoming quite the gentleman.

Turning abruptly away from the young people, Sally asked, "Well, when do I get to see Connie?"

"The nurse lets two people in once an hour for a few minutes," Fred said. He glanced at the clock. "And it's just about that time. You can go in with Allison."

She nodded, said softly, "No change?"

Allison shook her head. "Not really, although the nurse says she does make some movements from time to time."

"Moving is good. Next she'll be opening her eyes, and after that she'll be saying she's hungry." Sally picked up one of her tote bags and handed it to Dave. "In the meantime, I've brought some things for you kids—my laptop if they want to mess around with it—and some Georgia peanuts."

"Perfect. Something to keep our minds busy and our stomachs happy. I'll get Neil started on our project while Trina and I enjoy the nuts."

"Project?" Allison turned her gaze from Sally to Dave and back to her sister-n-law. "What project are you talking about?"

"Just a little something I came up with to lessen the tedium of waiting. It's my philosophy that young people need to have either their bodies or their brains busy at all times."

"I agree," Dave said as he started toward his friends. "We three will take turns working and eating."

Before Allison could come up with more questions about their project, the ICU door opened. This time it was the tall, bronzed nurse who beckoned them in. Allison had already decided the nurse worked the evening shift so she could spend her mornings getting baked on the beach and attracting the attention of every male strolling by. Dave may well have seen her there, but since he wouldn't have been concentrating on her face, it wasn't likely he'd recognize her.

Allison introduced Sally to the nurse since she knew Tuck had left instructions for only family and their housemates be allowed to visit. "I'll be spending the night," Sally told the nurse, "so her parents can get some sleep."

Even though Allison was accustomed to Sally's "take charge" persona, she still bristled at the assumption that sleep was even an option for either of the parents. But she didn't argue the point.

At the bedside, she watched as Sally spoke softly to Connie, rubbed her hands, brushed back her hair, muttered a prayer—exactly as Allison had done during every visit.

Back in the waiting room, Sally slipped down beside her brother, patted his hand, didn't say anything. Allison's liking for her soul sister shot up another notch. There were some situations that didn't call for words.

But she knew Sally's tolerance for silence was somewhat limited, so she wasn't surprised when she pulled her hand away, slapped Fred on the shoulder and said, "You smell like fish. Maybe you ought to go take a shower."

What did surprise her was his response. "You're

right. I need to get cleaned up and into some fresh clothes." He rose, pulled Allison to her feet. "And you need a break, too. Come on, Hon. Sally can cover for us here for a few minutes. We can both have showers and get back before the next visiting time. Tuck gave us the okay to go back into the house."

Fred didn't give Allison a chance to argue. "You got the keys to the van?"

Looking puzzled, she rummaged through her shoulder bag, came up empty. "Trina must have them. She drove us here."

After explaining their plan to the trio and getting the car keys, Fred added, "When we get back, both of you boys need to clean up, too. We should have done it sooner. Thank goodness, there's not another family waiting here to object to our fishy smell."

Dave nodded in agreement while Neil kept typing away on Sally's laptop.

Trina spoke up. "All right if I go with you now? I need to get into something more comfortable."

"That'll be fine, Trina. And you fellows keep Sally company. We won't be gone long."

The ride across town, over the bridge, and down Shoreline Drive was a quiet one. As he pulled into the garage area of the pink house, neither Allison nor Trina made a move to get out of the car. He figured they were both remembering the last time they entered the house and found Connie unconscious on the floor.

Going around the back of the car, he first opened the door for Trina and gave her a faint smile. She nodded in response, took a deep breath, and clambered out, but waited until he'd assisted Allison out of her seat before moving toward the steps.

Once they were in the house, Trina went about flipping on lights and then scooted into the room she and Connie shared. She quickly shut the door. Fred knew the girls had been best friends all through college and understood this ordeal was just as hard on Trina as it was for the family.

Turning his attention to Allison, he saw she was standing by the birdcage wiggling her index finger at Sidney. As he neared, he heard the pep talk she was giving to both the bird and herself. "Not to worry. Connie will be back soon, telling you how beautiful you are—maybe even singing along with you."

He gave her a brief hug before starting up the stairs. "While I'm getting cleaned up, you could check out the fridge. See if you can find something better than hospital snacks."

"Sure," she said while attempting a smile. "Got to keep my Big Boy fed."

As Fred lathered and shampooed and rinsed, he wished he could wash away the entire afternoon—in fact, he wouldn't mind erasing away the whole vacation. Not much had gone as planned. This was supposed to be a week of relaxation, of bonding, of making enduring memories for all of them—not murders and intruders and hospitals.

He emerged from the bathroom scrubbed and shaved, but with his spirits still in a slump. Seeing Allison, though, sitting on the side of the bed and holding out a Manwich to him along with a glass of iced tea put a grin on his face. "Thank you, Ma'am. You always know how to cheer me up."

He took the offerings, placed them on the bedside

stand, pulled her to her feet. "Now it your turn. Go get beautiful."

"I'll try, but I'm so exhausted I may fall asleep in there."

Slipping into the first pair of slacks he saw in the closet and grabbing a shirt that halfway matched, Fred was soon dressed and started on his lunch. He munched and sipped while listening to the running water, all the time wondering when their lives were going to get back to normal.

When he finished eating, he leaned back on the pillows and closed his eyes while he waited for the bathroom door to open. In the next instant, he was jerked upright by the clang of what sounded like falling metal—followed by an earsplitting shriek.

TWENTY-ONE

ALLISON'S BELLOW ECHOED in her own ears as Fred slammed through the door. "What happened? Are you all right?"

With one leg in the tub and the other leg over the edge, Allison tried to disentangle herself from the downed shower curtain. "I'm fine. Must have slipped on a soapy patch and grabbed the curtain. Now if I can just get out of this mess."

Turning her head to ascertain just what had happened, Allison saw the metal rod that held the shower curtain had split into two pieces. One section of the rod dangled above her head and was still holding most of the shower curtain. The other part of the rod rested on the tiled floor.

Allison peered through the painted seashells on the curtain as Fred stared at her. "And don't you dare laugh," she warned him.

"I wouldn't think of it." He started to push the dangling rod back up—then his arm stopped in midair and Allison saw his jaw drop an inch.

"What's the matter? What are you waiting for?"

It took a long moment before Fred answered and when he did, his voice was hushed as if he were whispering in church. "Turn your head very slowly up to the right."

Allison studied her husband's face a moment to determine if this was some kind of joke, but his wide eyes looked deadly serious. Following his instructions, she swiveled her neck over her right shoulder—and caught her breath.

"What do you see?"

Allison took a deep breath and stared for several more seconds before answering. "Green. Money green. I see a wad of money crammed into the shower rod."

"Good. I thought I might be hallucinating." He took a step back. "I've got to call Tuck. Now we know what the intruder was looking for. This money could be from the unsolved bank job in Atlanta."

Fred reached into his pocket, pulled out his phone, started punching numbers. Allison's frigid voice brought him to a halt.

"Stop right there." Her demand resounded around the bathroom and into the adjoining room. "You're not calling anybody until I get out of this tub and into some decent clothes."

A knock on the bedroom door surprised both of them. "Oh," Allison wailed, "I forgot Trina was here. She must think there's a war going on."

Fred headed for the door. "I'll explain to her—and then I'll call Tuck. You'll be dressed by the time he gets here."

But before starting to dress, Allison made a call to Sally. "Something's come up and we're going to be delayed. You and Dave go in to see Connie next visiting time."

She should have known Sally wasn't going to be put off without an explanation. "Delayed? Why? What's come up? Something I should know about?"

Since Fred was probably already telling Trina about

finding some hidden money, Allison knew she had to explain to Sally what had happened. Of course, she reasoned, Trina wouldn't waste any time calling Dave and telling him about the find, so she gave Sally a short version of the events.

Sally's response was about what Allison expected. "And where do you think the money came from and why was it hidden?"

"Fred says the cops here were talking about some robberies in Atlanta earlier in the year and the dead man under the pier fit the description of one of the thieves. So, the money may have been part of the loot and probably hidden to wait until the heat was off."

Sally laughed. "Loot? Heat? Really, Sis, you've got to stop reading those P.I. novels."

"They're better than the True Crime ones you read." Allison's voice broke. She couldn't keep up the silly banter. All she wanted was to get back to Connie's bedside.

"We have to wait here for the police to arrive. We'll be back to the hospital as soon as possible."

When she got off the phone with Sally and finished getting dressed, Allison trudged down the stairs. She slowed as she neared the bottom, closed her eyes, and again saw her unconscious daughter on the floor. It was too much for her. She hunched down on the last step, buried her face in her hands, and her shoulders heaved in quiet sobs.

FRED HURRIED DOWN the stairs to Allison, pulled her up, encircled her in his arms. "It'll be all right," he whispered. "Everything will be all right."

He felt her nod slightly against his chest. "I know. That's what I keep telling myself."

She drew back and tears glistened in her eyes. "Can we take a short walk on the beach?"

"Now?"

"Yes. I need it now."

Turning to where Trina sat hunched on the sofa, he said, "We're going outside for a little bit." He knew the respite would be short-lived, but it might be just what Allison needed. "Flip the porch light on when the officers get here."

Allison clung to his hand as they went down the front steps, strolled the well-worn path, came to the sand. The quarter moon gave enough light for them to avoid the abandoned sand castles, a forgotten ball, a lost towel.

As she lifted her face upward, Fred glimpsed a smile on her face. "My friends are still there," she said.

"Friends?"

"The stars." Her voice took on a far-away quality as she went on. "You know my dad died when I was still in high school."

"I know. You told me."

"Mom didn't do well after that, and I felt that it was up to me to be the strong one. There was a small knoll behind our house and I would go out there when life got too heavy and just stare at the stars. It seemed to help— as if the they were giving me part of their strength."

He put an arm around her shoulders. "Now you not only have the stars to help, but you have me and you have Dave—and soon, very soon, I'm sure, you'll have Connie back."

"Yes. That's what the stars are telling me, too."

As if on cue, the porch light came on. Fred took Allison's hand and they headed back to the pink house.

Trina had made a fresh pot of coffee and was busy pouring cups for the three officers who were pacing around the living room. Fred dropped Allison's hand, went into the kitchen area with the intention of fetching two more cups. Ed's commanding voice stopped him.

"Before we get comfortable, I want to see the money and the hiding place." He turned to Fred. "You haven't disturbed anything, have you?"

Slightly insulted, Fred kept his answer brief and civil. "Of course not." He headed for the stairs.

Apparently realizing he'd goofed, Ed patted Fred on the back. "Sorry. Just a routine investigator's question."

His detective ego placated, Fred grinned. "I understand. Have to cover all the bases. Been there, done that."

When they reached the bathroom, Fred stepped back to allow Ed and Sheila to enter. It wasn't easy for him to back off. For years, he'd led his team of investigators, had solved crimes, caught murderers, protected the innocent. Now he was just one of the masses. Not that he regretted retiring, but, as Hercule Poirot would put it, he still enjoyed using his "little gray cells." And those cells now told him the money hidden inside the shower rod went a long way to explain an intruder being in the house—an intruder who knew money was hidden somewhere but had no idea where. That same intruder either knew all the occupants of the pink house had intended to be gone that morning or assumed the house was empty. It was Connie's very bad luck she hadn't felt like going shopping.

Fred noted Ed putting on surgical gloves, but still not touching anything. The detective took a pen from his pocket, poked around in the wad of bills that was stuck in one end of the rod. "Sheila, you got the serial numbers from that bank job in Atlanta?"

Fred saw Sheila grin as she pulled a piece of paper from her shirt pocket, "Sure do, Boss. Fire away."

Ed shook his head slightly before he started to spout the letters and numbers on one of the bills in rapid succession—as if daring Sheila to keep up with him. Her fingers were as fast as his mouth and after capturing all the sequence, she quickly compared it with the range of numbers on the other paper in her hand.

She stood up straighter, gave Ed a pretend salute, "Sir, I would like to report that we have recovered the stolen money from the Third National Bank of Greater Atlanta."

Noting the detective's frown, Fred wasn't surprised when Ed said, "Aren't you ever serious?"

"No way," she said. "You've got that covered."

Fred held his breath for a second when Ed glared at his subordinate with a look that would have done in a new recruit. Sheila, though, simply gave him a motherly smile and turned her back.

Once again, Fred was glad to be far removed from office politics and petty rivalries. He was relieved when the techs arrived, did their fingerprint magic on the bills and placed the money in an evidence bag.

He was even more relieved when all the law enforcement people finally left. He found Allison on the front porch again staring at the stars. Putting an arm around her shoulders, Fred whispered, "Now we can get back to our gal."

After hearing Trina's excited spiel about the hidden money, Dave slid his phone into a pocket, and turned to see Sally coming in from the hallway. Since she still had her cell in her hand and was deep in thought, he figured she'd received the same news he had.

Coming up to the boys, Sally was shaking her head in apparent amazement. "You won't believe what just happened."

"I know," Dave said. "Trina called, too."

Neil jerked his head up from the laptop. "What? What just happened?"

When neither answered immediately, Neil slammed the computer shut, rose to his feet, put his hands on his waist, and lowered his voice to a near growl. "Well, are you going to tell me or am I going to have to beat it out of you?"

It was a common threat that both boys used on occasions, but one that neither took seriously.

Sally, though, wasn't in on the joke and had a worried look on her face, so Dave made the usual soothing platitude. "Don't get your shorts in a knot. It's nothing exciting—just that Mom found a hidden treasure chest—probably left over from one of Captain Kidd's forays."

Neil took his right hand and pounded his head three times and turned pleading eyes to Sally. "Please, Ma'am. Can you instill some sanity into this scene and tell me what it is that I won't believe?"

Before his aunt could comment, Dave decided the joke had gone far enough. "Sorry, Buddy, I just couldn't resist, but here's the real dope."

It took a while, but Dave told the story as he'd heard it: his mother in the shower, slipping, grabbing the curtain, the rod separating into two sections—and the hidden wads of money.

"Wow. Who would have thought to hide money in a shower curtain rod?"

"Probably a crook too dumb to take the money with him when he moved out."

"Or," Sally added, "a crook too dumb to make a reservation on the beach house when he was ready to retrieve it."

Neil pondered the information for a moment before commenting, "And that leads us back to the rental agency."

His forehead furrowed, Dave asked, "How's that?"

"The late Mrs. Platt. Maybe she was the partner-in-crime. Maybe she was supposed to make a reservation for this George Yates, but instead of doing so, she killed him."

Shaking his head like a run-a-way electric fan, Dave blurted out, "And then killed herself in a fit of remorse? That's a pretty lame scenario even for you, Neil."

Dave could tell Neil was trying to come up with a suitable retort when a nurse appeared at the ICU door. Glancing at the clock, Dave was surprised the visitation time had snuck up on them. He turned to Sally, "Wanna go in with me?"

She shook her head. "Not now. Take Neil with you. I need a little quiet time to get my brain working in the right direction."

"Come on, Pal. Maybe you can work your charm on my sister."

Neil shrugged. "She never took much to my charm, but one can only hope."

Both boys were completely somber when they pushed back the curtain and entered the cubicle. Dave went to the foot of the bed while Neil stayed at one side. Neither said anything until Neil reached over the railing and patted Connie's right hand. "Hey, Beautiful. You've got to wake up pretty soon. Dave's as grouchy as a nudist with a sunburn. I don't think I can stand much more of him wallowing in the pits."

Dave stared at his sister not sure of what he'd seen. "Keep talking, Neil. I think she may be coming around. It looked as if she fluttered her eyelashes."

Following orders, Neil kept up his silly prattle, while at the same time, he squeezed her hand. "You know, your brother had the gall to tell me my ideas were lame. He didn't actually call me stupid, but that's what he implied. But you don't think I'm stupid, do you, Con? I know you don't like me to call you Con, but since you insist on sleeping, I guess there's not much you can do about it. Now if you were awake, you'd probably call me 'Stony' because you know I hate it. But then I've heard you call Trina 'Little Miss Muffit' when you're irked with her. I bet if Trina were here right now, she'd tell you to stop being so lazy and get with the program."

Neil stopped to catch his breath, and at the same time, Dave gasped. "Omigawd, she's smiling. She's really smiling."

As he skidded over to the side of the bed opposite from Neil, Dave started talking directly to Connie. "Sis, you've got to listen to me. This is very important." He took her left hand, being careful not to disturb the IV fluids that flowed into her arm, and said, "If you can hear me, wriggle your fingers."

Dave held his breath as he stared at the flaccid hand. When nothing moved, he felt a tear slide down his cheek.

"Let me try." Neil cleared his throat and in his best

imitation of Humphrey Boggart, said, "Here's looking at you, Kid, and I'm waiting for your whistle."

Connie's eyelids and her mouth opened at the same time and she let out a low moan followed by "Water—please."

TWENTY-TWO

ALLISON'S PHONE RANG while she, Fred and Trina were on their way back to the hospital. When she noted that the caller was Dave, fear clutched at her heart. She knew the only reason he'd be calling was if there'd been a change in Connie's condition. Barely whispering, "Hello," she waited for the news.

Dave's voice bounced into her ear, "She's awake, Mom. Connie's awake and she's talking and she knows me and..." His words trailed off, but she didn't wait for him to continue as she closed her eyes and silently said a prayer of thankfulness.

Putting the phone on speaker, she grabbed Fred's arm and at the same time twisted around to Trina in the back seat and mouthed, *She's awake.*

Dave caught his breath and went on more somberly. "She's still pretty hazy—doesn't understand why she's in the hospital, doesn't remember being attacked at all. But she's awake. That's the important thing—awake and talking even though she can't remember what happened this morning."

"Thank the Lord," Allison said when she could stop crying long enough to find her voice. "She awake. That's all that matters."

"The nurse shooed us out and is calling the doctor now. Maybe she'll get her memory back soon, and be able to tell the police who attacked her."

"Or she may never remember," Fred said. "I still have no memory of that time last year when I was shot and nearly bit the dust."

"Maybe it's a blessing not to remember bad events," Allison said. "The important thing is she's awake now and going to be all right. Thank God."

Allison heard a timid "Amen" from the back seat. She turned around, saw Trina wiping tears from her cheeks, reached for her hand.

It took only a few minutes to get to the hospital, run in, and grab an elevator.

When they arrived in the waiting room, Allison grinned as Dave and Sally were dancing some kind of jig and Neil was clapping time.

Sally broke away, dashed across the room. "We just had to celebrate some way and since there's nothing here to drink except swamp coffee, we improvised our own victory dance."

"If I wasn't nearly dead on my feet, I would join you," Allison said. "Has the doctor been in? Is she really awake, coherent?"

Dave grabbed her around the waist, gave her a quick spin. "Mom, I don't know about coherent, but she knows her name and that this morning was Wednesday. That's enough for me."

"An intern is examining her now," Sally added.

Neil sauntered up and stuck out his chest. "And you all can thank me for bringing her back from la-la land."

Stepping forward, Fred snatched Dave's arm. "What's he talking about, Son?"

"I hate to admit it, but Neil's right. He was in there spewing his usual nonsensical chatter, and I guess Connie couldn't stand it any longer, so she woke up."

Allison grabbed Neil around his neck, gave him a peck on the cheek. "Neil, from now on, feel free to talk nonsense as much as you want."

A grin wider than the Mississippi River slid across his face. "I'll make a note of that."

Fred pounded Neil on the back, then snatched Allison's hand and headed for the ICU door. "Come on, Hon. We've got to see this miracle."

As he was about to knock, the intern on duty came out. Allison noted his smile was hesitant and his words cautious. "As you've heard, Miss Aldridge has regained consciousness. Her vital signs are normal, and she is lucid except for having no memory of a precipitating event. We'll continue to monitor her throughout the night and if she remains stable, we may transfer her to a regular room in the morning." He paused, smiled at Allison and Fred. "You may go in for a few minutes, then I suggest everyone should go home and get some rest."

Trina raised her hand at the doctor as if asking permission to speak but didn't wait for a response. "May I go in, too? We're best friends and she needs to know I'm here."

He shrugged. "Sure, why not?"

When they came out Sally was instructing the boys to clean up the trash that seemed to have accumulated around their chairs and to leave the notebooks they and Trina had been writing in.

Allison wasn't surprised when her sister-in-law announced that everyone else should go back to the beach house while she would be spending the night here—just in case something came up. "I'll get a blanket from the nurse, curl up on the couch, and catch a nap."

Knowing there was no use to argue, Allison agreed it was a good idea and five weary people headed for the elevator.

SALLY DID KNOCK on the ICU door and request a blanket, and she did curl up on the couch, but she had no intention of sleeping. Instead, she opened the notebooks the young people had written in. Per her earlier instructions, they had noted events of the past week, the local people with whom they'd come in contact or had heard about, and miscellaneous thoughts and impressions.

As she went through each of the notebooks, Sally scribbled notes and comments and questions in the margins. She began to get a good picture of Beacon Beach, its citizens and, to some extent, its law enforcement officers.

Somewhere in the middle of the night, she closed her laptop, the notebooks, and her eyes. She'd earned a little rest—because she now had three suspects. She didn't know any of them, but in the morning, she would try to find out more about them and perhaps she would quiz Fred as to what he thought of her conclusions.

The morning light was just beginning to come through the windows when Sally was awakened by a gentle nudge at her shoulder. Jerking up, she glared for a moment at the slim figure in green scrubs until her mind kicked in that the nurse was trying to tell her something.

Shaking her head to get the cobwebs out, Sally muttered an apology. "Sorry, forgot where I was for a minute. Is Connie all right? Has there been a change?"

The nurse nodded—and then smiled. "A change for the better. Except for some lost memory, she's doing very well. The doctor was just in and ordered her moved to a room on the medical hall. We'll be doing that shortly and you can come with her. She'll be in room 212. Should I call her parents about the move or do you want to?"

"Oh, let me do it. This is really great news."

Sally punched in numbers as she made her way to the restroom. Fred answered on the first ring and they rejoiced together as Sally splashed water on her face to fully wake her up and to wash away the happy tears.

WHEN FRED RELAYED the news to the breakfasters, the kitchen of the pink house resounded with cheers from Dave and Neil. But when Dave looked across the table, he saw both his mother and Trina wipe back slow tears that trickled down their cheeks. He shook his head as he despaired of ever understanding the female species. They cried in sadness when the news was bad and then cried with joy when the news was good. It didn't make much sense to him, but then he still had a lot to learn about women.

But right now, it didn't matter. The important thing was his sister was going to be fine. Maybe now their lives could return to normal. He was actually glad it was Thursday, that their week at the beach would be up the next day. Then another thought hit him and he blurted out, "But what if Connie's not able to travel by tomorrow? Are we going to stay on?"

His mother shook her head like a mad bull. "Absolutely not. If I have to I'll sign her out myself and hire an ambulance to take her home, we've leaving in the morning." Allison turned to Fred, gave him a peck on the cheek. "I'm sorry, Hon. You meant this to be a marvelous time for all of us. But I'm ready to leave Beacon Beach for good."

"I'm with you on that. Next summer we'll head in a different direction."

"Hey," Dave said. "I've got a great idea. How about Bermuda? That would be a nice change." Dave saw his mother roll her eyes and knew just what was coming.

"Oh, you're going to have a nice change, all right. The day you graduate you're going from being a student to a fully employed, self-sustaining, productive member of society." She gave him a wicked grin. "And Fred and I will be thinking of you while we're on a second honeymoon. Come to think of it, Bermuda might be a good destination."

Fred dangled his car keys. "Let's forget about next summer. We've got to get to the hospital before Connie thinks we've forgotten about her."

"You and Mom go ahead. Neil and I have some shopping to do."

Neil looked sidewise at his buddy. "We do?"

"Absolutely. We've got to get a gift for the patient."

"No flowers," Allison said. "We don't want to mess with flowers on the way home."

"No flowers, but she needs something she can cuddle."

Trina gave him a glare. "You're not going to get her a Teddy Bear, are you?"

"Don't know, but I'll find something she'll love. Want to go with us?"

"Sure. Someone's got to keep you straight."

A few minutes later both cars left the pink house—the van headed for the bridge that led to the hospital while Dave's car aimed for the two-block section of Beacon Beach euphemistically called "downtown." Trina remembered seeing a small gift shop where, hopefully, they could find something suitable for a recovering patient.

It took a while, but Trina found a flowered bag filled with miniature bottles of girlie products while Neil picked up the latest issue of a celeb-gossip magazine. Dave solemnly wandered the two aisles looking for the perfect gift, but it wasn't until he went into the toy section that he let out a loud, "Eureka!"

When he got behind Trina at the check-out counter, she gaped at the object in his arms. "You're giving her a doll?"

"Not just a doll—an authentic Raggedy Ann. She had one just like this as a kid, and she loved her scraggly red hair and the pinafore apron. She'll be thrilled."

Trina still looked doubtful. "If you say so."

On their way to the hospital, Neil kept the other two entertained by reading juicy items from the magazine.

"You two give her your gifts first," Dave said. "I want to save the best for last."

"Huh! She'll be so busy looking at the hunks in my mag, she won't have time for a baby doll."

"Or," Trina chimed in, "she'll swoon over my gift because she'll be so glad to get something that smells better than antiseptics."

When they arrived at room 212, Dave noticed it was a double room, but the bed closer to the door was empty. *Good thing*, he thought, *with all six of us here, there wouldn't be room for another patient.* He'd been surprised the receptionist had let them all in, but he figured since it was a small hospital the rules were pretty lax.

Fred was tilted back against the wall in one of the chairs while Sally sat in the other one looking as if she should be the one in the bed instead of Connie. Dave felt a pang of guilt for having slept so well while his Aunt Sally was on an all-night watch.

Connie, on the other hand, looked great. She welcomed them with a wide smile and wide-opened arms. Dave took the invitation, gave her a bear hug, and then couldn't resist a little teasing. "Just so you know, I'm keeping score and you owe me two dish-washing gigs."

Her little giggle was music to his ears. His sister was back. Life was good. Pulling back before things got too mushy, he said, "But to let you know we forgive you your dereliction of duty, we brought you some gifts."

Connie clapped her hands. "Oh, goodie. I love gifts."

Gently shoving Dave out of the way, Neil stepped forward, bowed, and handed her the glossy magazine. "Guaranteed to give you sweet dreams."

She studied the stud on the cover, blushed slightly. "Or to keep me awake all night. Either way, it's a fine gift, Neil, and I appreciate it."

Trina handed Connie the colorful bag brimming with lotions, colognes, and sweet-smelling soaps. "A scent for your every mood."

"Um-m-m," Connie murmured as she sorted through the vials. "Just what I need—a touch of Ecstasy to get me through an autopsy."

Giving her friend's hand a gentle slap, Trina shook her head. "Not exactly what I had in mind. I was thinking more of date nights." She stepped back, motioned for Dave.

Dave waved a plastic bag in front of her face. "And now may I present your new friend." He pulled Raggedy Ann out of the bag, swished the red hair around, and shoved the doll toward her.

Connie's face went ashen; she stopped breathing— and then she screamed and flailed her hands at the doll. "No! No! Get away from me."

TWENTY-THREE

FRED JERKED UP. What had happened? He'd been idly watching the gift giving scenario and thinking about how good things were going. Now the room was in chaos. Allison tore to Connie's side, patted her shoulder, made soothing sounds. Sally grabbed Raggedy Ann from Dave's hand and threw the doll on the floor. Trina retreated to a corner and seemed to be gasping for breath. Neil's eyes darted around the room while Dave seemed to be paralyzed.

The door flew open and a young nurse rushed into the room. She pushed past the young people, shoved Sally back, grabbed Connie's left wrist, felt her pulse. Glaring at the assemblage around the bed, she issued one order, "Out!"

At this point, Fred came alive. Tapping Dave's shoulder and looking at the other two kids, he motioned them out of the room. As if in a daze, they obeyed. Fred turned around, went over to Sally, took her hand. "You, too, Sis."

He could tell she wanted to argue the point, but then she nodded, grabbed the tote bag and headed toward the door. Pausing for a moment, Sally picked up the Raggedy Ann doll and crammed it into her bag alongside her laptop.

Connie lay with her eyes wide opened and with a haunted look on her face as the nurse checked her blood pressure.

Fred went over to Allison, gave her a reassuring hug, spoke to the nurse. "We're all leaving except for her mother. She's staying."

Looking up, the nurse hesitated, then gave a slight nod.

Once they were all out of the room, Fred gently closed the door, and motioned them to a group of chairs at the end of the hallway. The murmurings began. "I don't understand, she was fine one minute and then she went berserk."

"She's had a shock. It's going to take a while to get over it."

"Something set her off."

"We just have to be patient."

"Maybe she's got PTSD—you know, like soldiers after a battle."

Fred listened and agreed with all the comments—especially about something setting her off. But what was it? Something about the Raggedy Ann doll?

He shoved a twenty into Dave's hand and suggested he take the others down to the coffee shop for a while. "Sally and I will stand watch and let you know if anything comes up."

After the young people left, Sally sighed. "I don't mind telling you, Fred, I'm worried. That attack really traumatized Connie, and it's as if she's trying to block the whole thing—as if she's afraid to remember it."

"I agree. And that's not like the Connie I've come to know. Even though I've only been in the family for a year, I was amazed at how she jumped right into med school and never backed away from a challenge."

He watched as a man in a white lab coat entered Connie's room. "There's the doctor now." He rose, took a deep breath. "Let's catch him when he comes out. See if we can get some answers."

Fred waited with Sally in the hallway and was surprised when Allison stepped out. "What's going on?"

His wife shrugged. "I explained to him and the nurse about her panic reaction to the Raggedy Ann doll and he said he wanted to talk to Connie alone—that is, with just the nurse present—no family."

"I guess it makes sense," Fred said. "We detectives do it a lot if we think somebody will talk more freely."

Fred could sense Allison was getting riled. "And you think Connie is hiding something she doesn't want us to hear?"

"Of course not—not consciously anyway. But the doctor may be able to elicit information to throw some light on her response."

"There's definitely something about that doll," Sally said. "Her smile, her apron, her…" She pulled Raggedy Ann from the overcrowded bag and studied the doll's features closely. "I don't know, but there's something here."

It wasn't hard for Slink to keep up with the news of Connie Aldridge's condition. Like all small towns, locals delighted in asking their friends, their neighbors, their shop keepers, "Have you heard the latest about that young girl who was attacked?" And all the questioned person had to do would be to shake his or her head and the information flowed forth. "Seems that she's still in the hospital—has amnesia or something—can't remember a thing. Guess the cops will never be able to finger the jerk who did it. It's a crying shame. That's what it is."

And Slink was quick to voice agreement, while at the same time was thinking—*But what if the amnesia doesn't last? I can't take that chance.*

CONNIE LAY BACK on her pillow as the doctor gently questioned her. "Do remember your reaction to the doll?"

She nodded, but couldn't bring herself to say anything.

Earlier that morning the doctor had pronounced her physically fit and had even given her *bathroom privileges*. She thought it rather ironic to consider going to the bathroom by one's self as a privilege—something she'd been doing ever since passing the potty-training test.

But what did he think of her now? After her outburst, he might decide that even if she were physically fit, she might not be mentally fit. And maybe she wasn't. She could come up with no explanation as to the way she'd reacted to Dave's gift, just as she couldn't explain why she no memory of her attack. It didn't seem to make any sense at all to her battered brain. She poured out her anxieties to the doctor. "What's wrong with me? I shouldn't be falling apart like this?"

The kind doctor listened to her fear and told her not to worry about it. It wasn't her fault. The memory block regarding her attack could be due to lack of oxygenated blood to her brain and/or the force of striking her head. Her adverse reaction to the doll could have been a flashback to some childhood trauma. Nothing to worry about. She accepted the truth of his reassurance, but still felt the need to try harder to remember.

One attempt had been to visualize every aspect of Wednesday morning: waking up feeling fatigued because of nausea and vomiting during the night, staying in bed

while her mother and Trina went shopping, waking up
later feeling hungry and with the odd sensation that she'd
heard someone else in the house, getting up to investigate,
seeing Sidney in his cage, starting up the stairway and
then going back to pick up one of her horseshoe bookends.

At that point her memory wavered. Closing her eyes,
she imagined the bookend in her hand, her bare feet on
the carpeted stairs, then looking up—and seeing a figure catapulting toward her.

She squinted her eyes tighter, willing a clearer picture
to emerge. Yes, she could see someone—something—
a flash of color. But as soon as the image had appeared
it was gone again—scooting away faster than a rabbit
on the run.

A tear trickled down one cheek. It was no use. She
couldn't remember anything else about her attacker.
And she had no idea why Raggedy Ann had fright-
ened her.

SALLY STOOD NEXT to Fred and Allison as the doctor told
them he thought the best thing for Connie would be if
he discharged her that afternoon. "But she has to get
some rest first. The nurse has given her a mild seda-
tive, so she'll probably be napping soon. I'll come back
after lunch, check her over. However, I don't want her
to go to your rented beach house. It might be too traumatic for her to return to the scene of her attack. I recommend a quiet hotel room for the night."

"She can share my hotel room," Sally said. "Or," she
added, "her mother can share the room with her and I
can camp out at the beach house."

Fred shook his head at both suggestions. "Sir, the
minute you discharge Connie, her mother and I will

pile her into my van and head for home. Our son and his friends can go back to the beach house and pack up everything." He paused. "That is, if you think it would be safe for her to travel."

"I have no problem with that. But she definitely needs to be followed by a therapist for a while. Your daughter has undergone a lot of trauma and she'll need to talk it out."

"We'll see to that," Fred assured the doctor. "And since she'll be returning to med school the following week, I'll contact someone there and fill them in on her condition."

Sally was so proud of her brother—not only marrying into a ready-made family, but willing to take on all the responsibilities. "How about me tagging along when you go home?" she asked. "Think you could put up with me for a few days and I could spend some time with my niece?"

Allison slid close, put an arm around her. "We'd love to have you tag along."

"Sounds like you have everything covered," the doctor said. "So I'm going to scoot to my office and be back after lunch."

An inner voice nagged at Sally as the doctor walked down the hallway. *But we don't have everything covered. We still don't know who attacked Connie. And with the possibility that she might regain her memory of the attack, she could still be in danger.*

When they moved to the end of the hall, Sally urged Allison to take the most comfortable chair. "You'd better get some rest while Connie's napping. We can keep an eye on her door from here."

Fred agreed. "And I asked Dave to bring you something from the coffee shop. You didn't eat much of anything this morning."

Shaking her head, Allison said, "I doubt I can eat anything until we get Connie home." She attempted a smile and added, "Then you can make me some of your famous beef stew."

"Consider it done."

Several minute later, Sally glanced down the hallway, sat straight up, poked Fred in the ribs, and said in a strained voice, "There's a cop and someone else heading for Connie's door. Do you know them?"

Her brother swiveled around, smiled, nodded. "Yeah, that's Officer Tucker, the local cop, and his friend that works in the realty office."

"I remember her," Allison said. "That's Meg Freeman. She's the one who rescued me from the very rude Mrs. Platt."

Fred got up, let out a low whistle to get their attention, and strode toward them. The women kept their seats, but the conversation of the trio drifted down the hallway.

The officer greeted Fred with a wave. "Hi. Meg and I thought we would check and see how the little gal was doing."

"Nice of you to come. And she doing very well, but she's taking a nap right now. The doctor says she has to get her rest, so we don't want to disturb her."

Officer Tucker nodded. "I understand. Glad to hear she's doing okay."

Sally watched as the woman with the officer put her hand on the doorknob and gave Fred a sugary smile. "I'm so glad. We at the office were so worried about her." She turned the doorknob. "I promise I won't disturb her—just want to take a quick peek."

As Sally watched the tall redhead enter room 212 and close the door, something nudged at her brain—something she had to remember—something important. Glancing at her tote bag where she'd crammed Raggedy Ann in among her laptop and notebooks, it came to her.

She jumped to her feet. She grabbed the bag. She tore down the hall to Connie's room.

TWENTY-FOUR

Taking her eyes away from the two men in the hallway, Allison gaped at Sally as she raced toward Fred and Tuck. *What was her sister-in-law up to now?*

The men also had their eyes trained on the woman running toward them.

A frisson of terror swept through Allison's body. Sally was known to be impulsive, but she was also incredibly perceptive. Had she sensed Connie to be in danger?

Allison dashed down the hall. She had to check on her daughter.

As Sally flew by the men in the hallway, she motioned for them to follow her. When she slammed open Connie's door, Allison was right behind her while the men were still several yards behind.

Reaching the doorway and glimpsing into the room, she saw Meg bending over Connie and saw Sally coming up beside the realty agent. To her stark amazement, Allison witnessed Sally haul her tote bag above shoulder height and swing it full-force against the side of Meg's head.

"What the hell?" Meg screeched as she teetered sideways. Allison held her breath as she watched Meg grasp at the bed with her left hand and bring herself back to an upright position. But in the process, she dropped something from her right hand.

Allison heard a soft clunk as an object fell onto the

tile floor, and at the same time she saw Meg give Sally a shove backward. Her sister-in-law lost her footing, fell, and knocked over a chair. The commotion woke Connie and brought Fred and Tuck charging into the room.

As Sally struggled to get back on her feet, her right index finger pointed to Meg. Her voice was that of prosecuting attorney. "She did it! She's the one that attacked Connie."

Meg backed up against the wall, glared at Sally, gave Tuck a shrug. "That woman's crazy. I'm getting out of here."

Allison had great respect for Sally's detecting skills, but for her to accuse a respected realty agent who just happened to be the local cop's girlfriend was beyond belief. It just couldn't be.

But then she saw Connie cringe and clutch at her throat. Not a sound escaped her daughter's rigid lips, but her eyes were filled with terror. That was all it took for Allison to morph into a mama bear protecting her cub.

Scrambling over the empty bed that separated them, Allison pounced on the tall redhead. It didn't matter that Meg was inches taller and years younger, Allison resurrected all the tactics that as a kid she'd once used against schoolyard bullies. She scratched; she bit; she pulled hair. Meg had hurt her child, and the woman wasn't going to get away with it.

Somewhere in the background Allison heard Sally cheering her on with, "Way to go, Sis."

At the same time, Meg was flailing her hands as at a pesky fly.

FRED AND TUCK raced into the room. For a few seconds, Fred's brain vacillated between shock, amusement, and visions of a law suit. As a former detective, he knew that even if Meg was guilty of some crime, Allison was way out of line, and he had to stop her from getting into deep trouble. But he was more concerned of how all this was affecting Connie. She certainly didn't need the trauma of watching her mother in a wrestling match with her accused attacker.

Glancing over at Tuck, it looked as if the lawman was stumped as to how he was going to separate the two women and stop the fight.

Or was he wondering if Sally's accusation could possibly be valid? Fred wondered just how close the two of them were—more than just friends? It was something to think about later, but right now they had get the situation under control.

Fred slipped closer, spoke into his ear. "You take your gal and I'll take mine."

Tuck swallowed, nodded his head.

But before the men could put their plan into action, the door flew open. An irate nurse, who looked to be about Connie's age and dressed in hot pink scrubs, marched into the room. She confronted the man in uniform. "What's going on here, Tuck?"

Fred saw Tuck square his shoulders, paste on an artificial smile, give the nurse a small wave. "I'll take care of it."

"Good. See that you do."

Both men hurried over to the women. Fred came up behind Allison and enclosed her in a bear hug that he tried to make a combination of endearment along with containment.

But even though her arms were pinioned to her sides,

Allison wasn't giving up. She turned her wrath on the young officer. "Arrest that woman, Tuck."

At the same time, Meg grabbed Tuck's arm, pointed at Allison and said, "That wildcat attacked me. Arrest her."

Tuck stood motionless, his eyes darted from one woman to the other.

Fred couldn't stand it any longer. He released Allison, strode over behind the town cop, and snatched the handcuffs from his belt. In one swift movement, he cuffed one of Meg's wrists, pulled her across the room and out into the hallway. Once there, he hauled her up to one of the chairs and pushed her down. He didn't know if Meg had run out of energy or had given up, but she didn't fight against him. He closed the other cuff around the chair arm and pulled out his phone.

He ignored Tuck who had come up and kept saying, "I'm sorry. I'm sorry." Fred didn't know if the officer was talking to him or to Meg. It didn't matter. He was calling Ed to come down and make the official decisions.

He'd come to like Tuck in the short time they'd known each other, but right now, Fred was very disappointed in the young officer. On the other hand, he didn't know how he would react if a good friend of his was accused of a crime. It had to be tough.

As he was explaining the circumstances to the county detective over the phone, the elevator door opened and three young, munching machines exited. Fred finished his conversation, pocketed his cell, glared at Dave. "About time you got back here."

Dave stopped chewing long enough to say, "Huh?"

Fred didn't bother with explanations. "Just watch

her. Don't let her move. I've got to check on Connie and your mother."

When he reentered room 212, things seemed a little calmer. Allison was patting Connie's shoulder and trying to reassure her daughter that everything was all right. Connie was taking deep breaths in between sips of water. It took him a little while, though, to locate his sister. He crossed the room and spied Sally on her hands and knees examining the floor under Connie's bed.

Sally looked up at him as she pointed to an object on the floor. "There's something here you need to look at."

"What?"

"Might be evidence that will clinch the case against Miss Redhead."

Fred bent down and gave a low whistle. "Don't touch it."

"I wasn't going to."

Allison joined Fred in looking under the bed and whispered to him, "What is a syringe and needle doing there?"

TWENTY-FIVE

FRIDAY MORNING SALLY'S hotel room was crowded with her family and their friends as well as the two county detectives. All four of the young people sat cross-legged on one of the beds while Sidney bobbed around in his birdcage obviously delighted to have an audience around. Allison and Sally propped up against the headboard of the other bed. Not to be left out, Fred claimed the end of the bed by Allison's feet. That left the two chairs for Sheila and Ed.

Allison's mind flitted back over yesterdays' tumultuous afternoon. After finding the syringe filled with an unknown substance, she'd been frantic to get her daughter out of the hospital. In spite of the fact that Meg had been taken to the county sheriff's office for questioning, her mother's instinct told her to get Connie to a safe place. She knew well enough that being questioned was a long way from being arrested, and Allison had no intention of giving Meg another chance to hurt Connie.

The two girls had spent the night with Sally while the others tried to make the best of their last night of vacation in the pink house. In the morning, they went about their packing duties with glum faces. It hadn't been the kind of vacation any of them had dreamed about—better to simply let go of the memories and look to the future.

They were in the process of loading the cars, when

Ed called Fred and said he had some news. Fred suggested to the detective they meet in the hotel lobby where Sally was staying since the family had to pick up the girls. But when Fred called his sister, Sally insisted they and the detectives come up to her room as she had arranged for a late check-out. "No need for nosy people in the lobby to hear about our wretched week."

When they'd driven up to the hotel, Allison's heart was lighter than it had been in days. Her family was safe, and maybe now they would learn more of what had been behind the attack on Connie and about what charges were being brought against Meg Freeman.

But the detectives had barely gotten settled in their chairs when there was a knock on the door and a deep voice announced, "Room service."

Sally jumped up. "Hope you don't mind, but I ordered coffee and donuts. I figured we might need a little nourishment to go with the debriefing."

Dave pumped his right arm. "You're the best, Aunt Sally."

"Amen to that," Sheila said. "After the late night we had, I overslept and didn't get breakfast."

Allison sent a weak smile toward her sister-in-law and the detective with the rumpled uniform and graying hair. As much as she liked both of the women, Allison hoped the breakfast break wasn't going to take too long. She just wanted to hear the wrap-up and get on the road.

Ed must have felt the same way. He waited just long enough for each one to grab what they wanted and settle back down before he started his recitation. As a teacher, Allison recognized a memorized spiel, and that's just what Ed was delivering.

The detective's eyes focused on Connie first and then

circled the room. "I'm here because I know how important it is for those who have suffered traumatic events to have explanations—and a type of closure.

"As you probably know, we've arrested Meg Freeman for attempted assault. What you may not know is that we've also charged her with murder."

Soft gasps seem to echo around the room. Everyone sat up straighter: donuts were forgotten in mid-bite: coffee dribbled from neglected cups.

Ed sipped on his own coffee for a few moments before Sheila nudged him with her elbow.

Allison heard her low whisper, "Enough of the theatrics, Boss."

Nodding, Ed went on, "As you will recall, a week ago today, the body of a dead man was found under Sammy's Pier."

Giving a slight shudder, Allison knew the memory of that macabre discovery would probably always be with her, but she tried to focus on the detective's next words.

"Then on Sunday, Mrs. Naomi Platt was found dead in the realty office. This was followed on Wednesday with the attack on Miss Aldridge in the beach house you were renting." He paused to allow time for each one in the room to process the three events.

"Later, a cache of money was found hidden in a shower curtain rod in that same beach house. We were able to trace that money as coming from a bank robbery in Atlanta in February. We figured all of those events were related, but couldn't find the connection—until last evening.

"Yesterday, after Meg Freeman was taken into custody, we obtained a warrant to search her apartment."

Finally, Allison thought, some new information instead of simply rehashing old stuff.

"But first let me backtrack a little to the syringe found under Miss Aldridge's hospital bed. The fingerprints on the syringe were those of Meg Freeman. The syringe was filled with insulin and we found a bottle of insulin in her apartment along with the syringes and needles."

Connie stirred, asked, "Why would she have insulin?"

"Because she has diabetes and she had a prescription for it—took a small dosage every morning. However, the dosage in the syringe meant for you wasn't small. Our physician consultant called it a 'massive' dose."

"In other words, she wanted to kill me—or at least, put be back into another coma."

Allison was amazed at Connie's calm and matter-of-fact voice. No hesitation, no hysteria. Her daughter was back at being her usual strong self, able to face whatever came along.

"Seems that way," the detective agreed. He picked up his coffee cup, took a sip. "I'm going to let my partner take it from here while I indulge in a donut."

Sheila didn't miss a beat as she took over the narrative. "Our search of Meg's apartment answered a lot of our questions. There were several pictures of her with George Yates, the gentleman previously found deceased. Some of them were obviously selfies that had been developed while others appeared to have been made at various parties. There were newspaper clippings of the bank robbery in Atlanta as well as the liquor store robbery. And—there were clippings of robberies in Savannah and Charleston. None of these cases were ever solved, but I think we can assume the two of them were pretty busy filling their pockets."

Taking the last sip of her coffee, Sheila shoved her cup aside, and went on, "Since Meg has refused to say anything in response to our questioning, and since she now has a highly regarded defense attorney, it's not likely we'll learn much else. The grand larceny charge will be a slam dunk. We may not be able to prove she killed her partner, but our case for attempted murder against Connie is good and will be even better when we get her DNA to match the blood on the bookend."

Sheila grinned at Connie. "I've got to hand it to you, Girl, you put up some kind of fight."

"Yeah? Too bad I can't remember it."

"But you did remember her red hair. That's a biggie." Sheila hesitated. "You know you'll have to come back to testify at the trial."

"I know, and I'll be only too glad to do so."

Wanting to take the attention off from Connie and give her daughter a chance to relax, Allison came out with a question. "What about Mrs. Platt? Could you nail that on Meg?"

"Not yet. We're still working on it. We're assuming Mrs. Platt became suspicious about Meg's doings, and was killed to prevent her from talking. We had already confiscated her computer and will do the same with Meg's. Something may show up."

Allison's eyes grew wider. "I just remembered something. When I went in to pick up another key. I told Mrs. Platt that we were given two keys, but we needed three. That's when she became rude to me and said we must have been given three because there were three missing and I probably lost one. At that point Meg Freeman came over and sent Mrs. Platt out of the room."

"That must be it," Sheila said. "Meg must have taken the key to get access to your beach house. Maybe Mrs. Platt questioned Meg about it later—and it got her killed. That's so sad. The woman was just trying to do her job."

Shifting around in her chair, Sheila added, "Actually, Meg was one of our suspects from the git-go."

"One of your suspects?" Allison leaned closer. "Who were the others?"

Before Sheila had a chance to respond, Ed spoke up. "We're not at liberty to say."

Sally raised her eyebrows at the detectives. "Probably the same suspects I had."

"You had suspects?" Sheila asked.

"Of course. I've been working on the case ever since I got here. I'll tell you the names I had. You don't have to affirm or deny if they match your suspects."

Ed shrugged. Allison could tell he wanted to hear the names without actually asking for them.

"Here's goes. Ben Johansen, Clyde Johansen, Meg Freeman."

Ed's face remained stoic as he asked, "And what was your criteria?"

"Easy. Local, strong, access to keys of rental properties, able to leave place of employment during the day without raising suspicions."

"But," Sheila put in, "you've only been in town a short time and probably never met any of them. How did you come to your conclusions?"

"I had plenty of help." She pointed to three of the young people on the opposite bed. "Dave, Neil, and Trina are excellent observers. They told me all I needed to know."

For the first time that morning, a wide smile appeared on Ed's face. "Amazing. Could I hire you as a criminal consultant?"

Sally preened a little bit before answering. "I'll get back to you on that."

Ed got up from his chair. "Time for Sheila and me to get back to work."

Before the detectives could leave, Fred stood up with a question of his own. "How is Officer Tucker taking the news of Meg Freeman's involvement? I got the impression earlier that Tuck and Meg were pretty close friends. And, well, I like Tuck and hate to see him hurt."

Ed nodded. "I know he and Meg dated a time or two, even though she was older. And you're right, Tuck's taking it kind of hard. But he's a good cop, and in time he'll put it behind him. I don't think you have to worry about him."

"Good." Fred opened the door and stepped aside. Handshakes and best wishes made the rounds as the detectives headed out.

SLINK PACED AROUND the small cell, glared at her lawyer, brushed back her red hair. "Why in the world won't they let me out on bail?"

"Meg, judges seldom grant bail to accused murderers, especially one who was caught attempting another murder—and one they consider a flight risk. Not much I can do about it." The lawyer picked up his briefcase, motioned for the guard to let him out. "It might help if you would show a little remorse."

LATER, IN SALLY'S hotel room, Fred motioned to his charges. "And now we have to get back to real world— work and school."

"Sounds good to me," Connie said.

"Amen to that," Dave added.

Sally had decided to stay on for a few days and soak up some sun. "Once school starts back I won't have time to be lazy, but I'll drive up and see all of you before heading home."

It took a while, but finally, all the familiar phrases of "love you" and "good luck" and "drive safely" were said, and two cars headed inland leaving the beach for another year.

And, of course, Sidney had the choice seat with his cage stationed between Connie and Trina.

* * * * *

Get 2 Free Books,
Plus 2 Free Gifts—
just for trying the Reader Service!

HARLEQUIN™
I N T R I G U E

HI17R

Get 2 Free Books,
Plus 2 Free Gifts—
just for trying the Reader Service!

HARLEQUIN®
ROMANTIC suspense

Get 2 Free Books,
Plus 2 Free Gifts -
just for trying the Reader Service!

STRSJ7R

READERSERVICE.COM

Manage your account online!

- Review your order history
- Manage your payments
- Update your address

> *We've designed the*
> *Reader Service website*
> *just for you.*

Enjoy all the features!

- Discover new series available to you, and read excerpts from any series.
- Respond to mailings and special monthly offers.
- Browse the Bonus Bucks catalog and online-only exculsives.
- Share your feedback.

Visit us at:

ReaderService.com